MAFIA KING: MATTEO

BORRELLI MAFIA

BOOK ONE

ZOE BETH GELLER

KINKY INK PUBISHING

Mafia King: Matteo

INTRODUCTION

I loved bringing this book to life. It finishes Nanny for the Bodyguard and brings in Alena from Brutal Promise. There are many changes to the mafia world in NYC with this series.

This contains

Touch her and you …

Never let her go

Possessive alpha

FMC who brings light into his darkness

Suspense & Mystery

Spicy Scenes

and so much more!

XO,

Zoe

ACKNOWLEDGMENTS

Special thanks to Maureen Riley.

JOIN MY NEWSLETTER!

Visit shopzoebethgeller.com

Join my mafia newsletter! I share chapters as I write. See cover reveals first, and download free books here!

https://geni.us/MafiaNewslettersignup

Dirty: A Dark Mafia Romance Series (Also in Italian & German & Dutch)

Dirty: A Dark Mafia Romance Series (Micheli Mafia)

Italian King: Book 1

Dirty Vengeance: Book 2

Dirty Bargain: Book 3

Dirty Born: Book 4

Dirty Deals: Book 5

Micheli Mafia: A Dark Mafia Romance (Box Set)

Volkov Bratva Series

(also in Italian, Dutch, and German)

Bratva's Bride-Prequel-Italian and English

King's Promise

Brutal Promise

Sinful Promise

Borrelli Mafia Series

Nanny for the Bodyguard-Prequel

Mafia King: Matteo

Vengeance and Vows

Facebook Reader/Fan Group

ZBG Dark Mafia Romance

https://www.facebook.com/groups/478242870016630/?ref+share

Maine Megaladons (Football Series)

Faking it with the Football Star

The Player's Obsession

Maine Maulers Series (Pro Series)

Maine Maulers Hockey Series

Rookie in Love (now in audio)

Jagged Ice

Hotter than Puck

Benched by the Nanny

Puck in the Oven

Pucking the Team Captain

Pucking with the Goalie

Pucked Over by Cupie

Sin Bin Hockey Series (College Series)

Tyler: Hooked (Free prequel to the series)

The Sin Bin Hockey Series

Jackson: Against the Boards

Alan: Between the Pipes

Erik: Fire and Ice

Blayze: Slap Shot

Paavo: The Defender

Spencer: Penalty Box

Isak: Coach

Kaden: Game Time

Liam: The Enforcer

Jake: Roughing

The Sin Bin Hockey Series Box Sets

The Sin Bin Hockey Series Box Set Books 1-4

The Sin Bin Hockey Series Box Set Books 5-7

The Sin Bin Hockey Series Box Set Books 8-10

Facebook

Zoe Beth Geller's Hockey Pond Reader

CHAPTER 1

MATTEO

My father, Luciano, is dead. After years of wishing the man was six feet under, I finally got my wish. My only question is—why now? Last summer in New York, he was healthy. He returned to Sicily, and by January, he was dead.

I only say he died of cancer because I suspect his death was hastened by someone close to him. I can't tip my hand if that's the case. I shudder to think what this may imply for my younger brother should something happen to me.

After the Catholic church service and funeral, everyone gathers at my father's house. I've always hated this place. It's where my mother died, and today, it feels colder than a prison cell in Siberia.

I find a good vantage point in the living room and stand like a soldier at ease. Watching my three uncles move about the room, I can't help but wonder about their possible motives to eliminate my father.

They knew him best. It makes sense that one or more of them could easily poison his scotch. I hate its strong taste and smell, but it's a great way to conceal poison. But everyone knows that women, not men, typically use poison. When his health started to deteriorate rapidly, I had medical tests run. The results left me with more questions than answers.

My father being poisoned is not how I imagined myself becoming the next mafia boss. A killer needs a motive, and I don't know who has one strong enough to kill over it. The reasons for killing my father are too numerous to select only one. This makes the number of possible suspects limitless.

The men in 'the family' have dropped by to pay their respects. Most of the underbosses appear to be content with the pecking order. None of them have the drive to take over the organization. They stand around exchanging stories, but they aren't the type to linger all day.

Before leaving, our Sicilian friends and employees pledge their allegiance to me. I'll have to sleep with one eye open until I figure out who has the motive to take my birthright.

My mother died over twenty years ago, soon after the birth of my sister, Bianca. I remember it was a hot summer day. I came inside for the fresh lemonade Mom had made in the morning. I heard my parents arguing upstairs. I turned to leave when I heard the awful thud of her falling down the steps.

Her death was deemed an accident, but I have no doubt she was pushed. Believe me, my instincts are even stronger than the smell of my father's liquor.

With Mother gone, my only option was to create a family with my sister and three brothers as if Dad didn't exist. They needed me, and it was the only way to survive. I needed money to take care of them, so I had no choice but to follow in my father's footsteps. Hopefully, I will find redemption before I die.

I don't want or need a wife. The closeness I feel for my siblings suffices as companionship. Typically, an abusive situation either bonds families together or tears them apart. In a house with no parental love, we chose to bond. They are the glue that makes us a family. I'll need to be more vigilant than ever to keep them safe.

Unfortunately, even with my formal education, I lack the necessary work experience to secure a legitimate job in a corporation.

That's why I run my own. I've managed to obtain two properties. One is a casino in Atlantic City, and the other is an upscale hotel in New York City currently undergoing renovations. The next building I acquire from Wu will be demolished. I'll erect a colossal hotel there as well.

I aim to create and grow legitimate businesses so my siblings can escape the family curse. Dad was an old-school crime boss. Like the gangsters he grew up with, he liked extortion, fraudulent money-making scams, and racketeering.

My father clung to these business practices because they fed his ego. He was convinced he was the smartest man in the room. Even as a teenager, I knew he was full of shit. If I dared to challenge his opinion on anything, he beat me. Sometimes, he just beat me for no reason at all.

A good leader should never base their decisions on personal feelings. My father made the mistake of creating friction with other Sicilian clans over stupid bullshit here in Italy. Women wanted him for his money, but he never remarried, intent on keeping his wealth for himself.

As he got older, his sociopathic tendencies got worse, and he couldn't remember the promises he made to men he couldn't afford to piss off. To make matters worse, his alcohol abuse rotted his brain. When I looked into his eyes, I didn't recognize him anymore. I often wondered if he had lost his mind.

My sister would never have left the house if I didn't intervene. Had she remained under his thumb, he would have married her to someone undeserving. If any man abuses my sister, I will put a bullet in his head.

Now she attends college in England. Because her name is Borrelli, she uses a different last name and is always surrounded by heavy security. Sometimes, she tries to ditch her guards and go to the store or a club like a regular person. As a result, one guard plays the part of her best friend, and the other lives in the shadows to ward off suspicious eyes.

Like so many politicians who overstay their useful time in office, my father stayed at the helm too long and should have stepped aside years ago.

On the other hand, I'm glad he didn't hand over the reins too early. I've enjoyed my life in New York City without him hovering over my shoulder and micromanaging my every move. He had a flawed personality. I hope I never become him.

He left me a huge mess. We're in debt, and it's up to me to turn things around.

Dad believed every crime family was needed, even if it wasn't a fair deal. The Russians, the Albanians, the Irish, and others were able to outsmart him in the end. We've been on a sinking ship—not so much here in Sicily, but in New York. I spent enough time there to learn about the city, the players, and the way of life.

I have no desire to live in his relic of a house here or in New York. Every home is filled with outdated furniture. He's never redecorated since Nixon was president. I'm sure it's chock-full of clutter and reeks of the peppermint he took for his stomach. The basement is a fire hazard with a collection of old newspapers stacked from floor to ceiling. He was in his seventies and as outdated as a telephone landline.

Mom was too young when she was given to him, but he wanted to merge with her clan. I assume in the beginning, there was an attraction.

I'm not a trusting man. If I want to live to see tomorrow, trust is the last word that would be used to describe me. Trust gets men killed. It's pathetic how easy it is to lure those we want to kill to a remote location under false pretenses. Remembering I'm at my father's wake, I stifle my snicker.

My Uncle Giuseppe is making his way across the room towards me. He is my father's oldest brother, followed by Luca and Antonio. Luca loves money, and Antonio is like Dad, craving power, as only a younger sibling living with the two of them can understand. It's his way to survive, and being picked on for years makes him desire power more.

Uncle Giuseppe's gait is off, possibly due to a bad back or hip. His high-waisted dress pants and bow tie make him look old for his age. He may as well wear Velcro sneakers to complete the look. He's cheap, and he won't listen to anyone. Thank God he was never in line for my job. But who knows? Maybe he helped Dad along to the gates of hell, and I'm next.

"I'm sorry for your loss, Matteo. I know you don't give a shit, but he was my brother," he mumbles.

"I guess you'll miss him then," I quip. This lecherous man walks around with butterscotch candy in his pocket and goes out of his way to be around young girls. Even his wife thinks it's creepy.

My old man had me on the streets from the time I was seven, running numbers, and then it progressed to violence. I loved my time away at college and wish I could have milked it longer. I gave up on a law degree because my father wanted me to have a business background—so I took a few courses. It was pointless. We don't have to advertise to sell drugs or guns—those who want them know where to find me.

"As a matter of fact, I will miss Luciano. You, however, have never exhibited an ounce of empathy, even as a kid," he says. "One day, Matteo, you will find someone, and maybe it will make you a better person. Losing someone you love is a terrible experience."

"I doubt a woman can change me. I'm thirty-one, and I have no plans to settle down. I have my brothers and sister. That's enough."

"Eventually, you need an heir. Otherwise, there will be a power struggle, and the infighting will destroy us." He gives me a side-eye. He's right, and he knows it.

"Whatever helps you sleep at night, Giuseppe."

It won't be a fight from my siblings, but it would be a free-for-all for greedy outsiders who want to take us over. This is a legitimate situation that could put a target on the back of my beloved brother, Niccoló.

He would be next in line to lead if I were to die. To protect my family, I need an heir. History has taught us it's easier to assume a throne when it's not contested. There needs to be a direct path to the top. It's a rule as old as time, and wars have been fought over less.

I hoped I had more time before conceding to the age-old tradition of matrimony. It's a situation I dread.

"You're mean-spirited. I don't know who you got that from," he says through a mouthful of antipasti he's eating with his bare hands. I've seen five-year-olds with better manners. His creepy personality fits with his ugly mug. He didn't inherit the family genetics in the good looks department. Like my father, he's a schemer who always looks for an angle that benefits him. I never trusted him when he made deals with Dad. Whenever a deal went south, somehow Giuseppe came out without a scratch.

My father always bought his bullshit excuses. Before I left for college, I found a missing shipment in an old barn on his sister-in-law's farm. I'm sure he hijacked the cigarette container in what I refer to as the smoke screen heist. There was no use telling Dad. He would have believed his brother over me.

I didn't want to attend college with a black eye and split lip. I could have fought him, but it would only anger him more. Maybe Dad knew, and it was his way of throwing his brother a bone after Giuseppe took a bullet for him when they were teenagers running amuck in the streets.

I can't wait to get to New York City. I'm tired of this island and look forward to a change of scenery. God only knows I've screwed every single woman here over the age of twenty-one. Now that I'm older, I no longer go after the young ones who get clingy. The most gorgeous woman here left years ago, her name is Sophia. We talk from time to time. Maybe we'll have a fling if I run into her as she works for me.

Marriage has always been off the table. I'm a skeptic, always have been, and always will be. Why would any woman want to be involved in the life I live? My hours are erratic, and my life is complicated, not to mention dangerous as fuck. The moment a woman starts to call or text for anything other than sex, I block her number. I don't take pleasure in hurting women. I fuck like a buck—hard and fast. There are times when a woman is desired, and she serves a purpose. One purpose only—to get me off. Meaningless sex is safe.

I notice Niccoló. The women in the room flirt with him. The front door opens, and his girlfriend walks through it. The other women turn their backs in disappointment.

He is a handsome devil. He's madly in love with Chiara. Her father works the docks for us on the mainland. He turns the other way when our shipments of cocaine hidden in cans of pineapple come in from South America. We open the cans and transfer the cocaine to the inside of old machinery tires that we then transport to other countries.

"You should be happy that he's gone. You've hated him since Mom died. That's a long time to hate," Niccoló says softly, watching Chiara walk toward us.

"You were young. You didn't see how he treated her. If someone treated Bianca like that, I'd kill them. Mom was an angel."

"That's one thing we can agree on," Niccoló says. "I hope you're still going to join me in New York. You understand."

"Yes, I do. Maybe we'll run away and get married," he chuckles.

"Don't make any emotional decisions. Think things through. I have to speak with Bianca. We'll talk later," I say abruptly as I head to my sister.

She grew up with help from our mother's aunt. Dad had to have a girl, and Mom had a late-in-life baby that about killed her. I'm not sure about her death, injuries sustained from the fall, or possibly she broke her neck. The end result is the same. Money gets Dad out of trouble more times than I can count. It's what we do.

Dad didn't reserve his drinking for the evenings. As the child who took the brunt of the beatings, I could predict his moods from the number of empty wine and vodka bottles in the recycling bin.

I kiss my sister's soft cheek. She hugs me.

"Are you okay?"

"Sure, it was bound to happen, right?"

"Yes."

"I'm glad it wasn't by your hand."

"What do you mean?"

"I always saw the rage in your eyes and worried that one day you'd snap."

"Possibly, but it's important I remain in control of myself. Who else would be here for you?"

"Thank you for that. I love college."

"Good, I did, too. Stay vigilant. I'm investigating Dad's death quietly," I reply, moving away to work the room and shake hands. My presence commands the room.

I stop by a table with a hand-crocheted tablecloth, plates of cold cuts, and homemade delicacies. My other brothers, Renalto and Pietro, sip Grappa. I take a half-filled glass and raise it. We toast to the new era.

Who killed my father? Are they coming for me next?

CHAPTER 2

ALENA

$\mathcal{I}$ expected information on my arranged marriage tonight. Dad is stressed. He refused to come out of his office and missed dinner. I'm still in the dark about the family plans for my future—the uncertainty knots in my stomach. I'm free-falling into the abyss. Don't they know I'm in limbo?

"I don't think you are the pressing matter," Mom assures me as we clear the table. I follow her into the kitchen and stack the dishwasher. Her housekeeper made dinner and left early, which rarely happens. Sometimes, I think Mom doesn't want to be alone in this humongous house without Dad and keeps the housekeeper after hours so she has company. I'm sure nothing has changed over the years with Dad's unpredictable work schedule.

"When am I not the brunt of his disdain?" I joke. I'm feeling neglected without my father bellowing his political opinions at me. He talks like I have no life experience.

If he only knew what I did at night, he might discover other ways to go around the world—if you understand the underworld of single life.

Mom gives me a look that could turn our house cat, Pickles, into stone.

"Fine," I harrumph as I make a pot of hot tea. The kettle's scream is shrill. Mom is not one for the latest technology. When I was younger, she constantly needed to keep up with the other housewives in the family. They shopped in the same stores, went to the same spas, and took the same vacations.

There was always an undercurrent of competition between the women to find the newest thing on the social scene. Whether it was the latest luxury car or the best up-and-coming fashion designer, it was sweeter if someone scored an invitation to a new designer's show.

They would sometimes crash the venue using our guards to pave their way into his show with his newest collection if no invite came. Everyone was judged by who had the most toys, cars, and the best wardrobe. To be the first to discover the next fad before it became all the rage meant you were someone.

Granted, many of them had an unfair advantage because their husbands were manipulating the underworld by investing in designers. It was how they controlled the market, creating shortages, so the prices went up, and the profit margins were huge.

I pour two cups of black tea and skip the sugar. I have no butt, in my opinion, and my boobs are too large for my petite frame. However, I have no desire for my hips and thighs to get any bigger. I hand Mom a cup and follow her into the living room.

I put my cup on the stone-topped coffee table and sit with her on the overpriced couch a designer picked out years ago. It's stiff and uncomfortable, but the cream-colored leather goes well with the room's dark blue accent pillows and rugs, and it's an improvement over the teal in other rooms.

Mom turns on the TV to watch a reality show. One would never know she wasn't born here as she watches shows I can't be bothered to spend a year of my young life watching. I hate waiting for endings, so a serialized show with one weekly release would drive me insane.

"So, what is going on?" I pick up my tea and sip. My interest is piqued. After the drama with my roommate Izzy and her stalkers earlier this year, life has become boring. The stalkers turned out to be men who were hired to hunt her down. Since then, I've discovered that having more information is better than less, especially in my world, due to my family's connections. Secrets can be deadly. I wouldn't want a hitman chasing me without knowing why.

Izzy never knew she was the product of a forbidden marriage, a love child. It would have merged the Russians and the Italians decades ago. The future is uncertain for her Italian family because her biological grandfather is a demonic old man who gets off on the pain of others. Izzy has nothing to do with them, but that might change when the baby arrives. Until then, it's a wait-and-see situation that Izzy chooses to ignore. There are five leading Italian families in the city and the surrounding area. That pretty much covers my knowledge of the Italian mob, with the exception of the Morellis'. My best friend is related to them. It's a fucked-up story.

"You might want to get a job, Alena," Mom says during a commercial break. My mind wanders as I watch a woman in the show begin shopping. She obviously has an unhealthy addiction to her credit card. I can relate to some retail therapy being used to compensate for loneliness.

"Really? Dad would let me work?" This means I would have a reprieve from marrying until next year. These weddings are used as a showcase to the world that we're wealthy and powerful. However, the wait-and-see attitude of the situation has been looming over me like a plague.

I downplay my anxiousness when I'm with my best friend, Izzy. She's pregnant and basking in a love life that has recently upstaged mine. Something about hormones is all I remember. Besides, she's married to a hot-blooded, handsome, and mysterious Russian who saved her life numerous times. I can't fault her for falling in love with him. It would be impossible not to!

I'm relieved she found her family and will stay in New York City. She'll be the queen of the Russian mafia soon. I never knew she was part Russian even though she lived with me. I didn't mind giving her a place to stay. She has always been a loyal friend who keeps my life out of her conversations, and in exchange, she got to live with me for free while she obtained her fashion degree.

My mother's suggestion of work stymies me. Before getting overly excited, I press for more details.

"Did Dad approve this?"

"We've discussed it. There will be changes when Dmitry takes over, and we want to see what transpires before making any promises. The ever-changing environment and all that," she says with a shrug. "Why not give single life a go? God knows I don't like what I hear from your guards. Sex clubs? Really? I hope you use protection." Her judgmental comments tell me she gets very little action from Dad. Most of the men have a woman on the side. I think Dad is a workaholic with little sex drive.

I, on the other hand, am promiscuous. Whether Dad approves or not is of little concern. I have needs, and I love sex. It's one area where I'm in control. I decide where and when. It's liberating; maybe that's why I exercise my pussy muscles so much.

Unfortunately, I'm bored with the men in my sex life. Each man is just like the last. We play verbal poker, peppering each other with questions to see if there will be another hookup and if there is a potential future together.

It's getting older faster than I anticipated. Besides, all my college friends have moved on to jobs, so I don't get to see them as much. As a young woman in the city, I have too many openings in my social calendar.

In New York City, women outnumber men five to one. I size up my competition when I'm on dates. Most women lack fashion sense and don't wear outfits that flatter their figure. There's an art to it. Most designer brands have better quality control and tend to fit better. My secret weapon is a skilled tailor. Because of my large bust, I have to buy oversized tops, and have them altered to fit me perfectly.

A woman should show off her assets, and I do this tastefully. I assume my creative side leads me to judge others' fashion choices harshly. I can't help but laugh when I encounter women who wear heels to play putt-putt. The first rule of getting a date is to dress well. Second, one needs to dress appropriately for the activity.

The lack of fashion etiquette is ironic since we live in the city where the American fashion world lives and breathes. I have more room at the apartment now that Izzy has moved out and has a swanky place on the Upper East Side. It's not far from me, and I try to meet up with her as much as possible now that she's working on costumes for major Broadway productions.

"You've been quiet. What's on your mind?" Mom asks during a commercial break.

"Maybe I could find a job with my fashion degree. I love interior design."

"I can have your father look for opportunities," Mom volunteers.

"I don't want to bother him. I'll apply online and see if I can land interviews. How difficult can it be?" I shrug. The doors will fly open when they see my last name.

I'm flippant. I'm in the know as far as the beat of the city. However, I always concede that getting a great job without using my last name will be difficult. Names can either open or close doors. I've been raised on the premise that knowing the right person leads to securing a job. It's not talked about openly, but I know it's the mafia network that speaks volumes.

The commercials end, and the show picks up where it left off. I kick off my red-bottomed heels, curl my legs under me, and lean forward to pull the white and blue cashmere blanket from the ottoman. I wrap it around me before pulling it up to my chin. I love its softness of my skin.

Dad keeps the house as cold as the cold-blooded Russian he is. It is almost February, and it is snowing outside. The central heat is not on. Even though he moved here before I was born, it's another wheel of time that has never changed.

Dad's voice bellows down the hallway of the million-dollar house. I throw Mom a questioning look.

"He's fine. Nothing a heart attack can't cure," she teases, dismissing my concerns. The anger in his voice is unusual, even for him. However, it's been months since I temporarily shacked up with them for my safety during the wild adventures of Izzy discovering her past. Then, there was the explosion at her wedding. I must be suffering from post-traumatic stress disorder. I'm in the letdown phase after all the excitement this year. Maybe this is why I'm bored.

If Dad's yelling is any indication, I'd say things are not going his way this week. I wonder if I should use my real name on a job application. I need Kirill to look over my resume. Hell, I thought I'd be planning my wedding. It's all my parents talked about when I was in college. They made it sound like going to school was getting in the way of their plans for me.

I'm not oblivious to the fact I've been raised like a fatted calf, and the slaughter is imminent. It's unnerving not to be in control of my own life.

Izzy was terrified of my father when she lived with me. I'm not surprised. I'm sure he is to be feared. To me— he's Dad. I've never known him to be sentimental or affectionate. Maybe this is why I pursue men and play their games.

I'm seeking an all-consuming love from a man who will make me feel it in my bones because I'm numb inside. To my peers, I am enviable. I have everything a woman would want and more. But it's all material items. Sure, men flirt with me, and I turn heads when I enter a room. Izzy assumes it's my looks. I'll always be seen as my father's daughter. I associate the attention I get has more to do with my father's position than my big boobs and long legs.

Izzy tells me I'm beautiful. She doesn't know that I compare myself to women in fashion magazines. I wish I had higher cheekbones and a thinner waistline. I already fill my lips. It's exhausting how I constantly learn new makeup tricks to achieve different looks from online tutorials. I should have Dad sponsor a makeup line so I can cash in on my time using the products I research.

Who am I?

More importantly—who am I trying to be? Am I on an insatiable hunt for something unobtainable?

There is a hole inside of me I can't explain. Spending money is only a vehicle that fills it temporarily. Not having a relationship with the men I fuck appears to widen the chasm inside me. I've learned this because I find more peace in being alone than bouncing from one man to the next. I'm not satisfied even if I orgasm.

I also know that the dark beast inside me will emerge one day. I have no idea what that means. I assume I should make peace and accept myself for who I am, or I will fall into the black abyss. I don't want to lose myself to the darkness.

"I miss Izzy," I state.

"She's an important friend to have," Mom states as if I won the lottery. "Who could have guessed she was a mafia princess twice over and that she was penniless!"

The condo isn't the same without her. Now that she's met the love of her life, I'm a bit jealous. I never thought I wanted a serious boyfriend, but the men I've been with don't excite me. I get more satis-faction from the collection of dildos that I keep stashed in my night-stand. Perhaps it's the reason I like the sex clubs. There is a lot to be said for a handsome stranger manhandling me.

Being single in the city should be a dream come true. But my secret desire is to belong. I want someone I can trust. I desire a man who has my back and isn't afraid to stand up to me. I would love a companion who willingly goes home with me for the holidays and is not intimi-dated by my father.

I'm an only child. I'm used to doing things alone, but I've grown tired of it. A job would help fill my days. Maybe I'll make new friends and meet men who aren't in the mafia. I don't need to tell them about my family. It helps that my last name is not uncommon among Russians.

I've never had a serious relationship. Most of my friends assume that men are lined up to date me, maybe even marry me. I refuse to have sex with my best male friend, Kirill. We're close because we're both single and shared the past year hanging out together. He works for my father, doing the inner workings that only he and my father would know about, and the Don, of course.

Banging each other would be like incest. And I'm afraid it might jeopardize our friendship. My generation is more into sex. It seems men want to do it rough and get on with their day. Some expect me to put out on a first date, and if not, then definitely before the third date.

They never stick around long after they learn who I am. I think they are afraid my father would shoot them if they knew that we were together. Hence, I've never reached the envied hand-holding phase.

I'm opinionated, but I don't need to comment on every detail in life. I want a man who knows his mind.

Am I asking for too much?

Having a man hold my hand because he wants to mark his territory would be a turn-on. I fantasize about lying in bed on Sunday with a man who isn't afraid to snuggle me. It wouldn't be a bother. If anything, I'd like it.

"Izzy's great. I'll see her later this week."

"That's right, Roman is getting married soon. How is that going?"

"Good, as far as I know. Izzy is having a baby in a few months. That will mean I won't see her as much."

"Well, that's how it goes. You need to make new friends. You're so pretty. It should be easy for you."

"No, it's not easy. I have a tough time trusting anyone."

"I'm sure it will keep you safe," she replies without concern.

My family isn't overly endearing with words or affection. They never say, "I love you." I think my father compensates for this with the generous allowance he gives me and the fact he rarely complains about my spending on designer collections.

When I started school, I gave up on expecting any sign of affection from my parents. I noticed other kids getting hugs as their parents dropped them off. My parents love me, but if I have kids, I will smother them with affection.

Maybe I'm just being overly emotional. I called Izzy when she was at the engagement party in the city because I was having a panic attack. The attacks started before we graduated from the Fashion Institute when I thought I was being followed. I kept this information to myself. Everyone considers me impervious to fear and thinks I'm made of steel.

When we figured out Izzy was being hunted and that we were helpless without Dmitry's help, I realized how much of my life was out of my control.

I've lived on a need-to-know basis for my protection all my life. I am clueless about the inner workings of the family. It's expected that I accept this. And I do accept it—mostly. But my patience is growing thin. My birth dictates my life to be lived inside this family of criminals. I now fear the unknown. What if I'm kidnapped? What if I'm hit by a bus tomorrow?

I'm relieved Izzy gets to live here and hasn't been shipped off to Russia. I can't wait to hear her updates on what is happening in her world.

CHAPTER 3

MATTEO

*N*iccoló knows I'm leaving Sicily today and joins me for breakfast at my house overlooking the sea. It's a bitter-sweet moment as Federico serves us breakfast.

We eat together in the kitchen, overlooking the backyard filled with olive trees. Sitting here reminds me of our childhood. Without a mom to make us wash our hands before eating, we didn't think much about formal meals—except for dinner. Most of the time, we'd run around with a panini for lunch.

"I hope you'll tear yourself away from Chiara long enough to visit me in New York. I'm going to miss the hell out of you."

"I know, me too. We'll see how things go," Niccoló says as he sips orange juice.

"Dad's toxicology report showed lethal levels of thallium in his liver. Exactly when he was poisoned is unclear. I assume it started when he returned to Sicily for Christmas. But who knows?"

"A bullet to the head would have been more exact," he murmurs sarcastically. "I'm glad you didn't act on your impulses. I'm sure you would have offed him had he hurt any of us."

"True. The timeline on Dad is sketchy. However, I don't want to alert the entire family to this. It will make us look weak, and during the transition of power, I can't afford for us to lose the respect our name carries."

"Who do you suspect?"

"I'm keeping an eye on our uncles. They all have a motive, but they need men in their pockets to take over. I'm not sure if they'll try to take me out here or in New York. But I know it's coming. They might sabotage me to show I'm an ineffective leader. Then, I'd lose what I need—the men's loyalty."

"Shit. This sucks. I suppose we can't expect Dad's brothers to be civilized. But any self-respecting man who murders by poison is a coward. All three of them are too egotistical not to lay a claim to doing that, aren't they?"

"Not if there is a bigger play to be made. If the price is right, they might keep their mouths shut." I finish my eggs and toast, washing them down with coffee.

"Any idea what that might be?"

"Not yet. I'll have to be careful until I learn more. I have my men working on it. In the meantime, you need to be careful and discreet when telling others. Bianca is back at school, so that should take her off the game board. As for Pietro—I doubt he'll be an issue to anyone as long as he can spend all day in his vineyard."

"True. Jesus, I can't believe it's come to this, looking over our shoulders for a possible traitor in our own family."

"I could be wrong," I admit, pushing my plate to the center of the table.

"It makes sense. The men who work for us aren't overly ambitious. But who knows? Times are changing, and it could be the start of a takeover by any of them," Niccoló suggests.

"We shouldn't rule anyone out. Our best option is to keep our loyal men happy and know that our guards will give their lives for us."

"How long will it take for someone to get to them?"

I shrug. "I have no clue. However, if I'm taken out, make sure you find the bastards and make them suffer."

"I will. Let's hope it doesn't come to that," he replies.

I stand. Niccoló joins me. I hug him. "Good luck, brother," I say in Italian.

He returns my hug. "Good luck to you. I'll be in touch."

I stare out the floor-to-ceiling windows overlooking the gravel driveway and watch Niccoló climb into his white Ferrari. I'm humored by his refusal to drive the stereotypical red Ferrari most Italian men prefer. His security detail is split between two armored SUVs, one in front and one behind him as they pull onto the curvy road.

What surprises await me in New York? After packing, I call the service that coordinates the crew for my private jet. As a safety precaution, I give a vague departure time for later today. I'll show up unexpectedly.

I said my goodbyes to my siblings last night. Before closing the carry-on luggage, I shower and dress casually with loafers, jeans, and a dress shirt. September is warm—a reality of our changing environment.

When I was a kid, the tourist season in Italy used to end at the end of summer. Today, the tourist season lasts most of the year, with trains and ferries running more often during the summer months.

While my guard drives me to the airport, maneuvering the SUV expertly around the winding and hilly countryside, I text Gio.

Me: I'll be on the plane soon.

Gio: Good. The house is ready for you. Mr. Wu has been oddly quiet.

Fuck!

I should have let Antonio kill that motherfucker. I want his laundromat. We can clean money through it. But I want to turn it into a hotel and expand our empire. The building has height restrictions, but it's a potential goldmine without it.

The pilot greets me, and within minutes, I'm airborne. I haven't filled Gio in on what's transpired. I'm particular with the information I share over phones, even encrypted ones. I prefer to be cautious even if it's not as convenient. I'd rather discuss important matters in person when the timing is right.

Me: Have Antonio beef up security.

Gio: Trouble?

Me: Always.

I get up and mix myself a Manhattan. It's going to be a mind fuck switching from the laid-back lifestyle in Sicily to the busy streets of New York City.

* * *

Gio meets me at Teterboro airport with two SUVs to escort us into the city. It's a city with an incredible nightlife if one knows where to find it.

"True, so where to? Home?"

"I've been stuck on a flight for hours. I want to get into character, and by that I mean find an enticing woman to fuck. I'm sure you know where I can make that happen." Knowing Gio, who's in his forties and never married, I'm sure he knows exactly where to find what I want. He wouldn't be my best friend and advisor if he didn't.

"I know of a place. It's small, intimate, and by invitation only, but I can get you in. Don't worry, it's not a fuckfest of losers and one-timers."

"Great. Thanks."

"We are bachelors. We need to stick together. The city is filled with tons of women wanting to get married."

"I'm sure a large bank account is attractive as well."

"It never hurts. This place has a few rules, like no real names and safe sex only."

I nod. "Noted."

"How was the funeral?"

"Boring as hell. Between us, it looks like my father may have been murdered. His postmortem lab work showed poison commonly found in soil. The only consolation is that his death was quick. I don't want to show my hand to the person or persons responsible. The only people who know are you and my siblings. Be vigilant. It's an uncertain time to take my place at the top."

"I understand," he says. "I'll tell Antonio to keep his eyes open even when he sleeps."

"That will be me, too. How did I get stuck with the psychotic family? Given the family genetics, it's a wonder we kids turned out as well as we have. Pietro has always been the rebel. Is it really that terrible that he hates the family business and prefers to garden?"

"Not at all. He's probably the happiest of all of you, although I'm sure Bianca has all the men at school eating out of her hand. She's probably having a great time."

"Popularity isn't all it's cracked up to be, trust me." My years have been filled with women who want everything from a hard fuck to a ring on their finger. At times, it's as if my soul is being sucked instead of my cock. "Besides, her school is a bit unorthodox."

Gio nods. There is more to that story, but it's for another day.

Gio gives the driver an address, and the SUV winds down city streets with very little traffic.

"The theme tonight is Angels and Demons. They have one night a week for theme parties."

"Sounds organized."

"It's private. The owner is Madame M."

"It's not prostitutes, is it?"

"Hell no. Rumor has it Madame M loves sex and uses one of her large flats for friends to mingle, if you get my drift. An annual fee keeps the bar stocked and pays for staff on event nights. Trust me, you'll have a good time."

"Fine." The SUV rolls to a stop in front of a brick building.

"We'll wait," Gio says as he walks me to an unmarked door.

I feel the bite of the chill in the damp night air. All I care about is having a wet pussy dripping at the sight of my cock.

Gio punches in a code, and the door unlocks. We step inside to find an empty lobby with a single elevator. The doors are open, and Gio indicates that I should step inside.

"Penthouse. I'll be waiting here."

"Thank you, Gio."

I press the button with the letter P, and the elevator doors close. Due to the stress at home, my balls are tight. I'm not ready to sleep, and I want to get off.

The elevator lurches to a stop, and the doors open. I step out, not knowing what to expect. It's quiet, and I wonder if I'm at the right place. There's only one door, a red door. It opens, and a woman dressed in burlesque red and black lingerie, with pearls on her stockings and six-inch heels, steps out. She's tugging on a long black coat.

"Well, if I had known you were coming, I would have stayed longer," she purrs. She's tall, with alabaster skin and lips painted red like candy apples. She's wearing a platinum-blonde Marilyn Monroe wig.

"Maybe next time," I reply without an encouraging smile.

She grabs my balls as she passes me and gets into the elevator. The scent of her gardenia perfume tickles my nose.

"Nice package," she says as the door closes.

I hate the smell of gardenias. They are overpowering. I rub my hand over my face as if it will wipe away the perfume smell sooner rather than later.

I open the red door and step inside a dimly lit apartment. I can make out a bar in the center of the large room. Art Deco sconces, reminiscent of the Roaring Twenties, decorate the walls and provide the only lighting.

An older, attractive woman approaches and escorts me to the bar. She orders two Manhattans.

"Gio told me you'd be here. Nice to meet you," she extends a gloved hand. I shake it and notice the white gloves extend to her elbows. "I'm Madame M. Safe sex, condoms in every room. Gio said your membership forms and fees will be arriving."

"Yes, thank you." I lift my glass, and we tap them together before we drink.

She's smoking a thin cigarette at the end of a long cigarette holder. She looks like she stepped out of a silent film, but something tells me she dresses like this daily. She's still beautiful, especially for a woman in her sixties, if I had to guess. Her hair is silver, not grey, and styled in a short straight bob. Her floor-length gown is made of white sequins and sparkles like she is dressed to take the stage and sing a solo. She's classy and not at all dressed for sex.

"Nice to meet you. I'm Mr. Grey. Thank you for the imposition. I hate long flights."

"Darling," she purrs, "don't we all?"

I chuckle. I take another sip of my cocktail. My eyes are adjusting to the darkness, and I notice the walls are painted a dark teal, which shows off the cream-colored leather-backed furniture.

"This is an incredible penthouse."

"Thank you. It's a hobby. We all need one. Sex is my vice."

My eyes survey the crowd, which comprises mostly couples and a few single men and women. On my second sweep of the room, I see her.

The young, voluptuous woman is wearing a tight red and black bustier, with fishnet stockings up to her solid thighs and held in place by red garter belts. She's nursing a dirty martini, judging from the stick filled with olives in her hand. She suggestively eats one at a time, taking her time to savor them. She appears to be oblivious to how sexual this looks, and my cock is hard.

"Who's the girl?"

"That's Angelica to you. She's a sweet girl. I think the two of you would have a wild time. Now that my job here is done, I'll leave you to it," she says before floating away like a butterfly.

I ask for another Manhattan and a dirty martini. I grab both and approach Angelica.

She's a vision with her long brown hair with subtle highlights. Her cheeks are rounded, and her pouty royal red lips curl into a smile as I hand her the drink.

"Hm. Mama always told me to be leery of strangers bearing gifts."

"Oh, I hope I won't be a stranger for long."

"You must be new here," she states as she sets her empty glass on a nearby table. She takes a sip of the martini I hand her.

"Very new."

"I'm Angelica," she offers her hand.

"I'm Mr. Grey." I raise her soft hand to my lips and kiss it.

"Mr. 50 Shades, is it?"

"For the night, it appears so."

"Kinda unoriginal, don't you think?"

"Once you've been with me, I doubt you'd say I'm unoriginal."

She glances at my crotch and gives me a look—the one between a smile and an invitation to fuck her. I'm ready to come in my pants.

Madam M was right. The sexual tension between us is electrifying. I move closer when I glimpse a tall man with massive shoulders heading our way. He recognizes the universal move that declares she is mine and politely veers off.

"Do you come here often?"

"No, but tonight I wanted to be a little demon," she says giving me a token smile.

"Funny, your name implies angel."

"Trust me, Mr. Grey, I'm no angel. Follow me." She sashays like a model in her red-bottom stilettos and leads me to what I assume is a room. She pushes aside the beading hanging in the doorway.

I follow her into a room with dozens of candles burning. The wrought-iron bed takes up the entire room, and the scene reminds me of a shrine in a vampire movie.

She takes a few long sips of the martini before she sets the glass on the table. I toss back the rest of my drink and put my empty glass beside the bowl of condoms.

I slip my hand behind her neck and pull her into my chest. I cup her large tit, placing my hand between the fabric and her hard nipple.

My god, she's heavenly.

Her arms wrap around my neck. Her hand slips inside my shirt, and her other hand begins to unbutton it. I shrug out of it to help her undress me. If it were up to me, I'd shuck everything, but to a woman dying of thirst, the first few drops of water are always the sweetest.

She runs her soft hand slowly over my chest as if memorizing the contour. I'm starting to relax when she surprises me by grabbing my nipple and pinching it until it's hard.

My excitement is at an all-time high. She likes a bit of pain. So do I.

CHAPTER 4

I love a dirty martini and could make a meal from the green olives stuffed with blue cheese. I enjoy sucking on each one and rolling them around in my mouth before chewing and swallowing. I close my eyes to savor the last one and listen to the smooth jazz playing in the background. I get a whiff of bourbon and tobacco and open my eyes to see a handsome devil handing me a drink. I swallow hard when he introduces himself as Mr. Grey.

I recognized him from earlier when I saw him speaking with Madame M. He's not a regular and must be someone of importance to muscle his way in here. He's not at all dressed for tonight's Angels and Demons. It's a theme evening.

His clothes fit him well. He's handsome in the classic sense, with a strong jaw, piercing eyes, and sun-kissed skin. His tan is probably natural because he doesn't impress me as one of those city slickers who goes to a tanning salon. No, this man spends time outside and doesn't mind getting his hands dirty.

He's older, possibly in his thirties. It may be time I changed it up and stopped picking men my age. What do I have to lose? It's a chilly night—nothing will change if I go home and wall myself off in my condo.

Mr. Grey impresses me as the serious type who doesn't smile much. When I call him unconventional, I see the beginnings of a smile tug at the corners of his mouth.

Once inside our room, that same mouth ravages mine. I love the fullness of his lips. Warmth spreads down my body. He holds me by the neck, limiting my movement, but I can still stroke his chest and nipples.

He has strong hands, and I gasp when he rakes his fingers down my back and grabs my ass. As he sucks hard on my neck, I yearn for him to take me. I reach down and grab his hard cock. It's huge, and the thought of him inside me dampens my crotchless panties.

I can tell by the way he moves his fingers inside of me that he knows his way around a woman's body. Between his sensual touch and the threat of the unknown, I'm left trembling and hanging in the balance. Lost in the euphoria of his fingers moving inside my wet pussy, I dig my nails into his back to remain standing.

Sensing my needs, he pulls his fingers out and licks the juice off each one, then scoops me up and tosses me onto the bed. I land on my back. He grabs my stocking-covered legs and pulls me to the edge of the mattress. Running his fingers over the pearls on my fishnet stockings, he lets out a low growl.

He quickly kicks off his shoes and removes the rest of his clothes. I grab his hard cock and slowly stroke it while watching the light return to his eyes.

I can tell he's about to explode when he roughly pulls my hand from his cock, grabs a condom and sheaths himself. He rubs the large head of his cock in my opening, and I moan.

"Do you like that?"

"Mm."

"Tell me you want me to fuck you."

I shake my head. The tantric state I'm in has me feeling buzzed. He grabs my hands and pulls my arms over my head. He holds me immobile while his lips latch onto a nipple. He sucks hard, then releases it, flicking it with his tongue until my back arches off the mattress.

I squirm under him. Fuck, this is thrilling.

His free hand rips open the laces of the bustier, and my large breasts spill out. He grabs one and gives it a hearty squeeze. I pull my knees together and writhe under him.

"No! Legs apart."

"I can't," I manage to choke out.

"You can and you will," his deep voice fills the air between us.

"No," I refuse, pressing my knees together. It's futile as he easily spreads my legs and runs his fingers through my wetness and along the lace trim of my panties.

"I love this outfit," he murmurs as he buries his face between my breasts. My arms are numb from the fatigue of being immobile.

His cock is at my entrance. I lift my hips to reach it, but he moves away. He's punishing me.

"Tell me you want my hard cock to make you come."

"No," I answer to spite him. I can outlast him.

"Fine. Then it's my choice. Your arms are turning blue, so it's hard and fast."

Fuck. Yes. My pussy is pulsating. I'm wet for him and yearn for his large cock to fill me.

His first thrust is glorious. He's so large it takes longer than expected, and it's as if I'm a virgin again. He pushes harder, gaining ground until his cock is fully inside me.

I groan. This man was made to fuck and suck. He holds my wrists with one hand, and with the other, he tweaks my nipples until they are hard enough to cut cocaine.

I gasp and thrash about. He thrusts into me so hard that my hips respond by rising to meet his. My hips are suspended in the air as we grind on each other. His hard cock hitting places inside me that are so deep they've never been touched.

He pumps me harder, his cock slamming into me and pushing me up the bed. I want to touch him, but he's in control. I'm on the verge of coming. My mind is swimming when he pulls out.

"Not until I say you can come," he murmurs as he nibbles on my earlobe.

He releases my arms. I ball up my fists and beat at his chest.

"That's so mean," I say in frustration.

"It's just the beginning. Turn over," he commands.

I comply, and as soon as I do, he rips my panties. My bare pussy is facing the bed as he playfully slaps my ass. I feel the mattress dip as he kneels and places his palm on my lower back. "Brace yourself," he warns. I stiffen my arms to support my weight, knowing I better hang on to something.

He grabs my hips and rams his cock inside me without warning. I scream in ecstasy as my orgasm erupts. His balls slap into my ass as he continues to pound into me. He's in so deep that I gasp for air. Another orgasm crowns. I feel my vagina being ripped apart by his girth and friction. I come again, and this time, so does he, as I hear him growl and feel him shudder. He holds me to his muscular chest until his cock begins to relax. Then he releases me and lies down, rolling me to my back before pulling me to him. He skillfully pulls the used condom off. I hear it hit the trash can next to the bed.

"I just got off a long flight. Otherwise, I'd fuck you all night."

Weak from my orgasms and hoarse from the screaming, I can barely move or speak. No man has ever given me multiple orgasms.

I lie there in his strong arms with his cock tucked between us as he cuddles me from behind.

"That is a shame."

"I want to see you again."

"I don't know if that's a good idea."

"Is that a line, or is that how you feel?" His voice is deep and salty.

I ponder this briefly. "Men like you are an addiction, and there's no cure for it."

He surprises me with a warm chuckle. "You make it sound like it's a bad thing."

"Coming to places like this is to avoid entanglements."

"Fair enough," he concedes.

Wait, is he giving up already?

He pulls away and sits up, "I have to go." He stands and starts handing me my clothes. "Looks like I owe you a new outfit." He says as he hands me two pieces of black lace that used to be my panties.

"Don't worry about it."

He zips up his pants and searches for his shirt.

I scramble to get into my clothes so I'm not here alone—but pace myself to leave after him.

"I had a good time. Sorry, this was so brief," he apologizes. His dark eyes meet mine, and we're frozen, trapped by our mutual attraction. I don't want to be the first to look away, nor do I want him to leave, but that's not how this works.

"The number one house rule is that we do not 'date' our sex partners."

"Even if it's the most intriguing proposition in the world?"

"You're that sure of yourself?"

"Are you always this skeptical?"

"Pretty much."

"Well, I'll have to prove you wrong."

"You don't impress me as a man who has to prove himself to anyone."

"You're very astute for someone so young," he replies, slipping into his expensive Italian loafers.

"Am I?"

"You know you are. And you know that you own every room you walk into. I saw all those men eye-fucking you tonight."

"I wasn't interested in any of them." I hold onto his arm for balance, slipping one shoe on, then the other.

"It's obvious they're only boys. I'm not surprised," he says, turning to leave. "No regrets?"

"No. You?"

"None. Thank you for an incredible night, Angelica. Will you be back?"

"I'm undecided."

"Fair enough." He raises my hand to his lips and plants a warm kiss on my fingers before he turns to leave.

After the door closes, I flop onto the bed. Whew. He's the long drink of water I needed to put out the fire between my legs. Holy mother of God, he's huge, and I'm a bit sore, but I want more. I would never be able to say no if he wanted to see me again. I'm playing with fire and won't break the house rule. If it's meant to be, it will be. If not, I'm so screwed.

I leave the room, gather my belongings from a locker, grab my long coat, and go downstairs. I wait outside for my driver and look around for lurkers or strangers out of place. On the short ride home, I make minimal conversation. All I can think about is the handsome man with mysterious eyes and a reluctant smile.

The driver dropped me at my building and waited for me to safely get inside before leaving. I ride the elevator to my floor and unlock the door to my condo. I'm in a fog as I pour myself a glass of wine and fill the bathtub. The stranger has stirred up some buried feelings. Is it lust that made the sex so intense? Without words, he knew how to turn me on and get me off. That's a first.

As soon as I dried off from the bath, I texted Izzy that I got home safely. We do this as a safety precaution.

She calls.

"That's unoriginal."

"That's what I said."

"And?" she asks.

"Well, he wants to see me again but it's against the rules. It's probably a liability thing, but I wouldn't mind a repeat of tonight."

"That's strange."

"The fact you got married first is strange. This is scary."

"Right. Well, are you going to do what your mother said?"

"I'll try to get a job. I'm not sure what's out there, but why not? I'm bored off my ass without you, Dmitry, and Kirill running all over the place with a hitman looking for you."

"Sorry about that, but trust me, this is a safer option."

"I'm going to be an aunt. I'm still trying to get my head around this new development."

"You need to try harder. She'll be here soon."

"I know. I'm so excited for you."

"I know you are. I wish you could find someone manly enough to not only date you but also stand up to your dad."

"I know. I don't plan on that happening until the next ice age."

Izzy snickers.

"It's late. I better let you get some sleep," I say.

"Alright, call me tomorrow."

Izzy recently left her job on Broadway as she's getting close to her due date and wants to be a full-time mother. I respect that. Besides, I'm sure the men in the family will say it's bad for business if she doesn't quit her job. But she loves Dmitry, and I know he adores her.

I dress in warm pajamas, turn off the light, and crawl into bed. I've never been exhausted from sex until tonight. It's safe to assume my bodyguards are posted on the street below, but for some reason, the hair on the back of my neck raises as I drift to sleep.

CHAPTER 5

MATTEO

Gio and I wait outside the club for my Angel to come out. When the woman of my new obsession exits, she climbs into an SUV similar to mine. It pulls away from the curb, and before we follow, I notice it's followed by an identical vehicle—a security detail.

Growing up in Sicily, I can spot a paid guard a mile away. That's because death is inevitable and a way of life. Most mafia men don't worry about it. This is not the case with New York's criminal underworld.

Here, it's as if everyone wants to live as long as possible. Either the men have more to live for, or it's a cultural difference. For now, I'm undecided.

We followed her home and discovered the building she lived in. I put Gio in charge of finding out more.

With our mission complete, we head to my place for a nightcap in the study which also serves as an office. We light our cognac-laden cigars. Gio pours two bourbons and hands me one before sitting in high-back chairs beside a gas-lit fireplace. My den has a Gaudi meets Gotham look with dark colors and Art Deco lighting. Maybe that's why I felt so comfortable in the dimly lit sex club.

Gio leans back and puts his feet up on the ottoman. "Do I need to worry about this vixen?"

"How do you know she's hot?"

"You're never with a woman who's not."

"True, I deserve that."

Gio nods solemnly. "We need Councilman Addler to support our request for a height variance."

"Yes, I'm sure there is a function where I can talk to him. He's been known to hold out on these things before. My first project has to be successful. By the way, how is my cousin, Antonio? I heard he got married."

"Yes, to a nice Irish girl, Caitlin. She was his nanny briefly," he says.

I chuckle at this—happy he's found happiness. He's my cousin, and we've been best friends since we were kids.

"His wife, Caitlin, has a serious ex-boyfriend problem like he beat the shit out of her in Ireland. As soon as she recovered, she came here to escape him."

"He followed her here," I murmur thoughtfully. I tilt my head back and stare at the ceiling, focusing on the decorative medallion around the light. It looks so fake compared to the genuine art and sculptures in Italy.

"Yes, it took time, but he's here. Last week she was at the zoo with Rocco, and the bodyguards had to beat the shit out of him to make him go away. He's an abnormally strong man, and it took three of them to subdue him. Remember last year when we had to take down that heroin dealer on the street who was just released from prison? He was off his psych meds and had superhuman strength? Antonio had to put a bullet in his head. It was like putting down a rabid animal. This guy, Finn, is like that, small but strong. He's psychotic. Antonio is going to request permission to protect his family."

"What do we know about Finn?"

"He's a low-level dealer in Ireland. I'm not sure about his connections yet. Nothing has been flagged other than his criminal record and nearly killing Caitlin."

"We need to find out and evaluate the situation. He could be someone the Irish won't miss. See if he's connected, and if he is, who we'd piss off if we eliminate him."

If he came near Angelica, I'd kill him myself. No man should ever hit a woman.

Gio takes a puff of his cigar, blows it out slowly, and nods.

"Damn, it's been a long day. I'll have Antonio do a deep dive into Wu. We'll pick him up. He can't hide forever. Not with the way Antonio can hack into the street cameras and read car plates off the bridges."

"I'll break every bone in Wu's body if he doesn't sell to me. I needed this done last week."

"I'm sorry. Antonio thought he'd come through. Do you think someone else got to him?"

"It's very plausible. But we won't know until we pull the city records to make sure he still owns the building. If he double-crossed me, I'll kill him," I say, sending a smoke ring toward the ceiling.

"So, what do you think of Madame M?"

"I like her. She's an interesting character."

"Are you going back?"

"Not if you can find out who Angelica is. She intrigues me. I feel there is more to her than meets the eye." Her clothes weren't cheap. "I wonder what she does for a living," I muse.

"I don't like this. You're thinking too much about her. If you get involved with anyone, you are putting them in danger. Especially now," Gio reminds me.

"Perhaps. I wonder what Angelica's real name is." I have to admit I'm enjoying the mystery. It beats the family curse from my father's sins. To push a woman down the stairs is inexcusable. I wouldn't care if someone took my father out over some old beef. He was always cantankerous so it wouldn't be out of the question.

That being said, there doesn't seem to be a war on the horizon. It's too quiet. I don't trust it. My father's murder was designed to avoid detection. I'm ahead of the killer because he doesn't know I'm operating in the shadows. Poison may be the weapon of choice for women, but my sister is unlikely to be the next don as she has no desire to get her hands dirty. Besides, Bianca would have to take out everyone, and she is too timid to kill a spider. The psychotic gene in the family must have skipped her.

I wonder if I will turn into a man like my father. I don't think he knew what love felt like. I may have only had crushes in my past, but I love a smooth bourbon, a flavorful cigar, and a memorable fuck. With my rock glass empty, I stub out the cigar on the cut glass ashtray and place my hands on my knees.

"This was nice. Thank you, Gio. I think I'm ready for bed."

"It's about time," Gio chuckles.

"Don't forget about the girl."

"It's always a girl that gets you in trouble. You need a woman."

"She is. She doesn't know what it's like to be with a man. Goodnight, Gio," I murmur over my shoulder as I walk under the archway. I enter the spacious living area, and it's been so long since I've been here I didn't realize how massive it is for one person and some staff members. It's worth millions.

Will Angelica like it? Why am I asking myself this question?

Gio's right. I shouldn't drag anyone into the family until I've neutralized my father's killer. I want what I want when I want it. I will have Angelica. She may fight me, but in the end, she will submit.

After a hot shower, I slip into bed as the furnace kicks on. I don't mind cold weather when I'm skiing in the Alps. That's my idea of having fun in the snow. I am not thrilled about working in the bitter cold, but that's inevitable when one lives here. Thankfully, I won't be shoveling snow or scraping ice off a frozen windshield.

Having a soft, warm woman in my bed is another reason to pursue

Angelica. She seems harmless. I've never tried a relationship before, but she needs one. Maybe I do, too. Mindless unattached fucking is all I've ever wanted until now.

I prefer to be alone. When a woman starts leaving her undies on the bedroom doorknob, it's time to say goodbye. I'm not a big fan of change. My life is my job, and no woman would be happy with my long work weeks. She'd grow bored waiting for me to come home every night. I need a woman who can entertain herself and not complain about it.

Angelica strikes me as someone like-minded. I saw something familiar in her eyes—a frozen darkness that only another lonely soul would recognize. I'll keep this a secret. There is no need for her to know who I am. It's safer this way. I might have a soft spot for her, but I can't risk losing my focus while my empire and family are under attack.

I drift off to sleep with the memory of her arched back and screams of ecstasy as she squirted on my cock. It still turns me on, and my cock hardens at the thought. I can't wait to see her again.

* * *

I awake in the morning to noises from the kitchen and the strong smell of coffee. I pull on a pair of joggers and a T-shirt and walk barefoot downstairs.

Walking into the kitchen with its white walls and blue accents, I see a familiar tall, thin Italian. "Federico!" I exclaim. He's an incredible chef, and more importantly, I trust him. He also helps as a butler and takes care of the house. He's indispensable to a man who works too much to maintain a house this size.

"Mr. Borrelli, it's a pleasure to see you again. I slept like a baby on your jet." He gives me a warm smile as he turns on the espresso machine. "Thank you for bringing me with you."

"You know me and my routine. Besides, I don't have time to eat at the restaurant daily. I work late most nights. I love pasta, but once in a while, I crave a thick rib-eye steak cooked medium rare, of course. I don't have to tell you that overcooking meat ruins it."

"That it does. Please have a seat. I made hard-boiled eggs, buttered toast, and Italian bacon," he says, setting my breakfast on a table overlooking the massive lawn covered with snow.

In the middle of the spacious kitchen, pots and pans with copper bottoms hang from a wooden rack. He uses these to prepare five-star meals.

"I'm so glad you're here. Otherwise, I'd starve." I crack the egg and slide the shell off easily. I cut the eggs in half and drizzle olive oil over them before adding a dash of salt and pepper. I take a bite, close my eyes, and savor the flavor.

"I'm glad you like it," he replies, setting a cup of hot espresso beside my plate.

These are expensive comforts that compensate for my limited social life. I try to avoid the requisite social events where some elected official always has a hand out for a campaign contribution. It's an old boys' club if I ever saw one.

Here, I thought Italy had the lock on keeping women out of business and politics. We have rules over a hundred years old designed to keep wives at home. These same rules are often used in divorces to screw wives out of money.

I've learned that despite increased legislation for women's rights, women in Italy had more power before gaining the vote. It makes no sense. Men still earn more than women for the same work, and women who know how to play the game are rewarded with pay increases that aren't legal in government jobs meant to keep everyone equal.

Graft is everywhere. After years of experience in my father's operation, I've come to the conclusion that state government and big businesses are more corrupt than the mafia. At least I come at my enemies head-on. I'm too honest and direct for my own good. I need to finesse more and talk less. Politics is politicking, whether it's in government or big business. Everyone in these circles understands the main rule for survival is to take what you want or die slowly.

The competition today is like never before.

Right now, I have no idea who will attempt to usurp my position. If I'm to survive, I have to be more devious than my enemy. If my enemy is one or more of my uncles, they will go behind my back to undermine me and create dissension in the ranks.

Takeovers are never done single-handedly. No, power has to be taken, and their subordinates will support them. The question is, who wants me dead?

CHAPTER 6

ALENA

I wake up, and my first thought is about Mr. Grey.

Who is that sexy man who made my toes curl?

I curse him as I'm suffering from an orgasm hangover. My libido wants more, and my pussy is damp just thinking about him and the way he played my body like a fiddle last night.

I don't know the name of the man who gave me the greatest fuck of my life. He's handsome with a chiseled chin and eyes as dark as melted chocolate in a lava cake. I stand and pick up the bustier off my bedroom floor. I lift it to my nose and smell a cigar. It's not an ordinary cigar, but I wouldn't expect anything less from a man with expensive clothes and an Italian accent. I sniff my clothing again to pinpoint the odor. A light bulb goes off.

It's cognac.

He likes tobacco leaves dipped in cognac and rolled into a cigar. I've been around enough cigars to know these are special.

I didn't recognize him, but I'm not shocked in a city with millions of people. I know most of the elite in the city who travel in our circles, but they have Russian accents or are Americans. The man has an Italian accent that comes and goes when he speaks English. Italian is his first language, but his English is perfect. I love men with accents. I wonder why our paths haven't crossed before.

I pick up the rest of my outfit and dump it in the hamper for the laundromat. I enjoy a long hot shower. Damn it. I'm horny. As hot water pounds my shoulders, I run my hands over my breasts and grab myself. I think of his sultry eyes and deep-throated voice when he ordered me to turn over.

Fuck it was hot. He's hot.

I grab the showerhead that is affixed to the wall, lift it, and hold it to spray water over my breasts. I slide two fingers over my clit and circle them over and over until my clit hardens. Oh, fuck me. I move my hips ever so slightly. I feel the beginning of an orgasm. I shudder, and tingling sensations run up my back as I come. Placing my hand on the shower wall to maintain balance, I gasp as thoughts of him make me come again. My legs are weak.

After I rinse off and step out of the shower, I grab a rolled towel off the rack. I dry myself off and wrap the towel around my waist before I stand in front of the granite vanity. I look at my reflection in the bathroom mirror. I glow. It's that after-sex glow. I'm sure it's from last night. Sex toys are great, but they aren't a substitution, especially when he has a massive dick and knows how to use it. The way he took me so completely makes me want to break the house rules.

But how will I find him?

And if I find him, what am I going to say? I want another hookup? I can't let him know I like him. I'm sure he's a man with women who willingly give themselves to him, and I'm sure he takes advantage of zero commitment.

What if he's married?

That would be the reason for the anonymity. It's possible I exchanged sex with a stranger, and now he's lost to me. Madame M will never disclose personal information. But I'd like to pick her brain about what they discussed while drinking at the bar.

I apply my facial cream and wrestle with whether to go back to the club to see if he's there or wait until he's bored with the women there and let him find me. I finish with my makeup and stand. I take myself in. He's right. I turn heads when I walk into a room, but I don't take it seriously. My father would demand nothing less from me.

I'm meeting Izzy for brunch in an hour. I will leave early as I no longer have a personal guard to drive me. My father will insist on one of his men driving me when it's late or a special event. I could call a driver, but I decided I would walk today. The restaurant is nearby, and it's a nice day.

I grab my phone on the nightstand and head to my closet to pick an outfit. My sick closet and everything in it screams money. I'm no longer self-conscious about it, knowing that Izzy has the same kick-ass wardrobe and shoe collection. Now that she's part of the family—she went from rags to riches and has an enviable family lineage.

I slip into a belted Fendi mini dress resembling a trench coat, step into my favorite black boot knee-high boots, and zip them. Grabbing my purse and coat from last night, I leave my apartment.

As I walk to the restaurant, appropriately named The Brunchery, the crisp winter air fills my lungs and clears my head. I check my peripheral vision to make sure no one is following me. I'm not overly concerned, but my Spidey senses tell me I'm being watched. I cross a bridge that provides a good vantage point and stop to look around the park, pretending to take in the scenery. I resume my walk, seeing nothing unusual and nobody lurking in the shadows.

The leaves smell of fall, reminding me of the holidays ahead and that I'll be alone for them—again. When I arrive at The Brunchery, I'm relieved to see Izzy waiting outside.

It's only now that my senses fire. My Spidey sense tells me I'm being watched. I move to overlook the park as a pretense to see if I can find any strangers lurking around. Nothing happens. It must be the past catching up to me. I resume my walk and am relieved when Izzy is waiting outside because we have a reservation.

"Izzy," I call her with relief in my voice.

"Alena," she hugs me, and we enter the establishment to be seated.

The hostess leads us to a bistro table for two near the windows. As I drape my coat over the back of my chair, I wonder if the table will be big enough to hold both plates. The server arrives to take our drink order. Izzy asks for water with lemon, and I order a mimosa.

"Izzy," I lean over the small table as she struggles to fit with her pregnant belly. "I'm into the mystery man. I have no idea who he is. What do I do?"

"I have no clue. Do you want Dmitry to find out? Why not ask Kirill?"

"He likes me. I can't use my best friend to hunt down the man I want to fuck me until I can no longer walk."

"Oh, so it's like that?" Her eyes grow wide. She gives me a reassuring smile. "How do you know he won't find you?"

"Doubtful. Hence, anonymous sex club," I whisper before the waitress reappears. Izzy orders the daily gyro omelet special.

"I'll take the New York Strip omelet, tomatoes, no potatoes, and another mimosa, please."

"Alena, are you sure? You're used to straight vodka, but it's early, and there's tons of sugar in the orange juice."

I'm not pencil-thin, it's true. I'm Russian, and like many Russian women, I'm big-boned and big-breasted. If a man is looking for a woman with a ballerina body, I'm not it. My ass could be bigger and my hands smaller, but I make the best of it. I wear clothes that draw attention to my cleavage, but the look is not slutty.

My butt is too small for a woman with huge breasts, but I've learned to cope with disappointments. I'm not waif-like, so if a man wants a petite woman, I'm not it. I'm not tall, and I don't think my fingers are pretty at all. I flip my hair straightened hair over my shoulder. I'm lucky I don't have to fuss with it much to make it look professional.

"It's fine. I'm not developing a drinking habit," I reassure her. "Although, there is something I might be addicted to..."

Izzy giggles. "I know. So, we're back to talking about Mr. Grey."

"I can't get him out of my head. This is insane," I say as I finish the mimosa before the second one arrives. "I don't know how to get him out of my head," I say as my head sinks into my hands. "Of all the men I wished I had met over the years, I finally found one who knows what he's doing, and he's gone."

"You could go back to the club."

"I'd look desperate. He impresses me as a man who's all business. I'm sure he doesn't want attachment. I don't blame him, but if I continue to settle for hookups, I might never get married. It doesn't help that Dad is dragging his feet when it comes to finding me a husband. He would let me pick my own."

"Yeah, lately, everyone is now waiting to see when my father will turn the empire over to Dmitry."

"So, my father isn't the only one in a wait-and-see approach?"

"Not at all. Don't get worked up over it. It's just business. There's always a bit of uncertainty before the next don takes over. Hopefully, it won't take my father's dying before my husband will take over as the new don."

"Good to know."

Izzy nods and sips her water as our food is delivered.

"So, how are you feeling?"

"Amazing. However, pregnancy is getting old. Soon, I won't be able to reach my feet," she replies, rubbing her belly.

"You must be so excited," I squeal with happiness. My best friend is in love with her husband, and they are perfect for each other. Dmitry's gruff, take-charge demeanor softens when Izzy enters the room. She's his princess.

"I am. I didn't expect to be a mother so young, but my mom had me young, too. I am so happy I found my father. It's given me so much to be grateful for."

"Yeah, like surviving the hunt of being a deer in winter," I reply sarcastically.

"Yeah, there's that. I try not to think about it. How are you doing with your panic attacks?"

I shrug. "As well as can be expected, I guess."

"Do you have your resume? I mean, are you going to join the workforce?"

"Yes," I emphasize the "y." "It's a great idea to have my independence nailed down before I get married, right?"

"Great. I like this newfound independence to seize the day that doesn't involve men." Izzy nibbles at her omelet and fruit.

"It's good to try on your own before you call in favors," Izzy says, speaking like the mafia-savvy wife she's become. Funny, if anyone should know how the mafia life works, it should have been me.

Today, I realize too late that I should have taken more notes growing up with my father as the don's advisor. I spent my time rebelling through men. I should have been sharpening my wits about how the mafia men finesse and manipulate others to get what they want. Those are the skills I need to compete in the business world.

Art, music, and modeling are all cutthroat businesses. I'm used to being taken care of and took it for granted. Now, I realize how fierce the competition will be. I feel inadequate and ill-prepared for the quest I'm about to undertake.

Sex has made me insanely hungry, and I have no problem finishing everything on my plate. Izzy insists on picking up the check. I thank her and toss back the last of my mimosa before we leave.

"Izzy, what did it feel like when you were being followed?"

"Creepy." She pulls her fur-trimmed hood over her fluffy jacket that looks like a white shag rug, and I love it.

I shrug into my long coat.

"I'll drive you home," Izzy says as her driver approaches the curb.

"There's no need. It's just my imagination and nothing to worry about," I argue.

"Get in the car. This is not negotiable. If we learned anything this past year, it's to trust our instincts," she says in a maternal tone that I can't argue with. Damn, she already has her mothering voice down, and the baby girl hasn't even arrived!

She gets in first and slides over. Then I get in next to her.

"Kirill, I didn't know you drove," I say, surprised to see him.

"It seems it's the only way I get to see you now that you have the condo to yourself."

He's not kidding. It's so true. I feel vulnerable inviting a man into my condo, so I choose to meet people out. Besides, it gives me an excuse to get out. Without school or a job, I get bored staring at four walls. It gets so bad that I exercise to pass the time. I do lunges, combine Pilates and yoga during TV commercials, and throw in a few sit-ups. I have a membership at the yoga studio around the corner from me. I just need to walk there and use it. I tend to work out harder if I have someone to compete with.

"What's up, Kirill? I'm sorry. I've been preoccupied with the marriage that has been put on hold. And now, I've been told to get a job."

He laughs. "You're kidding."

"No, it's not funny. Besides, I find it empowering," I reply, defending my right to work. I never thought it would happen, but who knows? Maybe I'll like it and make new friends.

"Sure, you do. All this from the woman who's centered her life around making daddy happy," he teases.

"Seeing as how you are here, what do you know? Anything going on?"

"Nothing I can talk about, and you know that," he quips as he maneuvers the G-Wagon through bumper-to-bumper traffic.

"Right. You know what, Kirill? I need a suit for interviews. Can you drop me at the Chanel store?"

"Is that okay with you, Mrs. Volkov?" Kirill asks, glancing at her reflection in the rearview mirror.

"You know it's Izzy to you," she replies as she reaches out and tussles his hair like he's a teenager and not a man approaching thirty.

"Yes, it's fine. But I have to get home after that. I'm sure I'll be ready for a nap. Growing a human inside requires tons of sleep."

I can't wait to find out about that personally. However, I have no inclination to give my body to a tiny human just yet. I need to use my education and start a career.

"I would have never finished school without you," I tap Izzy's leg affectionately. "You made me stick it out."

Kirill pulls up in front of Chanel and turns to say, "Call me, Alena. I mean it. We can get drinks at the club."

Yeah, and have a panic attack over the bar where Dmitry stabbed a hitman? Maybe it will help to erase the traumas if I face them head-on and see if I can exercise the demons.

I leave the store and realize I forgot to call my driver.

Shit.

Just then, a limousine stops in front of me. A tinted window in the back glides down.

"Do you need a lift?"

Even though I can't see him, I know that voice. Chills run up my spine. I lean down, and of course, it's the man from last night.

"If it's not an imposition," I answer casually. I mean, we've already had sex. How dangerous could it be? Besides, we're not alone. He has a driver, like everyone with money here. I can't blame them. It's the easiest way to navigate the city traffic, allowing passengers time to multitask. When you're making hundreds of dollars an hour, every minute adds another zero to the bank account.

The driver, a handsome middle-aged man in his forties, collects my bags and the zippered cloth travel bag. He opens the door for me, and I slide in as Mr. Grey slides over to make room.

"You're shocked," he says. His whiskey voice makes me wet with the warmth, and it resonates long after he finishes speaking.

"Surprised. It's difficult to shock me," I state. I'm self-conscious that I might be oversharing.

"I find that difficult to believe. You seem quite competent."

I'm blushing as if I've had too much alcohol. I feel the warmth on my face. I hate it when that happens.

"What are you doing here?"

"I have to shop, don't I?"

He wasn't in the store. *Has he been following me?* I would have felt his presence if he was that close. I wonder how he found me. Judging from his impeccable suit that looks far more expensive than anything my father wears, he has enough money to pay for information.

"Have you spoken to Madame M?"

"No, the fact we're both here is pure coincidence. Where can my driver take you?"

"Are you not coming?" My eyes beg the question.

"Relax, I won't leave you alone with him. I'm a possessive man, and I don't share."

I don't even know where to begin with that declaration. But what I do know is that I want him to fuck me, and now.

CHAPTER 7

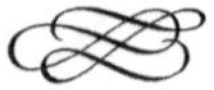

MATTEO

I want to say it was a coincidence that Alena and I happened to meet, but I'm too calculating. I leave very little up to chance.

"Are we on a first-name basis yet, Mr. Grey?" She flirts.

"Not yet. But soon." I know not knowing my real name drives her crazy, but I like the mystique of it.

"A true man of mystery," she says with a smile and lights up the dark interior of the limo. It's a dreary day filled with gray skies.

I push a button, and the one-way glass between us and Gio closes. I wasn't prepared for her to sit so close to me in the warm, confined space. She smells fresh and sweet.

"Why don't you tell me what's on your mind, Angelica?" I refrain from smiling. I'm not overly affectionate with women I fuck.

"It's your limo," she states, evading the question.

"So it is," I reply before I lean down and claim her red lips. They are soft, like pillows.

She eagerly meets my increasing demand on her lips, and her arms snake around my neck. I loosen my tie before I pull her into my broad chest. I inhale her soft, scented perfume as I run my hand through her long hair. Her lips are sublime, and my cock grows hard.

She rubs over the zipper that contains my stallion and moans softly as I suck on her neck.

I should be dealing with Mr. Wu, but I can't resist my desire to be with her. I like the name Angelica, but I can't help but wonder what her legal name is. One of my guys is gathering intel on her, so her real name is forthcoming.

"What will it be, Angel?" I ask. "I have a meeting to attend. I don't have a lot of time."

She unzips my pants, and my cock salutes her. She helps me push down my boxers and sinks to her knees on the limo floor. Wrapping her manicured red nails around my cock, she strokes the shaft and takes my tip in her mouth.

Fuck! Her lips are gorgeous, and I stare, fascinated by this well-dressed socialite with a sex drive. I find her thrilling.

"That feels so good. I love watching you fuck me with your gorgeous lips," I say, placing my hand on her head. I want to toss her like a rag doll and explore her body.

I'm oblivious to the limo starting or stopping in traffic. Time has no meaning. I'm experiencing the most exquisite euphoria, surpassed only by her warm pussy milking me last night.

Her mouth moves expertly, sucking my balls and filling her throat with my cock. I groan and fist her thick hair.

I'm on the verge of coming.

"Stop," I order her.

Her lips freeze on my cock. It takes all my willpower not to explode.

I place my hands on her shapely sides and lift her off the floorboards.

"I want to fuck you now."

"You have a meeting."

"Fuck the meeting. I have to have you," I reply. I begin to undress her, peeling off layers of clothing. Her hands are on my suit, pushing my jacket off my shoulders. I shrug out of my jacket and fling it on the seat across from us.

"You're wearing too much," I complain.

"Will people see us?" she asks, shrugging out of her coat.

"Do you care?"

"Not really," she murmurs between kisses on my neck. I pull my thin T-shirt over my head and toss it. Her nails gently rake over my back before she moves a hand to caress my face. I unbutton her blouse and tug it off. I unhook her bra, and her boobs spring forth like a fountain of youth. I promptly take a nipple between my teeth, giving her a nip that makes her squeal. I massage her boobs as I repeatedly flick a thumb over her pert nipples.

Her blue eyes remind me of the azure water off Italy's coast. I'm sinking into them as I pull her skirt up and sink two fingers into her pussy.

"You're wet for me," I murmur against her cheek. My mouth descends on hers, ravaging her plump lips. She meets me with equal intensity and her breathing quickens. I move my fingers in and out of her pussy while rubbing her nub with my thumb.

"Ah," she moans, pulling her lips away from me as she takes a breath.

"Do you like this?"

"Hmm."

"What does my Angel want?"

"I want you to fuck me."

I suck on her breasts and then move to her hard nipple. The car is warm. I love the fact her body responds to me without having to touch her. She was dripping for me the minute our eyes met.

I can't point fingers. My cock was hard the minute she stepped out of the store.

"I don't have a condom," I say. "I'm clean."

"I'm on the pill."

I've always practiced safe sex and worn condoms. It's my way to avoid pregnancy and getting trapped in a marriage. With Angelica, my need to feel her skin on my skin without protection supersedes precaution. I'm so excited my cock is ready to explode.

I pull my fingers out and place them in her partially open mouth. She sucks on them, and it's sexy as hell.

I position her so she's flat on the seat. Her boobs are on full display. With one foot planted on the floor and the other foot on the seat, I angle myself over her and line up my cock with her pink pussy. I gently slide into her and feel every muscle squeeze around me. God, she's tight.

Using my leg as leverage, I thrust deeper. She grabs at the door and back of the seat to brace herself, but it's useless. There's nothing to grab. Instead, she clings to my shoulders. Her nails digging into my skin as I fuck her hard and harder.

Her hands clamp onto my shoulders, and her nails are leveraged as I continue to thrust into her. She moves over the slippery leather. I continue to pound her with my huge cock. She wails, making a loud and extended "Ahs." She writhes under me as she climaxes. Her body consumes me. Her pussy clenches around my cock. When she's finished with one last shudder, she opens her eyes. I meet her gaze. I explode, filling her with my seed.

I collapse, careful not to put all my weight on her. My legs are shot. Once I've regained my breath, I lean backward and grab white square napkins from the bar. I gently clean her and dispose of the napkins.

She pulls her skirt down and straightens herself, looking for her clothing.

"Where can I take you?" I ask.

"Out to dinner."

I look at her in question, contemplating a date. She gives me an impish smile that turns me inside out.

"That would mean we'd no longer have hot, meaningless sex," I respond.

"Don't you just hate that?" she replies as she quickly dresses, and I search for my shirt.

"I'd hate for you to see who I really am. I might be different at night."

"Unless you're a vampire, I doubt it."

I chuckle.

"That's an intriguing offer—dinner. I'll consider it."

"Great. You can drop me off at 59th Street."

"I can drop you off at your place," I offer. I know where she lives. But that would be presumptuous of me to intrude on her perceived anonymity.

"And ruin chance encounters?"

"You have a point."

Angelica dons her coat and makes herself presentable as I speak to Gio through the open window and give him instructions.

Gio pulls to the side of the road, opens the door facing the sidewalk, and retrieves the bags from the trunk.

"Thank you for the lift," she says, thanking my driver.

"No problem at all," Gio says before returning to the driver's seat.

I stick my head out the window.

"What about me?"

She leans down and kisses my lips. It's a kiss that could easily lead to round two.

"Behave yourself," she says before she turns on her boot heels and walks away.

"Damn, that's cold," I murmur to Gio.

"It's safer this way. Besides, we need to get to Wu," he says.

"Right. Let's go. Any word on her real name?"

"I'll tell you as soon as I find out."

It takes thirty minutes to get to the building, where Antonio has Mr. Wu strapped to a chair. He's been worked over, yet he's determined to defy me.

"Mr. Wu. You're being disrespectful." I take off my suit jacket and roll up the sleeves on my shirt.

I punch him in the gut.

"Who owns your property?"

"I not tell you," he replies in broken English before spitting in my face.

"That's the last time you get to do that." I look to Antonio.

"It appears his property has been signed over to a shell corporation. However, we've loosely linked it to the Sidovo family over the years."

"The Russians?" I exclaim. "How the fuck did that happen?" I glare at Antonio. Love made him weak. He lost his focus. He should have killed Wu before Christmas.

Wu is chuckling.

"I'm sorry, Matteo. We had him under surveillance and didn't pick up any meeting with our rivals."

I extend my hand. Antonio places a 9mm in it.

"I hope you hid your family well, or I'll kill them all," I say, enjoying the terrified look on his face before I squeeze the trigger.

"You didn't want to torture him?" Gio asks.

"He's been through more torture than I could ever deliver. Did you see the scars on his hands and arms? He most likely escaped a work camp as a child in China. They survived on will alone. You're talking about communist work camps," I say.

I pick up a rag from the floor, wipe my prints off the gun, and hand it to Antonio. "Clean this shit up, and don't be lazy. Trouble is coming, and I need you to be alert, or it will cost us our lives. Do I need to be concerned about your future performance?"

"No, sir. I'll make sure I don't make any more mistakes," Antonio says.

His father, Carlo, is the youngest of my father's brothers. He's the only uncle I like. I have to keep an eye on Antonio and his old man. Art of War—keep your friends close, your enemies closer. Looks like we're going to be fucking—kissing cousins.

I've considered Carlo the least threatening as he was mothered more than the others and only had slight infractions with the family. He likes to bet but has the lock on running numbers, like a lottery and illegal betting. He runs numbers in his head and has a photographic memory, so nothing is written down. With no paper trail, everything he does is deniable.

In essence, we have a walking money machine. He knows when to lay off bets and knows every client on the island. He maintains a low profile and causes me no grief—or so I assume.

Have things changed?

I turn to Gio.

"What the fuck? How did the Russians find out what we were buying? It's a huge fucking city. It's an attempt by someone to make me look bad." This building is under construction, and I pass a fold-up chair as we leave. I kick a random folding chair in anger. It sails through the chilly air only to crash with the sounds of cheap metal to console me.

"We'll figure it out. We always do. Wu might have been fucking you over. He knows anyone connected would pay over what it's worth to fuck you. It could have been someone who followed your old man. Maybe someone overheard him, or one of your uncles sold us out."

"You're right. We're where we are now. I need to do damage control."

My phone rings. It's a guard tasked with Angelica.

"I have information for you. Her name is Alena Pasnov. She's Russian. Her father is the consigliere to Alexsei Sidovo—of the Russian bratva."

"Thank you, Leo. You've been most helpful."

I turn to Gio.

"I think I found a way to even things with the Russians."

My lips curl into a rare smile. Not only is Alena someone, but she will be my someone, and it will keep her father in line. Men who piss me off have a debt to pay.

CHAPTER 8

ALENA

I'm breathless by the time I make it into my condo. How did Mr. Grey know where I was? Do men hang out in the parking lot of a woman's designer store to wait for them? No man does that unless he wants points or, realistically—sex. Unless he has the makings of a stalker.

Do I believe in coincidence?

No. The fact that my mystery man knew where I could be found is a concern. However, I also find it thrilling. If he's following me, then he likes me. We definitely have the hots for each other. I'm just not sure it will evolve into anything more than steamy sex.

I should call my father. I've always called him when something felt off. But he would put me under house arrest to keep me safe. I'm sure I'm overreacting.

Izzy is right. I need to call Kirill. He is a trusted friend, and he can be discreet. There's not much information I can provide him. The limo is probably leased, and I was too busy fucking Mr. Grey to get the license plate.

I drop my shopping bags inside the condo and toss my coat on the couch.

Perhaps Madame M's computer can be hacked. She must own one to keep records of all the patrons of the sex club. She loves the roaring '20s, but certainly, she's using the 21st century to run her business—I hope.

Kirill is a great hacker. Unfortunately, Tito is gone after Don's wife bought his loyalty. Kirill knows all the players inside the bratva. He also has access to the legit businesses and players we exploit for our gain. It could be a councilman we need to vote for a contract to go through, or the favor might be as simple as a variance on a building. We always need those to add additional floors to an apartment complex or office building. Sometimes, the family needs an invitation to a social function that allows my father, or the Don, to have access to a judge we need to get a legal case dropped or deliver a bribe.

These wheels need to stay greased to make our organization function. I'm not privy to the nitty-gritty details of how it gets accomplished. As Mom always says, the less we know, the safer we will be.

But is that true? The Don had to execute his wife over her betrayal to overthrow him. I cringe to think of what it's like being married to anyone who would screw over their partner so ruthlessly.

I text Kirill and he agrees to meet for drinks later. He's picking me up in his new sports car. I'm not surprised. He's such a showboat. If he could pick his occupation, he'd choose to be a Formula 1 race car driver.

I undress, putting my boots on the closet shelf. I walk to the bathroom to take a shower. As I pass the mirror over the sink, I notice hickeys on my neck.

I should be pissed that he marred my alabaster skin but instead I'm glad to have the bruises as a visual reminder of his passion. It means he's real, even if I don't know who he is. Besides, it's not every day a woman gets fucked by the most fuckable man in the city. Sex in a limo was a first for me, and the thrill of being caught added to the excitement.

We've carried the anonymous charade off effortlessly at the sex club. But what was fun in the beginning is now wearing on me. Who is this mystery man, and why is it such a mystery? He could be nobody. He could be somebody.

I'm not sure what to think of Mr. Grey. What was he referring to when he mentioned I might not like him at night? Is he a monster? The only monster I can think of is blue and in a children's movie that's as old as me.

I turn on the water and undress while I wait for it to warm. Thank goodness my dad put in an expensive heat-on-demand unit when he remodeled this unit for me. In older buildings like this, getting hot water in winter can take forever.

The fragrance of my mystery man clings to my blouse, and after one sniff, I toss my clothes into the hamper. I take my time washing myself in the shower before I realize I need to send out resumes. I sent a draft of my resume to an acquaintance of my mother, who works in human resources. She emailed me suggestions on how to improve it. I'm not great at finessing sentences. In my opinion, resumes make you sound great and provide very little information.

Resumes are like political speeches. The politician will talk for ten minutes and say nothing. I call it word salad. I wouldn't know how to converse without stating my opinion. It's unnatural that so many people talk about things that won't matter in a few years. Meanwhile, the most important questions that will shape our world for the next ten years are the ones that are never asked or discussed.

I dry myself off and wear a comfy jogger that my mom gifted to me for Christmas. It feels like silk, and the dark blue accentuates my eyes.

I texted Izzy and thanked her for brunch. I also informed her I got home okay after banging the mystery man in his limo.

My phone rings immediately.

"Yes?" I tease her.

"You just hooked up with him again?" Izzy squeals excitedly.

"Yes, I did. He picked me up in a limo after I finished shopping, and his driver drove us around the city while we fucked and sucked in the back."

"How did he even find you? I mean, no one knew you were shopping at Chanel. I think you need a guard to keep you safe."

"You mean to cock block me? No way. I'm not doing anything to scare him off. It's the most incredible sex of my life."

"Promise me you'll put Kirill on it today, or I'll tell Dmitry."

"Relax. I'm meeting Kirill tonight for drinks at the club. I'm sure he'll get to the bottom of it."

Maybe the limo was caught on a surveillance camera, and Kirill can get the license plate number. That would make it easy for him to track down his true identity.

On the other hand, I doubt someone hiding their identity is riding around in limos that can be traced back to his real name. Why is he still playing the game? I'm nobody important in the hierarchy of the bratva.

"True, but please be safe. I worry about you."

"I will. I gotta go work on my resume, so wish me luck."

"Luck," she says before saying goodbye and hanging up.

I open my state-of-the-art electronic device Dad bought me for college. It has all the design software I needed for college. If I get a job and need to work at home, I am equipped to do it. Most designer jobs have teams who share ideas, and each person gets a portion of the workload to find what needs to be purchased.

In college, we spent a night at an Airbnb to get the area's vibe. Then, we worked together to make the colors neutral so the paint on the walls wouldn't annoy anyone. It also makes maintenance easy. We throw in a few pillows that are the same color, repeating it a minimum of three times to tie in the color throughout the rooms, and voilà, it's finished.

That's how it worked in fashion school. I'm conflicted about working with a team because group dynamics can be cutthroat. I had to take some business classes in school. I found the students were mean and withheld assignments from me. Those students had the attitude that they knew everything, and no group discussions were held as outlined in the syllabus. Not only was I cut out of that loop, but emails with my portion of the assignment never made it to my inbox.

To my horror, the group petitioned the teacher to remove me from the group for nonparticipation. I spoke to the teacher, who wasn't sympathetic. I realized all of this two weeks before a website had to be live for the professor to grade it. I took matters into my own hands and hired a web designer to outdo these petty classmates. I handed in the written paper with a grad student's help and got an A in the class.

I could have done without the drama, but I'll make the impossible possible when push comes to shove.

With my resume, I searched online for job openings. I found cabinet sales, window treatment sales, and furniture. Ugh. There is no way I'll be a floor salesperson. How is that even related to design? I'm about to give up when I see an interior design assistant opening.

The job requirements are for conceptualizing design projects, scheduling oversight, and overseeing the delivery of goods and installations as required.

I'm qualified, and the pay is adequate. I have very little experience, but I'm not asking for a lead position. The company's name, Indio Designs, sounds legitimate, and their location is nearby. I filled out the application, attached my resume, and clicked the submit button. I admit my odds of success aren't good. I have no work experience outside my internship. The position will likely go to some seasoned professional.

I have time to kill before I meet Kirill, so I pull on yoga pants and a T-shirt and head to the yoga studio. The weather outside is brisk but warm enough to walk to the studio with my yoga mat tucked under my arm and my gym bag holding my wallet, phone, and towel slung over my shoulder.

Just my luck, when I get to the studio, they're in between yoga classes, so I wind up waiting for the next class. It seems I spend my life waiting in lines or waiting for something to happen.

The prior class finally finished and rushed out of the room, and those of us waiting politely entered the stuffy studio. The wooden floor is shiny, and floor fans are blowing the air because many bodies moving around have warmed the room.

I pick a spot and pull the yoga mat from my shoulder. I unroll it before I walk to the cubby to grab blocks and the straps needed for stretching.

Once everyone is situated, the instructor begins. I focus on my breathing and watch others in the class to make sure my form is correct. However, as much as I try to concentrate, the dark eyes of my lover aren't far from my thoughts.

I glance around the room briefly when the woman next to me puts herself into a headstand from the pose we're in. Shit, that's impressive. She makes it look effortless. If I tried that, I'm sure I'd break my neck. After forty-five minutes, I'm sweating, and class comes to an end. I wipe the sweat off my brow with my small towel, wrap up my mat, and hit the water cooler with paper cups on my way out, grabbing my coat off the peg.

When I get home, I have nothing better to do, so I cook. I fry up ground sausage and add herbs and old wine to the red sauce in a pot. I sprinkle herbs from the cabinet before pulling out mozzarella cheese, ricotta, and no-boil noodles. The sauce simmers for hours, and I breathe in the aroma of herbs that fills the air.

I curl up to watch an older movie that Izzy and I love, and then it's time to put the lasagna together before I slide it into the oven. I'm never sure how long to cook this dish, but I assume when the noodles are soft —it's edible.

I checked my emails out of curiosity and to my surprise, Indigo Designs replied. They request an interview and want to know if I'm available tomorrow. I replied yes, and they sent me a location with a room number.

I'm not getting my hopes up. I'm sure there will be fifty people, and it will take a month or more for them to decide who the lucky winner will be. Huge companies are fat cats, and they play with job applicants like they are catnip.

* * *

It's eleven at night by the time I take a cab to the club where Kirill is meeting me. The club is owned by the Bratva and since it's relatively new, it's always busy. Tonight will be no exception. I hear the heavy bass before I even reach the VIP door. I enter the code and open the door to a blast of dance music. My eardrums hate me. The DJ is on the microphone yelling for the crowd to get on the dance floor.

I spot Kirill immediately. He's dressed in a dark suit.

"Kirill," I call, throwing my arms around his neck. "You're too official."

"Tell me about it." He hugs me, and when he pulls back, his hands are still on my arms. He looks me over, and he smiles. "You're looking very official."

"Tell me about it." He hugs me, and his hands are still on my arms when he pulls back. He looks me over, smiling. "You clean up well."

I shouldn't have worn such a skimpy dress, but I would have looked out of place otherwise.

"Well, thank you," I reply, as he places my hand in the crook of his elbow and escorts me to a VIP table away from all the noise from the dance floor.

"How is the job search going?"

"I have an interview tomorrow. It's not far from the condo. Most of the jobs out there are shit, like, low-level sales positions. I'm no sales-person," I complain.

"No, you are not. You should be a model. Look around you. The men are staring at you as if you're the only woman in the room," he says.

I glance around the room and blush. "Men are staring, but not because they want me. They probably see me sitting in VIP and wonder who I am. Or they do know who my father is."

The bouncers, servers, and bartenders all work for the families. Knowing who butters their bread keeps them from reporting drug activity in the club. Once the DJ starts, the cover charge to enter is collected in cash only.

"Don't be so sure about that. There are plenty of men here who have no clue who you are. So, what's so important we had to meet? Not that I'm complaining," he teases.

Kirill has always been direct. I'm sure my father loves this about him. There is no beating around the bush with him. Russians are usually all business and don't bother sugar-coating their answers. Their manner of speaking is very primal.

"No, and you're not to tell him. Don't be angry, but I don't know his name."

Kirill slams his fist down on the table and curses in Russian.

Shit. I quickly stand and grab the waitress and order a bottle of Vodka.

"Relax, the bouncers will be here if you continue to act like this," I say, tugging at his arm.

He quietly seethes as the waitress returns with vodka and sets two glasses on the table. I twist off the cap and pour for us, sliding one to him.

"Drink," I demand.

He tosses it back, and he pours another.

"Your father will have my hide. You are supposed to be behaving now that we've taken your guards off you. What the fuck are you doing? Where did you meet him?"

"At Madame M's sex club, the penthouse."

"That really exists?" He all but chokes on his third shot of vodka.

"Yes," I sheepishly answer, embarrassed to have my casual sex life exposed. I feel naked and, even worse, vulnerable. I despise vulnerability. "I'm not proud of my behavior, but let me explain. I don't know his name because the club requires us to use fake names. But I like this man, and I wanna find out who he is."

"And you're still fucking him?" It's more of a statement than a question.

"Yes." My shoulders slump in defeat. His sharp eyes study me. I hold my breath and wait for him to criticize my risky behavior. Instead, his eyes fill with disappointment. Ugh. This was a bad idea. I should have asked someone else who doesn't care about me. I can't handle his judgment.

"Sorry to sound harsh. I'm not surprised you go to sex clubs. I just don't understand it when you could have me 24/7."

"You know why," I reply. "It would fuck up our friendship."

"I know, I know," he says and rubs his hand over his thick black hair. "You're probably right. If you were mine, I wouldn't let you out of my sight."

"Yeah, I know, you are extremely possessive. What mafioso man isn't?" I chuckle.

"That goes without saying. Any man who is near you feels the same way. But if this man hurts you, I'll kill him with my bare hands."

"He hasn't," I assure him. "It's a rule at the club that we remain anonymous, but I have a feeling he figured out who I am. I mean, it's not that difficult. All he has to do is follow me home. It's not like I'm in witness protection," I shrug. "Who am I kidding? Even those guys get whacked eventually."

"I'm calling Dima. He will guard and follow you so we can gather intel the next time you meet this guy."

"Fine."

"Fine? You aren't fighting this?"

"My will to find out who he is supersedes my willpower for privacy, so for the foreseeable time being, I'm not going to fight you on this. But don't tell my father," I warn.

"Got you," he replies as he pours more vodka. We clink our glasses together, and I toss back my second shot.

"Now that we're done with business, how have you been?" I ask.

"Busy with stuff, you know."

"I heard my father being irate this week. What the hell is that about?"

"He's making deals, and we had an issue. It's all been settled. I'm sure he'll return to his cold and indifferent self the next time you see him."

"I love you, Kirill. You understand me, and you definitely have my father figured out."

"Maybe, maybe not. But for now, everything is good except for you living dangerously and meeting up with strangers we haven't vetted. We're not at war, but that can change without warning." He sets his glass on the table with a thunk. He grips the glass tightly while he gives me a stern look. "Please, don't do this alone again. Let Dima know next time you go on a mission of self-destruction."

I nod.

Kirill knows me well, and he's right. My meaningless hook-ups feed the hole of darkness in me. I proceeded to defy my family by not having a guard and doing whatever the fuck I wanted with no thought about possible consequences. I know one day—this will catch up to me.

CHAPTER 9

MATTEO

I toss Angelica's dossier on my desk and collapse into the well-worn leather chair. I lean back with my fingers laced behind my head, satisfied that whoever sold me out didn't plan on us having a chance encounter. If it was a one-time fuck, I might never have known she's a precious gem, a gem that belongs to my enemy, a gem that will soon be mine.

He took what was mine. Now, I'll take what is his.

When I ask Gio for a status report on Alena, it's no surprise she's currently at the hottest club in the city. This makes my blood boil, knowing the place is full of wolves, worse than the likes of me.

What is her father thinking, allowing her out at this time of night with no protection? Obviously, no one watches her as much as I do—otherwise, they would be onto me.

Gio's phone rings.

"Pronto?" There's a pause while he listens. "Yes, I'll be sure to tell him."

"What now?" I grumble when he hangs up.

"That was our Human Resources person calling to say Alena Pasnov has applied for the design consultant job at Indio Designs. She has an interview tomorrow."

"Perfect timing. I was hoping she would see the ad. It was a long shot, but she's taken the bait."

"Hook, line, and sinker."

"Make sure she's hired and starts immediately."

"Yes sir," Gio says as he leaves to pass on my instructions.

Knowing Alena is out at a club in the middle of the night has my blood boiling with jealousy. Unable to sit still, I start pacing back and forth, hoping it will help me focus. I need to put a stop to these extracurricular activities. Just thinking about her with another man makes me angry. She won't have time for anything else if I can keep her busy at her new job.

I rub a hand over the ten o'clock shadow on my jaw. I have an idea.

Alena will join the team I have in place at Indio. She will be working alongside Sophia, a woman I used to fuck until she made the mistake of thinking our casual sex was going to lead to something more permanent and exclusive. She was wrong, of course, and I've been ghosting her. When Sophia finds out I'm engaged to Alena, her claws will come out, and she will make Alena's life a living hell as retribution for me taking her out of the marriage equation.

Alena won't know what hit her.

Gio returns to tell me it's done.

"Great. Sophia has been nagging me to give her more staff to help re-decorate the hotel. This will shut her up."

"Are you sure you want Sophia around Alena? What if something happens? You know how she gets when she's pissed off."

"That can be said for just about every woman," I chuckle. Someone used Wu to fuck me over my first week as the don. That won't happen again. "I can control Sophia if she gets out of hand."

Satisfied my plan is in motion, I return to the leather chair and light a cigar. We need to discuss the marriage contract.

"Alena will be pissed when she figures everything out. She won't like being a pawn in my game. The contract needs to stipulate the marriage has to be consummated and Alena needs to be pregnant within a year. I need an heir."

"She's not gonna be happy about being told what to do. Her father has spoiled her by allowing excessive freedom."

"It wasn't intentional. He's just an old prick, too busy working, to pay attention to his daughter. He has no clue what he's been given, but he'll learn when I take her. I will make sure she has enough guards to fight off an army if necessary."

Mandating a shared marital bed in the contract will make her unable to resist me. I can't wait to fill her with my cum. My cock twitches just thinking about it.

Fuck.

Now I have to see her. Why wait? I'm the don. I can fuck who I want—when I want.

I order Gio to get the car.

"We're going to the club."

"That's not a good idea. You have a plan, a perfect plan. Why risk screwing it up?"

"You don't get a vote." I'm quick to remind him. Gio is my best friend, but we have clear boundaries. I rely on his wisdom, and he helps me run an empire, but tonight, I'm a man first, a don second.

"Fine, but I'm going with you to run interference if needed. That place is crawling with every mafia family in the city. We don't know who will come for you next."

"Fine, get your gun."

Gio nods, then calls for the car to be brought up. Within minutes we're in the G-wagon. I sit in the back and Gio sits up front with the driver. It's a painstakingly long ride to get from Long Island to Manhattan.

Alena loves the limelight, that much is obvious. She lives in a condo overlooking Central Park. If I know anything about New York-ers, they'd rather give up sex than give up life in the city. If I take Alena away from this lifestyle, she may become restless and resentful.

"Have the penthouse floor of the Central Park hotel prepared for me."

"Are you planning to live there?"

"I might need it to keep Alena happy during the engagement period. Its location will ease her into a more secluded lifestyle after we're married."

"Speaking of marriage, will you be taking a honeymoon?"

"Doubtful. It's not safe to travel as long as someone is trying to unseat me."

"Any idea who it might be?"

"My best guess is it's one of my uncles. I'm not worried about Carlo so much, but the other two," my voice trails off, and I shrug. "There's always the possibility it's one of the other Italian families here. Santino Moretti is Cosa Nostra, and he's well-connected in Chicago, Detroit, Boston, and Philadelphia. The Morettis' have the most to gain from taking over our territory."

"No one has seen the old man in some time."

"It's better that way, isn't it? It keeps your enemies guessing. I'm surprised his son isn't running the business by now. Santino's getting up there in age."

"There is no age limit on crime. Besides, many of these guys end up in prison or sickly."

"Speak for yourself," I growl under my breath.

"Oh, well. You, my friend, are the exception," Gio adds to recover from his unintended insult.

As the driver pulls up to the club, Gio pulls his gun from the holster under his jacket and puts it in the glove box. Then he gets out and opens my door. I step out and button my Armani suit jacket as we walk straight to the front of the line. Bouncers, knowing we mean business and have money to spend, let us in immediately.

Once inside, I glance around the cavernous club. There are two levels: the top, no doubt, the VIP level. I size up the competition dressed in expensive suits with personal security as their wingman.

Some of these men are local officials or politicians, but I don't recognize anyone I've bribed recently.

"Alena will be at a VIP table," I say, scanning the faces on the second floor. "There she is," I point out, spotting my future queen in a skin-tight red dress. "Who's that with her?"

"His name is Kirill. He works for Pasnov. He's a low-level threat and probably just her friend."

"Or are they something more?" I growl, pushing past people to cross the dance floor. At the bottom of the steps, I stop abruptly.

"What's the matter?" Gio asks.

"I need to lay low until the deal is sealed. Get me a napkin and a pen."

Gio snatches a cocktail napkin off a nearby table, and the couple sitting there looks annoyed, but when I glare at them, they get up and leave. Good.

Gio hands me the napkin and fishes a pen from inside his coat pocket. I write, "Meet me by the restrooms. Mr. Grey." I fold it in half and slip it to Gio.

"Find a way to give it to her without tipping off Kirill. And make sure she's not followed."

"Got it." Gio leaves to carry out my mission. I watch him climb the steps and bump into their table like he's drunk. It's a classic move and one I've used a few times myself.

Message delivered. I make my way towards the bar, and my heart races. What the fuck am I doing chasing after a woman in a club? Then I remember we met in a sex club and that we have a pattern of fucking in new places.

That's what's turning me on, the adrenaline rush of having sex in public. It's the risk of getting caught that makes me horny.

Needing a drink, I have the bartender make me a vodka martini and take it with me as I explore the club. Spotting a short corridor, I walk down the dark hallway until I find a door with a sign that reads Manager. I check the doorknob, and it's locked.

I backtrack to a spot near the restrooms and wait, hidden behind a fat man who could use a gastric bypass.

My pulse quickens as she approaches. When she's within reach, I grab her arm and pull her towards me.

"Oh," she gasps before she realizes it's me.

"Someone's out late," I say, sipping my drink.

"I'm beginning to think you're following me," she replies and playfully tugs on my tie.

I take a mouthful of martini and close my lips around hers so I can funnel the drink into her mouth. She swallows and sucks the vodka off my lips.

Our tongues merge in a deep kiss that leaves my cock so hard I could use it as a kickstand. I lean against her, pinning her to the wall. Her body melts into mine, and she slides her arms around my neck.

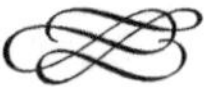

ALENA

Some drunk practically falls in my lap, and after he's gone, I realize he passed me a note. I cautiously open the napkin under the table.

My heart pounds in my ears. Mr. Grey is here. I'm immediately soaking at the mere thought of seeing him. I can't wear panties with this dress, which is a problem.

I'm convinced Mr. Grey knows more than he should about me. I'm thrilled to hear from him and unsurprised when the note implies he doesn't want me to be followed.

I excused myself, telling Kirill I needed to pee.

What does Grey want? My heart is filled with anticipation, which leaves me slick between my thighs. I ball the napkin into my fist before tossing it under a table as I pass.

I reach the stairs, glance over the railing, and see Kirill chatting up the waitress. I sigh in relief. Good. He has no idea what I'm up to.

The line waiting for the bathroom is long and can't just be girls needing to use the toilet. I'm aware that cocaine is still the drug of choice for those who can afford it. Those who can't wait any longer can be seen snorting white powder off the back of their hand. Others are blatantly popping pills or smoking legalized marijuana. These people remind me of a bunch of junkies outside a methadone clinic.

I walk down the corridor to the bathrooms lined with A-listers who frequent the posh place. This is the hottest place to be, but it doesn't look so pretty right now.

Without warning, someone grabs my wrist and pulls me into the darkness. As soon as I smell the familiar cologne, I know it's Grey. I part my lips to say something, but his lips cover mine, and a cold liquor fills my mouth and slides down my throat. The alcohol relaxes me, and I melt into his strong arms.

I'm lost in the darkness I see in his dark eyes. I parted my lips to say something, but his lips covered mine. The kiss is soft and my knees grow weak. His arms pull me safely into his chest.

He puts his empty glass on a nearby table and takes me by the hand.

He pulls away from our kiss, which has intensified.

"This way," he says as he leads me back through the crowd, and we enter a dimly lit hallway. "Who are you with?" His voice is hostile and accusing.

"A friend."

"I suggest you don't go out with other men. You're mine."

"You don't own me," I snap back.

"We'll see about that, Il Mio piccolo angelo," he replies, pinning me against the wall.

I'm sure that last word is angel. One can't live in New York City and not pick up some words in another language.

"You're sexy as fuck in high heels. I can't wait to make your toes curl when you come on my cock."

I'm breathless with my need for his cock to be inside me. I've wanted him to thrust himself into my wet pussy from the second I received his note.

"You are mine," he mutters against my ear. His warm breath brushes the tiny hair on my neck, causing goosebumps to spread like fire up my back. "From now on, you can only wear this dress when I'm with you," he says as his hand slides under my dress and his fingers slip inside me. He fingerfucks me until the noise of the club fades into the background. "You're dripping for me," he murmurs.

His teeth nip at my neck, and his hand grabs my breast, and he massages it through the fabric. I writhe under his attention. My nipple betrays me as it forms into a hard nub when he rubs his thumb over it. My knees buckle in submission.

He grabs the back of my thighs and lifts me off the floor. Grinding his pelvis into mine, I feel his hard cock between my legs and cling to his shoulders, bracing myself to be fucked.

I'm helpless, pinned against the wall. It's exhilarating to give myself to him when he forces his porn star-sized cock into me. I moan and bite my lower lip to keep the noise muffled.

He moves in and out of me, faster and faster, until he's pounding my pussy into a tantric state that makes my toes clench inside my shoes. Fuck him for being right about that.

His hands are under my butt cheeks, holding me as he continues to thrust inside me. My back is riding the wall, and my dress is shoved to my waist. With all the friction he creates, I wouldn't be surprised to have my back torn up from riding the wall. I've had carpet burns before; wall burns—no. A cold draft caresses my naked ass. It's exhilarating and liberating.

What if we're caught?

My hand clenches the hair on the back of his head. The other hand grabs his suit lapel like a vice grip.

His cock strokes the walls of my pussy, and I moan and groan with each thrust. My clit is shredded by the sheer size of him, and I wonder if I'll bleed afterward, like the last time.

One of his hands moves to my lower back as I arch and climax. I bite his neck to keep my screams from entering the stale air encapsulating us. He groans into my neck as he fills me with his cum. His forehead briefly rests on my shoulder.

He pulls out and gently eases me to the floor. I'm unsteady on my heels as I try to stand. I'm dizzy from the head rush. My leg muscles are fatigued. He holds me to him, sensing my predicament. I'm still getting my balance and recovering from the head rush when I hear him zip up his pants. I guess we're done.

"I'm very possessive. If you value your friend, keep him a safe distance from you. I protect what's mine," he threatens, then he's gone.

Fuck!

That was hot, and all my senses were reeling. I make my way to the women's room and enter a stall where I ball up toilet paper and clean up all his denied children running down my leg. I toss it into the toilet and hit the button to flush. I pull my dress down and walk like I've just been fucked.

After I splash cold water on my face, I grab a paper towel and dry my face, blotting it so my makeup won't run. I use my fingers to fluff my hair into place and hope Kirill doesn't notice.

Dammit. I should have insisted Mr. Grey give me his real name tonight. Next time he wants me, I'll demand information first. It's unfair that he knows more about me than I do about him.

Maybe Izzy is right. I need a guard. Mr. Grey is a dangerous man. He's not the type to show emotion, judging from his detached style of fucking me at will and then leaving as if it was nothing. He's not one for cuddles or handholding. I know that much. His hands are strong but smooth. I wonder what he does for a living.

I quickly return to the table to make up for the time I've been gone and find Kirill pouring me another vodka.

"There was such a line," I lie my ass off.

"I would have sent a search party, but I know you can hold your own."

"Yes, I can," I say as I sit and promptly down the vodka.

His gaze lingers on my face longer than usual, watching me.

"Are you okay?"

"Yes, why wouldn't I be?"

"I don't know. You seem distracted."

"I'm fine. Just a bit nervous about a job interview tomorrow. I'm sure that's all it is. I can't stay out too late."

"Okay." He finishes the bottle.

"The noise is getting to me. I'm ready to go," I say. It's true. The noise is making my ears ring.

"No problem," he says, holding two hundred dollars and tossing them on the table.

"Did you get her number?" I tease.

"Wouldn't you love to know," he replies as he escorts me to his Lamborghini the valet has brought to the front door for us. He helps me get in.

Kirill drives me home as we chit-chat, and then he waits for me to enter my building before leaving. Inside my condo, I slump against the door, dropping my purse and taking off my heels. More cum trickles out of me. I slip my dress off and use it to wipe away the cum as I walk naked into the bathroom.

I take a long hot shower to wash off the smoke and smells of the nightclub. Once I'm dried off and in my pajamas, I turn off the light in my room and look at the city below.

Where are you, Mr. Grey?

* * *

I take a cab to my interview. There's no way I'm walking ten city blocks in heels. I'm wearing my new outfit and hope I'm not over-dressed. I was surprised to find the address is a huge building. I make my way to the security man standing at the front desk. It's not unusual after 9/11.

I look at the electronic screen on the marble counter displaying company names. The guard at the desk asks what floor and lifts the phone. He nods to me, saying twelfth floor, and I step toward the metal detectors. The man in uniform motions for me to walk through. I put my purse in the container to my left and walked through the scanner. He looks in my purse to check for weapons and hands it back. I make my way to the elevator. When I step off on the twelfth floor, I discover that Elementi Decor takes up the entire floor. That costs a fortune in rent. I wonder what else this company does.

I give my name to the receptionist, who instructs me to take a seat. She's pretty and answers the phone in Italian. It's such a pretty language. I wish I knew how to speak it, but that will only happen if I have someone to speak it with. Izzy is half-Italian, but she knows more Russian words than Italian ones.

I fire her a quick text to keep her updated and tell her my guard's name is Dima. I know him. He's in the family, so to speak. Izzy wishes me luck and types stay safe.

A woman enters the waiting room I've been relegated to. She introduces herself as Doris. She's here to collect me, and leads me to an interview room. Then, I sit in a blue plastic chair like the ones found in a school. She asks me about my degree and experience as she types, and she's all business. When she asks about job references, I'm ready with a reply.

"I haven't been working because my future was up in the air until recently," I state. My hands are folded on my lap, and my ankles are crossed and tucked under the chair.

She pushes the large-rimmed glasses up her nose. She's wearing a matching plaid wool suit, and her silver hair is coiffed perfectly atop her head. She's so striking that I look at her longer than what would be considered polite.

"Your records appear to be in order. Do you have ID with you?"

"Yes, why? Is something wrong?"

"No, in fact, we're short on staffing, and we need you to start tomorrow," she says, typing into her computer.

I'm speechless.

"Is that too soon?" she asks when I don't respond.

"Oh. No, that's fine," I reply.

"Your driver's license, please."

"Oh, right." I pull my purse to my lap and, with apprehension, dig into my wallet before I hand it to her.

"You will have full medical and dental insurance after thirty days. You have two weeks of vacation after a year. I can give you the salary as posted."

"That's fine." The money is extra income for me as Dad gives me an allowance.

I spend time answering questions, sign forms, and am given an address for the Palazzo Romano Hotel. It's downtown. I don't remember it, but considering the fact I secured a job, it is reassuring. The address makes it real. I push the paperwork she gave me into my purse. It's information on the company's website and a list of benefits. Everything is so impersonal today. I'm impressed the interview wasn't a Zoom call.

When Doris finishes the process, she stands, putting her hand out.

I mimic her as it must be my cue to leave. I take her outstretched hand in mine as we shake like a business deal has been concluded. She gives me a quick smile.

I guess, in a way, it is a business arrangement. She congratulates me and walks me to the front door.

By the time I reach the street, I recognize the SUV that stopped in front of me as one in my dad's fleet. Dima has the window down so I can see him. He's here to collect me. I am stunned to see him, but that's on me. I forget my life changed last night when I asked Kirill for help.

Dima is doing his job. I forgot he was tailing me this morning. I'm perplexed by the interview as I found it too perfect. There was no drug test, and I expected it to take months to be vetted. It's as if Doris was expecting me.

Dima makes casual conversation and asks where I need to go. I tell him home. He complains about the traffic the entire drive. I swear the man uses his horn more than the gas pedal. Finally, he rolls up to my building's parking garage.

"I'll be down here checking things out. Just text me if you're going anywhere. I'll drive you."

"Thank you, Dima," I say as he pulls up to the secure door to the building.

There is no cell phone reception in the elevator. Before walking to my condo, I check the hallway to see if anyone is in it. I'm suddenly overwhelmed by recent events. I have a job. I have responsibilities. My days are no longer my own.

I drop my purse on the counter and look the hotel up on my phone. Indigo Holdings owns the hotel. The address is in the city. It's a nondescript name. There are no details as to who the owner of this company is. It has to be legit if they are renting out floors inside buildings. A design company hired me to work on the hotel project. With my luck, the place is owned by some asshole with lots of money.

I have no clue if the hotel is privately owned, so I decide it doesn't matter.

I am employed. I might be the first mob daughter ever to work a day in her life.

I text Izzy. She must be busy as she doesn't respond.

I'm relieved Dima is downstairs. I don't want Mr. Grey to know where I live. A shiver runs up my spine. *What if he already knows? Is he a lover or a stalker?*

What game are you playing, Mr. Grey?

CHAPTER 11

MATTEO

Gio pulls up in front of the home Alena grew up in. Her father's mansion looks like a winter greeting card with a fresh blanket of snow on it, and the circular driveway is cleared. On this part of Long Island, each home is like every other house next to it. Leave it to Russian newcomers to lack imagination. And why not, after spending most of their life in communist Russia, they have little to go by. Compared to Italy, where we have thousands of years of civilization and skilled artisans.

Gio opens my car door and accompanies me, while another guard remains with the vehicle. As soon as we step inside, we're both searched for weapons. The place is massive, but the décor could use an update. Someone, probably the wife, is stuck in the '80s by the look of the worn mauve carpet and dated Nagel artwork.

We follow some guy dressed like a butler to the back of the house and into a man cave with lots of dark wood and the smell of decades-old cigar smoke. The lighting is terrible, but the floor-to-ceiling windows offer a spectacular view of a tree-lined backyard that stretches to the water.

It's obvious this room has been decorated by someone other than the wife. I'm gonna go out on a limb and say it's the man we're here to see, a man who wields considerable power in the Russian bratva.

Speak of the devil, Mikhail Pasnov steps out of the shadows. He's tall, over six feet, with broad shoulders and a big belly. Some would be intimidated, but not me. I think he looks old, tired, and out of shape. According to Gio, he's in his fifties, but he looks more like a man in his sixties. He approaches, and we shake hands.

"Matteo, welcome to the city. I'm sorry to hear about your father."

"Thank you."

"Have a seat. I hear you like bourbon."

"I do," I reply as Gio stands behind me. The butler enters the room carrying a tray of unopened bottles of high-end bourbon and vodka. He opens them and gently lays the caps down before pouring a bourbon for me and a vodka for Mikhail.

He hands me the rock glass with amber-colored liquid. I take it and swirl the contents as I watch Mikhail take a shot of vodka and pour a second. The butler asks if there's anything else we need. Mikhail dismisses him with a wave of his hand. The man quietly leaves, closing the double doors behind him. Gio takes up a defensive post next to the doors.

Mikhail, still holding his drink, walks across the room to a fireplace and pokes at the embers with a metal rod. Satisfied with the renewed flames, he stows the poker and collapses, as if exhausted, in one of the high-back chairs in front of the fireplace. I sit in the matching chair opposite him.

"I understand your request to meet is over a dispute. I assure you I meant no harm. The laundromat has been on our radar for some time."

Bullshit.

His opening statement sounds rehearsed. I don't trust him. He's acting way too calm, but that's to be expected of anyone who used to work for the KGB. The man has been trained to pass a lie detector test and withstand all sorts of torture without so much as flinching.

"Let's just agree to disagree. I'm prepared to reimburse you whatever you paid for the lot. It's on my territory and should have never been sold to you."

I pause, letting this sink in. His calm demeanor fades as his pale blue eyes narrow and eyebrows like Brezhnev's furrow.

"That's preposterous."

"Oh, I don't think it is. That property is more than a building to me, and as my first action as a Don, I won't be fucked out of it. Wu used you to get to me. He never should have sold to you, and he paid for his sin."

I take a sip of the bourbon and lean back in the chair, waiting for his next move,

"What are you after?" he asks as he leans forward in his chair. Gio steps forward protectively but relaxes when Mikhail reaches for the poker and stabs at the embers in the fireplace, not me.

"I'll forgive your overreaching in exchange for an arranged marriage with your daughter, Alena. Alena has to marry someone. It might as well be me." I sneer condescendingly at him.

It's tough to pick up, but the man's forehead creases. I see the corner of his mouth twitch. It's subtle but enough to know I got to him.

"Alena is young, full of life, and she's no virgin. Don't you want someone who hasn't been touched?"

Ah, a polite rebuff.

I sip my bourbon. "I want Alena. In fact," I reach into my jacket and whip out an envelope. "I've already drawn up the terms of the marriage contract. I'll leave these with you and return in a few days to sign the papers. The engagement will be announced on Page Six, and the wedding ceremony needs to be extravagant."

I stand, toss what's left of the bourbon into the back of my throat, and swallow.

"This marriage ensures there will be no confusion going forward," I say, handing him my empty glass and turning to leave.

I nod to Gio as he opens the door and follows me out. Mikhail's men hurry past us to check on their boss. What's the rush? They'd be too late if we'd killed him.

As soon as we leave the house, I take a deep breath of cold air to clear my head.

"Damn, that house was gloomy. If we stayed any longer, we would have seen the ghost of Gorbachev. Thank God Alena is not like her father. Having met him, I can see why she's so defensive and has so many trust issues."

I know what it's like to be ignored until a parent needs something. Her life was probably much the same and still is. Her father considers her his property until she is someone else's. All he wants from her is an arranged marriage that benefits him.

"What are the odds he'll take the deal?"

"I'd say the odds are good, very good. I doubt Mikhail wants the Don to know he negotiated this deal behind his back."

"Yes, you have the upper hand. So you're going through with this?"

"I want this fucking building. And I want to add floors so it will be the tallest hotel in the city. I'm riled up. Until I reach the sky, nothing is too much.

"The hotels our family owns make money. The only problem is that a councilman previously voted against a height variance for someone else. Find out who the holdout is and take care of it. I need this to go smoothly. If my uncles smell blood in the water, they will eat me like a shark."

My focus has been on fucking Alena when I should have been focused on my enemies.

"I need Alena. She'll be an asset. It doesn't hurt she's our enemy's daughter."

"Are you sure that's all it is? Marriage?" I feel his eyes observe me as he waits for an answer.

"Of course, besides, a marriage will get the uncles off my back and will provide an heir. I hope it will take the target off my brother, Niccoló."

"Yeah, it's no secret the family is unhappy about your bachelor status, especially at your age."

I scoff as I slide into the SUV. The door is closed behind me.

"Alena will be useful at social functions. She'll run interference with the lonely women desperate for attention. She'll be helpful to me in networking among the city's power brokers. Marriage will give me approval and will deem me a trustworthy person. Her pretty face and charming personality will soften my opponents and expedite my deals."

"Now, you sound like a Don." Gio chuckles in relief, and we head to lunch.

CHAPTER 12

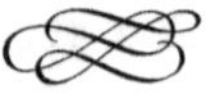

ALENA

I dress in my favorite Ralph Lauren outfit for my first day on the job. The skirt and jacket are black suede, and the turtleneck is forest green. I tug on black leather boots that come up to my thighs. I bet Mr. Grey would love this outfit.

I approach the mirror over my sofa and apply lipstick before dropping it in my purse. Now, where the hell did I leave my phone? Damnit. I'm not old enough to forget where I left it.

I tell myself it's first-day jitters, not dementia, and use my watch to ping my phone. I follow the ringing sound to my bedroom, grab the phone and my coat, and leave, locking the door behind me.

When I step outside the building, Dima jumps out of a black Escalade and opens the door for me.

"Thank you, Dima."

"My pleasure, Ms. Pasnov."

"You know that makes me feel so old, don't you?"

"Yes, I do. But it's your father's directions."

"Of course. He's ex-KGB. This means somewhere in the recesses

of his reptilian brain, he's still fighting the Cold War. That's why he trusts no one and treats me like I'm trying to defect. The man has no idea what my generation thinks."

"He does know your generation, and he chooses to ignore it," he replies as he starts the engine.

"By the way, congratulations on your new job. Am I still taking you to the Plazzo Romano Hotel?"

"Yes, thank you. Don't say anything to Mom and Dad. I haven't told them. I want to make sure things work out first."

"Of course. I will take your secrets to my grave." I look in the rearview mirror, and he gives me a Cheshire grin. I almost giggle at the thought of him burping up a feathery canary.

"You can say that until your boss threatens to use the jumper cables."

"Ouch. That would never happen. Your dad's a teddy bear," he jokes. I'm glad Dima isn't easily offended.

He says he has more fun driving me around rather than my mother. Her idea of fun is to stop at every store and look for bargains. The only other time she gets out is once a month when she meets with other Bratva wives to organize charity events.

I admire her dedication to helping the disadvantaged youth in the inner city. It's a source of conflict for me because all the syndicates use the less fortunate communities to sell drugs and run rackets, like gambling and prostitution. It's so hypocritical. I'd rather help kids in hospitals.

Dima is not the enforcer type. He's a tall, muscular man, and he carries a weapon. He is trained to defend me and to keep me safe. But under it all, he's not what I'd call intimidating.

Kidnappings were a huge ordeal when I was in elementary school. Due to that, my mother and others freaked out. I did the kidnapping drill like others my age who have similar backgrounds. Some in the class were just wealthy assholes in private schools.

I was thrown in a truck and taught what to do if I'm ever taken as a hostage. Our parents thought the training would save our lives. In reality, it only gave them a false sense of security. I was more concerned over the occasional gang hits spilling over into middle and upper-class neighborhoods.

I wouldn't mind knowing how to use a gun. I mean, I can pull a trigger, but I have no clue as to what I'd hit with a bullet. Dad believes it's his job to protect me, so my teen and high school years were filled with countless versions of Dima.

"Well, Russian leaders are known for torturing people and keeping the truth from citizens. In this country, it's called selective denial," I say to break the silence as we sit in bumper-to-bumper traffic.

"This is what you learn in college?"

"No, it's what I've observed."

"Kirill has instructed me to follow you everywhere. We need to find out who Mr. Grey is. You said he speaks Italian?"

"I think so. His face isn't familiar. It's odd. It's not like I don't frequent enough high-end places around town. I'm surprised I haven't bumped into him before. Maybe he's a new arrival."

"Just because he's not on the cover of one of those shitty gossip magazines doesn't mean he was living in Siberia. Have you checked Instagram and other social media?" He says to poke fun at my culture.

"I checked. He doesn't have a social media presence." *Shit, I just proved to Dima how much social media dictates my life.*

"If anyone knows how to cyberstalk, it's you," he laughs, "That phone never leaves your hand. No way am I letting my daughter have a smartphone. I don't want her comparing herself to those so-called influencers with their fake breasts and butt implants. And no fake nails, fake eyelashes, and fake hair. When did women decide they want to look like porn stars? My daughter needs to concentrate on getting good grades and earning her allowance."

"Good for you, Dima. I'm sure she's smart and level-headed."

"Thank you. She is, and I want to keep her that way."

"Wow, is that the hotel?"

"Yep. I'll drop you off and come up."

"No, I can't have you hovering over me my first day," I complain. "This isn't the bring your bodyguard to work day."

"You're always so defensive of your space. Nothing has changed with age."

"Nope," I say, popping the 'p.'

"Very well. I will hide in plain sight. I have a book I can read to make it look like I'm waiting for someone. I might check out the indoor pool."

"Thank you," I graciously reply.

"But you have to keep me apprised of everything concerning the mystery man."

"Deal," I say as I let myself out of the vehicle.

I may have lied.

Will I tell him?

Will I let Mr. Grey suffer with a case of blue balls until he gives me his name?

I check my surroundings before I step into the elevator. I push the button for the 10th floor. The doors move, and then— *thunk*. An arm is jammed between them, making the doors stop abruptly before it retracts.

The familiar cologne hits my nose, and I raise my head.

It can't be.

"Good morning, my little Angel." Mr. Grey is clean-shaven. His cologne mixes with the clean scent of goat's milk soap—a light, clean fragrance filling the elevator.

My heart stops.

"You're quiet today," he says, stepping in, and the doors close behind him.

"Um, this is twice in two days. Am I your new bad habit, Mr. Grey?"

His lips curl into a sexy smirk that makes my pussy tingle.

"I have an affinity for close encounters with you," His eyes bore into mine. "Only you," rolls off his tongue like a summer heatwave.

I meet his gaze, mesmerized. Our eyes lock. I'm powerless against him. Our eyes communicate with a language of its own.

We can't look away from each other. Neither of us is willing to give up the other. If we were about to have a head-on collision, I wonder if we would break our gaze or die.

The universe stops spinning when he's in my orbit. Without a word, he controls me. He has command of my mind, body, and soul. I'm completely enamored with him. His presence speaks more than words because he's a busy man. Time is money to a businessman, and yet he's here making time for me.

My pussy throbs. My ovaries drop eggs like an overproductive hen.

"What is on your agenda today?"

"You," he murmurs, pushing the button for the 8th floor. The elevator lurches upward. When we pass the 7th floor, he hits the emergency stop button. The elevator suddenly stops, knocking me off balance and sending me into his strong arms.

His warm lips cover mine. I respond without thinking. I can't get enough of him. His bedroom eyes and slicked-back hair beg to be tugged. In my excitement, I've forgotten the oath of celibacy I swore to maintain. That oath went right out the window, or should I say—the elevator door.

His kisses are as sweet as sun-ripened strawberries. All coherent thoughts leave my head. My pussy feels like an active volcano bubbling and boiling with hot lava.

My leg naturally wraps around his. I breathe, drinking him in as my eyes close and melt into his arms.

I gasp. He's a man who likes control, and with him, I welcome it, trusting him implicitly.

I massage his hard cock through the silky feel of his suit.

He pins me against the steel elevator wall. The alarm's blaring is distracting until he slips his fingers deeper into me. I gasp in pleasure and let out a moan as I shift my skirt to give him more access.

I want more of him.

I plant my feet on the metal floor. His fingers inch deeper. I swoon as he hits my secret spots. He needs no instruction. He knows exactly how to press my buttons.

I swoon and wrap my arms around his neck to anchor myself and pull him closer, but he holds me at bay. My eyes open, begging the question, why?

There is no answer. He's a fortress—his eyes are as cold as a frozen lake. His walls are impenetrable and indestructible.

I know he's seen death. He could kill me with the flick of his wrist.

His long fingers snake around my neck. Panic turns to excitement. He holds me in a death grip, one hand on my neck, the other finger-fucking me. I can't move. I'm on my tiptoes, gasping for air and moaning with pleasure. He strokes a new G-spot, and suddenly, I'm limp with pleasure.

I'm in a tantric state, teetering on the cusp of my pleasure, not knowing which way I should fall. Do I come now? Or hold out for a more incredible rush?

"Don't come yet," he murmurs as his lips brush my neck. "I'm going to choke you, and you'll love it."

Choke?

With his hand on my throat, I can't protest. I can't speak. It's as if I've been given an injection to paralyze me.

What the fuck?

Men have tried this move before, but it never did anything special.

His fingers ravage my pussy, pumping me faster and faster. My nub turns hard, as do my nipples inside my bra. I long for him to rip off my clothing and grab my breasts. I want to tug at them and make them hurt, but it isn't easy to breathe.

Oh my God, will I die?

"Come now, Angel," he says as he finishes me. I'm overcome by an intense wave of euphoria that leaves me reeling. I come again and again. These are the most intense orgasms I've ever had.

How did he know that would happen?

He hits the button to release the emergency stop. In my post-coital bliss, I lean against the wall and watch the elevator door open. The doors open and shut—he's gone.

I take a deep breath.

Fuck, that was intense.

I'm powerless against him. I can't hold out for answers. I'm a victim of falling under the spell of Mr. Grey.

I press the number 10 and pull my skirt down. I fluff my hair, smooth my modest skirt with the palms of my hands, and pick my purse off the floor as the elevator door opens.

When I stand upright, I find myself face-to-face with Dima. He's a Russian wall, standing tall before me. There's no getting around a confrontation.

"What the hell happened?" he asks in Russian.

"I'm flustered. I was stuck. I don't know what happened. It jerked, and I kept hitting the buttons, and then it started to move. So here I am!"

"Your cheeks are flushed. Are you okay? Was anyone in there with you? I saw it stopped before the eighth floor."

I say, "No," and hope there is no video feed of the inside elevator.

"Well, I reported it to maintenance. I was in a panic. Did you see him?" He asks in Russian.

"No. I'm sorry if I worried you. I'll wait for you next time," I offer in an attempt to console him. I have to throw him off Mr. Grey's scent as quickly as possible.

"I think that's best. I don't trust this situation with your mystery man. Every day that passes is a reason for concern. You should have never let it get out of control," he adds as he gruffly takes me by the arm and leads me to the office like a child.

"Fine," I snap as he opens the glass doors to the office. I sail through it, and my face is still pink with the afterglow of my sexual encounter.

I walk toward the sound of muffled voices and find myself in a huge conference room surrounded by glass. This feels like a fishbowl.

"You must be the new girl," a chipper voice says behind me. When

I turn I see a woman a few years older than me. She's wearing an argyle sweater, black slacks, and brown ankle boots.

"Yes, I'm Alena Pasnov. I was hired yesterday."

"I'm Penny. I'm Sophia's assistant. She's our boss. Follow me. I'll introduce you." She's shorter than me but walks faster, and I practically jog to keep up.

"Thank you," I reply as I follow her. We pass three partitions that each house a chair and a laptop. I notice a main printer in an office station to the left with shelving for supplies. There is a room with fabrics and color scheme templates.

The office concept is an open work environment to facilitate collaboration. The overstuffed floor pillows and spa music playing in the background help to stimulate creativity. There's no need for artificial lighting because a wall of windows allows plenty of natural light. I'm surprised at how comfortable I feel already in this new environment.

At the end of the hall, Penny stops at a frosted glass door and knocks lightly before opening it.

"Here she is! Sophia, this is Alena," she says, stepping out of the way.

I take this as my cue and walk to extend my hand. "Nice to meet you," I say.

She places her soft hand in mine. "Welcome. I see my request for staff hasn't fallen on deaf ears after all. Make yourself acquainted with the staff. We work primarily in groups, so make friends."

"Thank you," I say as Penny nods toward the door.

"She's gorgeous," I mumble to Penny as she shuts the door to Sophia's office.

"She's Italian, as in Sicilian. She's nice if you're on her good side."

"How do I manage to do that?"

"Don't be late and never say anything bad about anyone is a good start."

"That's not so difficult, is it?"

"Give it time," she chuckles. "You're new. Everyone will be nice at first."

"This isn't as cutthroat as working in the fashion industry, is it?"

"I'll let you be the judge of that," she says, and I detect her English accent.

"Where are you from?" I ask before we enter a room where my co-workers are gathered.

"London. We have a design office there as well. Otherwise, I'd never be approved for a visa to work in the States."

We're standing outside the break room when Sophia comes to get us and points to the big-screen monitor. It looks like we're having a staff meeting. We gather in front of the screen to watch a video showcasing several five-star resorts worldwide. We're supposed to see what the competition is doing and develop something just as impressive. How much money is spent on lobbies and amenities to impress guests and win awards is amazing.

"Nice to meet you, Alena. Welcome to the team," Nathan says.

"Thank you," I reply as I take his hand, and we shake. The pitch of his voice is higher than I expected, and as soon as he moves to grab material off a shelf, I realize women probably aren't on his menu.

"This is Cindy. She's worked on movie sets, and she can help you coordinate the vendors," Penny says.

"Hi, Cindy," I say.

"Hi. You were a quick hire," she states before looking at Penny. "Haven't we been waiting months for a new hire?" She throws a questioning look at Penny.

Penny shrugs. "We have. Isn't it great we have more help?" she replies enthusiastically.

"Just peachy," Cindy replies. She has red hair, is under five feet five, and stares down at her black-rimmed glasses to study me.

Looking around at my co-workers, I'm the youngest person here. It doesn't take long to figure out that most have years of experience with Fortune 500 companies. I am in rare company, and no one will take me seriously.

This leads me to wonder why I was hired when there had to be more qualified applicants. On the bright side, I have a job, and by the end of the day, I conceptualize the project. We're redoing the hotel floor, which will be replicated when the rumored new hotel is built. No one mentions a location, but I'm not concerned. I have a job and a purpose.

After Dima drives me home, I have dinner for one in my condo after I shower and change. I pour myself a glass of wine before calling my mother. I assume she'll be happy to hear I've been self-sufficient when I inform her that her daughter is the newest member of the working class.

She congratulates me, and she appears to be preoccupied. I assume she's in a mood. Then my father starts screaming obscenities in Russian.

I hold the phone away from my ear.

What the fuck?

"I don't want you working at that hotel. Those Italian bastards, the Borrellis, own it."

Mom grabs the phone. "Sorry, dear. He's in a mood," she says.

"Mom, I didn't do anything wrong. I thought he would be proud of me."

"I know, dear. Don't mind him. Come by for an informal dinner party next week. I'll send you the date and time. It's casual, but do your hair and dress nicely. Gotta go."

She hung up before I could say goodbye.

Dinner? What is going on? The two of them are behaving strangely. I was just there for dinner.

If this isn't cryptic, I don't know what is. Dad has not been himself, and it sounds like he's still stressed out.

I call Izzy. Neither of us has a clue what is going on with my father.

To forget my family's weirdness, I changed the discussion to my first day at work and Izzy's naps.

CHAPTER 13

MATTEO

"*I* have good news, boss," Gio says. "Antonio found your father's retired advisor, Mr. Gambino. I have his address and thought we'd pay him a visit."

"Great idea. Maybe this guy can shed light on my father's transgressions and whereabouts before he left the city. That information could potentially lead us to the person or persons behind his suspicious death."

My phone rings. Sicily.

"Fuck."

Like I don't have enough going on.

I answer and listen to Uncle Luca drone on about how he needs a vacation. He's warming up for the real reason behind his call. Leave it to my uncles to never get to the point. He thinks I have all the time in the world while all he does is sit around drinking grappa all day.

"Yeah, well, if that damn Chinaman continues to drag his feet, you need to use an ice pick and chop things off one at a time."

"Okay, Uncle Luca. I get the picture. Remember, this is New York, not Sicily."

I chuckle. He doesn't know Wu is dead. I'm keeping a playbook in my head of who knows what and when. One has to be sharp and a step ahead of the others to stay alive.

"Good. I'll let you get on with that then," he says. "Good luck getting anything done in that shithole," he says, making a gagging sound to show his disdain for the city.

I hang up. I don't have the energy to remind him my businesses in New York make more money for the family than anything he has going on in Sicily.

It's lunchtime, and I follow Gio into the solarium where Federico has laid out a spread. We sit at the table and start with chicken gnocchi soup, followed by pane con la milza, a lamb innards and ricotta dish. I bite into a toasted tomato and cheese sandwich that tastes like it came off a panini press in Italy.

"Everything tastes incredible, Federico," I say as he refills my wine.

"I'm glad you like it. Can I get you anything else?"

"Thank you, that'll be all. And I won't be here for dinner tonight."

"Very well," he says before leaving.

"We need to get a move on if we want to see Gambino today," I say.

"I agree. He's probably eating as well. He was old school like your father."

"You mean old. He's past retirement age. We were supposed to visit him last week. We can't put it off any longer," I elaborate.

"True. I hope he will give us answers. The sooner we neutralize the threat, the safer you and Alena will be. Maybe hold off a bit on the announcement?" Gio nudges me to use better judgment.

"You worry too much."

"Well, considering I have to keep you alive. You should be appreciative."

"Noted."

After we finish eating, Gio calls for a car and driver. I put on my suit jacket and grab my long overcoat. I make sure the gun I put in my belt clip earlier is still there. It would be stupid not to carry a weapon, especially since we're heading to a place we've never been.

Gio has the driver pull up, and I follow behind him as fresh snow falls. It will be nice to have Alena warming me at night. Well, depending on how pissed she is over our meeting. I haven't seen her in days and wonder if she misses me.

I had paperwork with her father regarding the building and marriage contract. Now, Antonio wants to speak to me about his issue with Finn. It never stops. Put out one fire, start another, rinse, repeat.

We both know he wants to kill Finn. I don't mind one less dealer dead. It's easy to make his death look like an overdose. However, I can't risk any blowback over it.

We make our way into the city's Lower East Side near Soho. We walk up flights of steps as the elevator has a sign "Out of Order," which seems odd as it's in a well-kept neighborhood.

"What moron designs a building with only one elevator?" I grumble as we head to the stairwell. Gio pulls his gun and goes first before opening the stairwell door. He looks up and clears the corner before he motions for me to follow. "What floor?"

"Third."

Why does it always smell like dead mice and urine in a stairwell?

On the third floor, we walk down an empty corridor until we arrive at number 323, Gambino's apartment.

"You'd think he'd be living in a nice house with all the money he's made over the years," Gio stops when he notices the door is cracked open. Sensing a setup, he immediately goes into defense mode. His head is on a swivel as he checks our surroundings.

I peer across the railing behind me, and as far as I can see—I don't notice anything unusual. Window cleaners are working; horns honk below, and there are snow-covered rooftops as far as I can see.

Satisfied we're not being watched, I nod for Gio to open the door. Thankful for the cold that led him to wear leather gloves, he nudges the door open with his foot and enters the room.

We find Mr. Gambino in his recliner with a shot to the head.

We exchange looks of concern.

"That's a hit. But why?" I ask.

In the distance, we hear the loud horn of an ambulance followed by the sirens of emergency vehicles.

"If an ambulance is coming, so are the cops," Gio murmurs, voicing his concerns.

"Someone wanted us to find him."

"We need to go," he says.

"Fuck."

What if someone saw us?

"Have Antonio hack the surveillance and erase all the footage," I order. It helps that he's a great hacker, and has others to help.

"Sure thing, we need to go that way," Gio points and takes the lead.

We walk to the opposite end of the building to avoid running into the rescue crew and discover dangling cameras on both floors.

"They want us to know they were here," I mumble.

"Whoever killed Gambino came this way," I propose.

"The question is, who?" Gio says as we jog to our waiting vehicle a block over to avoid detection. The plates are all listed to offshore companies. It's not impossible for someone to build a profile and start connecting pieces that might point to us at some point in time. In order to defeat our enemies, we keep an ear to the ground. I wish our sources were as good as those in the Red Keep in Game of Thrones. We do our best to know what's happening in our families and what might affect our business by way of government intervention or newcomers who think they can usurp our power.

Today, the Feds make all businesses register with the Bureau of Financial Crime and provide identification. All the big players know how to get around the rules. Gone are the days of hiding money in the Cayman Islands.

Nowadays, smart criminals deal in cryptocurrency and operate out of underground bunkers with water-cooled computers or hide in abandoned buildings in places like Kosovo. You will find call centers with hundreds of people working on dating sites everywhere. Hackers are constantly creating new ways to trick people into clicking links to viruses that steal money from a victim's bank account.

We made our getaway, and once inside the vehicle, we close the privacy divider between us and our driver.

"Someone knows our moves."

"Antonio?" Gio asks.

"He's in love and working on the details to stage Finn's overdose," I mutter as I stare out the window.

"There's no way they're tracking us. Just to be sure, I'll have all the cars swept for bugs and have someone other than Antonio look at all our security footage," Gio says.

"Let's check the location of Antonio's phone and car. My gut is telling me it won't be easy to find the rat. Gambino knew something that someone wanted to cover up."

"Like a murder," Gio adds. "There is no reason to kill a retired mobster. His execution is meant to send a message. But why? We don't even know what it's supposed to mean."

"True. I think it means my father's death was orchestrated, and if one person knows why, someone else has to know, too. Unless we run into a string of dead bodies and all possible witnesses have been neutralized—this could be part of a huge cover-up. There's no way a syndicate would kill off a retired man of the last regime unless there is a motive to do so."

"I'll have one of our forensic guys go through your father's phone. We need to reconstruct your father's last months, if not the entire past year of his life."

"His house sold for more than the listed price, which isn't surprising." I run my hand over my head. "His stuff is in storage. Do we need to go through his personal stuff? I never thought there might be crucial information buried in his crap."

Gio shrugs. "Let's start with the phone and his computer. We might uncover something. Then again, he might have used a burner phone for everything with a clue. He had numerous phones, and Gambino was in charge of keeping track of them."

"He didn't like computers. It's possible something was written in his mess of papers in my study or the boxes I threw in my garage."

"Hmm, we would be further along in solving this mystery if you hadn't started sleeping with that sexy Russian."

"Well, that's a pleasure you should consider so you aren't stuck growing old alone."

* * *

I snap the box shut. She will love the ring. I wonder how she will react when her father tells her she has to marry me, share my bed, and have my children. I hope our daughter takes after her with blue eyes and a sassy tongue.

I love how Alena's eyes flicker with fear and simmer with lust when she banters with me. I'm not sure why I want to marry her. It's not like I have time for a wife and kids.

I wonder if I'll regret marrying an American-Russian woman instead of marrying an Italian. Italy's mainland culture has changed drastically compared to the island of Sicily. The more remote the area, the more we remain the same, and time moves slower. Small seaside Sicilian towns are the same as when I was a child.

I'm sure she'll forgive me for surprising her. I have no idea why I've been toying. That's not true, either. I find her to be a worthy opponent. I love her banter. Her snappy retorts amuse me. She even makes me laugh.

It's not as if I have time for a wife. However, some doors need to be opened, and I'm confident she will be helpful.

I grab a tie and drape it around my neck before tying it. I look at myself in the mirror before I slip into my Italian shoes.

There is a quick knock on my open door.

"Ah, Federico," I say as he hurries into the room.

"I just want to know if you need anything before you leave."

"No, I'm fine. Thanks. However, there will be a woman here shortly. I think you'll like her. Her name is Alena. She's going to be my wife."

His eyes open wider in surprise.

"Very well, sir. I look forward to getting to know her." He nods.

"Take the night off. I'll see you at breakfast."

"Thank you." His heels tap together before he leaves the room, and Gio sails into my room.

"Are you sure about this?"

"Yes."

"This is a ballsy move if I ever saw one," he says with concern.

"Did a black cat walk in front of you today?"

"No, why?"

"You are brooding, and it reeks of pessimism. Do you doubt my ability to control my wife?" I turn away from the bureau mirror to observe him.

"No, I'm afraid she'll be your greatest weakness," he replies.

"I seriously doubt that. I find her body to be perfect for fucking. She'll be moving in, so please make sure Federico has someone make the room look a bit less manly. I don't know, maybe add some flowers or whatever shit women like."

"Have you considered Alena's safety? You could always get the building back by using negotiation or war, but she's a liability that isn't made of bricks."

I turn and narrow my eyes on Gio. "I am aware of this. I'm the one who runs his hand over her firm and supple body. Everyone needs to know that I'm the only man who will fuck her until she's limp and filled with my cum. She's mine, and anyone who touches her will die."

"In that case, I'm sure she'll like it here. It's not the dank museum she grew up in."

I shudder at the memory. "That mausoleum needs to be torched, and if her father does anything to undermine me, I'll torch it myself," my voice raises in anger. The thought of seeing him again so soon is not a pleasant one.

"It will be a short dinner, I assume," Gio states.

"It better be short. The only pretty thing in the house is Alena." I turn on my heels. "She is the crown jewel. Who knows? Maybe in time, we will conduct business with the Russians."

"Stranger things have been known to occur," he grins as he strokes his goatee.

"Good. I'm glad you're on board. We'll make sure she has a guard with her at all times. Her days of gallivanting around the city like a cat in heat are over. As my fiancée, that behavior is… unacceptable. She has to pay more attention to her surroundings and realize she lives in a world where men will harm her to get to me. Her father had her on a long leash. If I have to, I will keep her chained to the damn bed."

"I'll have Antonio put someone on her."

"No, I want Vito on it," I snap, surprising myself.

Lately, I've thought more about Alena's safety than my own. Damn. I can't get enough of her. I spend half the night figuring out how to fit her into my next day without it appearing obvious.

"You don't trust Antonio?" Gio is quick to discern what I'm implying.

"I do. However, his father is my uncle, and it would be an easy avenue to undermine me if Antonio didn't know he was being manipulated. With my family, I have more questions than answers. For now, I'd rather err on the side of caution. I want someone who is removed from the clutches of Sicily. Vito is American-Italian, which makes it more difficult for someone back home to reach him."

"That makes sense. I see you thought this through," Gio replies tersely. I'm sure his nose is out of joint because he feels left out.

"It just came to me—honestly, I like the kid."

"Exactly, a kid," Gio points out.

"You're getting up there, old man," I tease.

Gio's dark hair is shorter than he used to wear it, and silver is beginning to outweigh the darker hair on his head and goatee.

I nod in the direction of the door. "Time to get this deal finalized. Let's go."

CHAPTER 14

ALENA

When Dima pulls into my parents' driveway, the house is lit up like a Christmas tree.

"That's odd. They usually sit in the doom and gloom," I say. "Like a Russian gulag in winter."

"Sarcasm? Already?" Dima tries not to laugh.

"Haven't you heard? Sarcasm is just an insult delivered as a joke. You have to admit my parents have been acting weird lately. What's going on with them? You must know something. I don't want to walk into an ambush or spend all night getting waterboarded with personal questions."

"I can't help you. What about Kirill? Have you asked him?"

"He would have texted me if it was news that I needed to know."

"True."

"I wonder if Dad's business is in trouble." His entire life is wrapped up in the family business—and he's not even the Don!"

"Be mindful of what you say, Alena. I'd hate for you to piss off your father."

"As if he could be in a pissier mood than last week when he found out I was working at a hotel owned by the Borelli family."

"Why does he care? He okayed you finding a job."

"Apparently, he doesn't like the Borellis. Who are they?"

"Their name has been around for years. They are another well-connected family."

"Wait, I work for a company owned by the mob? Why didn't you tell me?" No wonder Dad is pissed.

There has to be bad blood with the Borellis for Dad to get so riled up.

"I have no clue. The design company, Indigo, is owned by a shell company, but the hotel is legit and in the Borelli name."

"I've never heard of them. I thought the Morellis were the feared Italians. That old man is bonkers if you ask me."

I mostly hang out with Kirill rather than other girls my age from other syndicates because it's too easy to become involved with the wrong person. Besides, I rarely travel to Brooklyn. I never mingle with young adults from other syndicates because it's too easy to get involved with the wrong person.

Izzy is from the Moretti family, and when her mother fell for a Russian, her family was all pissy about it. They forbade Izzy's mother from seeing her boyfriend. It all ended tragically when they got caught in the crossfire between the Russians and the Italians.

I don't want the same thing to happen to me. It's bad enough that someday, I will be forced to marry some stranger who controls my every move for the rest of my life. I can't understand why people bother to flee oppression and move to the United States only to impose their restrictive customs on their children.

I'm lucky Dad let me attend college, and it bought me some time for myself before I was married off in a barbaric tradition. I don't know why my parents bothered coming to the United States if they are still committed to maintaining the good old ways of repression.

"Prearranged marriages between our families are meant to build trust and form alliances that prevent conflicts. There hasn't been a mafia war in years," I am quick to point out.

"The problem is it's too easy to offend everyone nowadays. Territory lines get blurred. One never knows when there's a beef until someone ends up in the hospital or the morgue. Then a meeting is called," he says. "These things happen all the time, and you never hear about it."

I take his words to heart and will study them later. I need to learn more about my world before I marry. If no one will tell me what's going on, I'll investigate it myself.

"I better get going." I resign myself to the fact that my parents are probably entertaining friends and want to show me off. I hope tonight's worst-case scenario is that their friends are shopping for a new car, not a wife.

Double yuck.

I was prepared for that life until Mr. Grey showed up. Now, I'm not so sure. I've never had my toes curl during an orgasm. I've never had a man's voice make me wet between the legs. I've never been so excited to see his face as his lips hover dangerously over mine, to the point I'm panting with anticipation.

Who is this stranger, who fucks the hell out of me and leaves me wanting more?

The hand necklace he gave me was my first, leaving me wanting to know what else he had in his sexual toolbox.

No, I can't settle for the average Joe. I won't go down without a fight. Mr. Grey has taken me to new heights. Fucking with him all over the city is exciting. I'm not sure another man will ever measure up to him. I wonder what he's like in real life.

I tug my coat around me to make the long walk up the sidewalk. I'm early as usual when I open the unlocked door and step into the warm foyer. I can hear voices in the kitchen. I hang my coat on the rack and walk past the formal dining room.

The antique chandelier over my head is beautiful, but one bulb is burned out. I roll my eyes and question why I'm even surprised. At least the table is set with my grandmother's bone china, silver utensils, and crystal glasses. There are also bottles of vodka, bourbon, and white wine. Strange, as Russians, we drink vodka. Who's drinking the bourbon?

"Mom, Dad? What's going on?" I ask, interrupting their conversation. They are huddled together. Mom is still wearing her apron. From the look of casseroles, side dishes, and appetizers, she's been cooking all day. Mom rushes to greet me.

"There you are," she says as she hugs me. A hug—after all these years?

She's wearing a new dress, a pearl necklace, and matching earrings that dangle as she moves. Why is she dressed up? This is not a casual dinner with friends.

"Dad?" I ask as I pull away from her and find a lasagna on the counter. Dad is pouring a shot of vodka. I doubt it's his first.

"I like your outfit," Dad says.

This is peculiar. My father never notices me or compliments me on anything I wear.

"Thanks," I reply, stunned. "Can you tell me who's coming to dinner?"

"Someone special," he says as he turns to the counter and downs a shot of vodka. I'm irritable. Just when I think this night will never end, the doorbell chimes.

"I'll get it," Mom exclaims, making a beeline for the front door.

I don't even recognize my parents. I'm perplexed, but concern takes over. Oh God, I hope Kirill and I aren't being matched. We're friends.

What the hell is going on?

If something happened to the Don, Izzy would have told me. It must not be him, so why are they fussing so much?

I follow Mom to the door but try to hang in the shadows, but it's difficult to hide when every damn light in the house is on! I can't wait to discover who our guest is.

Dad only jumps for the Don. And he's paid to do that! My curiosity was piqued as the door opened, and there stood a handsome Italian with a perfect complexion and dark eyes.

I know those eyes, that face, and that muscular body under his expensive suit. My breath catches in my throat.

The man I know only as Mr. Grey. He acknowledges my mother and glances in my direction as if he knows I'll be here.

Fuck.

He's noticed me already. It's as if our bodies seek each other out without us being cognizant of it.

His presence turns me on.

I casually wipe my sweaty palms on my outfit before I step out of the shadows and confidently walk toward him.

He shakes my father's hand, but his eyes remain transfixed on mine.

"You must be Alena," he says with an air of confidence that I find polite, if somewhat condescending. He knows damn well who I am.

It wouldn't be difficult for him to use his contacts to track me down. It dawns on me that all of our sexual encounters were meticulously planned. How did he know I'd be at the sex club that night?

I've been manipulated and deceived. Or was I just lost in the allure of his huge cock and a thirst to have my sexual needs satiated?

He's used the information he gained to his advantage.

Shit, Dima said the Borrelli's are connected. Am I being married off to the Italian? He said they are mobbed up, and holy fuck, I work in his hotel. Dad was furious when he found out. There is more than meets the eye going on in this room. I thought I had a clear understanding of my world and my future. How is it that I'm the last to know Mr. Borrelli has entered our lives?

I should have learned the ruthlessness of others from that business class where the girls manipulated the class events to make themselves look superior.

But what is Matteo gaining through his connection to my father? Is it a business deal? What could be their reason for becoming so chummy overnight? He's never mentioned the Italians except for the older retired ones he runs into at the liquor store. They are harmless, but he believes they talk behind his back.

Behind Mr. Grey is a tall man in his forties who remains inside the foyer with his back to the front door.

"This is Gio. He'll wait outside in the car now that we've all met." He turns his strong neck, which I've bitten, and nods for Gio to excuse himself.

This is too formal. I'm flustered. This is out of control. I'm vulnerable. I enter a flight-or-fight survival mode. I have to get out of here before the room caves in.

I'm about to escape when Mr. Grey grabs my hand and passes the roughness of his grip off as an introduction.

"I'm Matteo Borrelli. Call me Matteo." He announces this as if he's the newest king in the city. Maybe he is. My father is already kissing his ass. What has my father done? He's a wolf father let into our home.

Matteo and I lock eyes.

This is war.

He used me to get to my father. Does Dad have something Matteo wants?

My mother claps her hands to get everyone's attention. "Let's have a drink."

Father grabs the bottles from the adjoining dining room. Mom collects the glasses. She pads behind him like he has her on a leash. It's as if they've rehearsed tonight.

I'm worried about the arrogance displayed on Matteo's stern face. His features softened when he looked at me.

What does he want from us? Is this a doomsday movie I recently watched where all the electric cars drive themselves into dumps as if they are possessed?

It was a surreal movie experience I didn't care for, but I found myself in my own altered reality, unfolding before my eyes in real-time.

Matteo extends his arm, indicating that I should go first.

How chivalrous. It's the least he can do, I suppose. All I want to do is mutter obscenities at him to protest his presence. I know now is not the time, and keep my lips sealed.

We adjourn to the formal living room that is only used on holidays when we entertain family and close friends. If Alexsei Sidovo, the Russian Don, were here, this is where we'd sit.

Oddly, Sidovo isn't here. What are we doing?

I sit cautiously on the edge of a cushioned chair built for looks, not function or comfort. The only thing making me more uncomfortable is Matteo's virile presence.

He makes no secret of the fact he's taking in my body. He started with my legs, and now he's lifting his gaze to my lips. Then our eyes meet. I defy him as I look at my mom and mumble something insignificant about the weather.

The drinks are handed out, and Dad stands and proposes a toast.

I look at my father with veiled eyes. What the fuck is going on?

"Matteo, we want to thank you for your generous offer to marry our daughter. We wish you both a long life of happiness."

What the fuck?

Matteo stands, and they touch glasses. Dad isn't smiling.

This isn't what he envisioned for me. I was supposed to marry a Russian and strengthen the bloodline. I never considered being married off to the enemy.

My jaw drops. My mother's expression gives nothing away. She's had a lifetime to perfect her poker face. After years of tolerating her husband's drunkenness and verbal abuse, she is a shell of the person I remember as a child.

Our men can put a glossy spin on our lives, but it's not always pretty behind the public eye. Maybe this is why I'm a rebel.

Everything promised has been a lie. I'm hurt that my father did not speak to me first. Mom is broken. Maybe that's my future. I will be broken, too.

I'm dying to text Izzy for details but discover I'm stuck. My father has me under his watchful eye. He would not hesitate to embarrass me if I stepped out of line, and given the fact that his current look could kill a spider, I couldn't move an inch if I wanted to. Without my phone, I am helpless. It's hanging with my coat in the foyer.

And if looks could kill—Matteo would be dead.

"Alena, Matteo has requested that you move into his mansion before the engagement is announced to the public," Dad says. It's not a suggestion. "It's for your protection."

The orders are starting, and now I will be exiled into the enemy's territory.

What did I do to be subjected to such torture? I'm angry at Matteo. And at the same time, I hate myself because my body yearns for him. My body aches for him to be inside of me.

"Alena, take a drink," Mom says as she pours two vodkas, and the men refill their glasses. We all toast, and I knock it back without a blink.

"Where do you live, Matteo?" I ask. "There are a few Italian families in the city, and I wonder where we'll be living," she adds a curious undertone to words meant to challenge me.

"I have a home you should find comfortable on Long Island. And, if it's not to your liking, I can sell it and buy something different. We can also live at the penthouse on the Upper East Side."

"How will I get to work if we live on the Island?"

"Work? You don't need to work," he says, dismissing my concern without any thought about how I feel about it.

"I want to work. I have a job at your hotel," I say, stressing the word "your." "I'd like to keep it."

"Now, now, there is time to iron out the details later," Dad states, ending the argument before it gains traction.

"Dinner is ready." Mom stands. "Alena, come help me in the kitchen," We head into the kitchen while the men move into the dining room.

Mom and I carry plates of food to the table. Dad and Matteo are having a quiet conversation and are waiting for us to join them. Mom passes food to Matteo first. He politely takes some of the dumplings before he passes them to me.

This is going to be a long night.

I need vodka.

CHAPTER 15

MATTEO

I know women. I can tell Alena is seething under her calm
exterior. This is the calm before the storm. Like a dragon,
Alena has fire in her belly and is ready to torch this place.

Her eyes are colder than the Bering Sea, and she's giving me a
guarded glare. I wouldn't be surprised if I went home with a case of
frostbite on my balls. Her eyes travel to my crotch as if to imply she'd
snip them off if given the chance.

She's biding her time. War has been declared, but she has to pick
her place to retaliate. She can't undermine her father as it would bring a
physical punishment, which would be carried out in front of me. I'm
not one to hit a woman, but the old guard is different.

Alena is proud. She will exact her revenge when we are behind
closed doors. I'm looking forward to the encounter. I'm a sick man. I
played her like a fiddle; now she knows I have her against the ropes.

I hope this doesn't affect our sex life. I'm not immune to the fact
that some objects might be hurled at my head.

Dinner continues painfully slow. It's a meal served with undercurrents and back-handed innuendos.

"I take it you're from Sicily?" Alena asks.

"Yes, my father recently passed. I'm taking over the family empire. I'm more than happy to have you at my side as my fiancée."

"How long have you been here?"

"I've traveled here over the years to learn English and the customs here." I eye her as my brows furrow slightly. It's as if I'm asking how many questions she intends to ask.

"How is work, Alena?" Dad asks.

He's obviously trying to validate her recent accomplishment by feigning interest.

She wouldn't have a job if it weren't for me. It looks like this might be a thorn in my side. It sounds as if she likes her job. I imagine a woman who was raised to be cared for would have been happy with the arranged marriage she knew would be happening.

She's of marriageable age and was raised to be cared for in exchange for a life of leisure. So why would she choose to work?

The novelty of the job will wear off in a month. She'll crumble like a shortbread cookie. I can never eat one without wearing it. They are best if they crumble in a cold glass of milk. That way, I drink them both together, and it's not messy.

Alena is doing her best to ignore me. My balls tighten at the thought of her in my bed, riding my massive cock as I make her mine.

"I'm sure you know everything there is to know about me," Alena states.

Fair enough.

I nod. "Tell me something I don't know."

"I've been hooking up and having anonymous sex with a hot Italian. What are you going to do about him?"

Her mom gasps and drops her fork. Her father's hand slams the table as he jumps to his feet.

I put a hand up to calm everyone.

"I'm sure he'd love to see more of you." I chuckle. She's boxed into a corner.

Alena is quiet, and her father takes his seat. Her mother begins to clear the table, and Alena follows her lead.

"Forgive her. I don't know what has gotten into her tonight. I'm sure she'll be faithful. I don't know of any Italian. I think she only intended to cause an issue with the arranged marriage," her father suggests.

"Don't worry, I'll make sure the marriage happens," I murmur. "Make no mistake about that. The wedding will be extravagant. All the important players will be invited. I trust Alena will open access to people I need to network with. How is she at social events?"

"She's not one to carry on conversations with women who don't have their own opinions and can be a bit of a wild card."

"I like that about her," I say as we stand and enter the living room. The women rejoin us, and I thank my hosts for the evening. Before I turn to go, I ask Alena to follow me to the foyer alone.

"What are you doing?" Alena whispers in an accusatory voice.

"Putting a ring on it. No woman of mine will be seen with another man's hand on her. Ever. If anyone touches you, they will die, so warn Kirill," I sneer.

"You're mean. I won't marry you," she blurts out.

"You will if you value your father's life. He took something of mine. Now I've taken something of his," I reply jovially. "Besides, we have a marriage contract."

"I'm not an inanimate object!"

"No," I concede as I run my hand down her beautiful face. "You are not. But you are mine, and I suggest you don't forget it."

"This isn't over," she spits.

"Oh, but it is," I say as I pull the box out of my pocket. Inside is an emerald-cut diamond, the largest canary diamond on the market. It has the most intense color of yellow ever seen by man.

I pluck the ring out of the box before I take her hand into mine. I slip the ring on her finger.

"We're official," I state as I watch her eyes grow wide.

"This is too much. It's too big."

"That's not what you say when you marry the most eligible man in New York. I want every man to know you are mine."

I raise her hand to my lips and kiss it before I let go.

"You really shouldn't have..." Her voice is softer now and trails off as she looks at her ring finger. I think she likes it.

Her voice is softer than before. Does my Angel like jewels?

I can't imagine she's submitting, but she's wearing my ring, and for now, it's enough.

"I have to be going. Pack what you want from your condo. You'll move in this week. I'm looking forward to seeing you soon." I drop a phone in her hand and enjoy the surprised look on her face. "This is your phone from now on. Shortly, I'll have my guard, Vito, with you at all times. If you want to live to see the honeymoon, you have to be safer than you've been," I reply frankly.

"When will I see you?" she asks, but I close the door without giving her an answer.

Outside, Gio steps out of the vehicle and opens my door. It's started to snow, and I'm grateful for the heated seats when I slide in.

"How did it go?" he asks.

"It went. She has my ring on her finger. It's not the romantic gesture it should be. It's nothing like in the movies— but I don't want her to get the wrong impression. This is a business deal, not a romance novel. She'll learn her place."

"I hope so for your sake. American women are different. They don't like to follow the man. They like to be equals."

"Home, Gio. I trust the staff has made the house ready for her."

"Yes, there are flowers in vases for the first time, and your room has a less intimidating vibe with throw pillows on your bed and a huge fluffy comforter. Federico says girls like that shit. I must admit it makes your room look less... spartan."

"Great. Whatever makes her happy. I'm sure she'll need time to adjust. She said she wants to work. I don't like the idea. It gives the wrong impression. She's to be my queen. What do you think about that?"

"It's admirable, considering she's never done so before. But it's a risk. When the news of your engagement gets out, your enemies will target her to get to you."

"True, but that would happen no matter when I married. Have you gained any leads on Mr. Gambino?"

"No. He's still dead, if that's what you mean. Might I remind you that you have a mountain of his papers to go through?"

"I hate tedious tasks. That's why I do what I do. Every day has a new challenge, and my adrenaline rushes. Make sure Antonio is looking into any digital accounts Gambino might have had. His house still has a phone jack, but it's worth a shot."

I sit back in the leather seat and stare at the snow falling. The falling snow, illuminated by the streetlights, is mesmerizing.

"I managed to lift the SIM card from the advisor's phone. It was old, but it might be worth a shot. You said he carried your father's phone. We might get lucky."

"I'm sure it's backed up to an encrypted file, but see what Antonio can do."

Gio nods as he drives, and I reflect on the night's events. Alena is gorgeous. It might be beneficial for her to continue working. I'm sure I'll put a baby in her quickly. I don't want her to have too much time on her hands. I'm sure she'll tire of the commute from the Island and give up working soon.

My phone dings.

Alena. Hmm. She misses me already.

Alena: This isn't over.

CHAPTER 16

ALENA

I stare at the masssive diamond on my finger. It's exquisite. It's not like any ring I've ever seen. I'm giddy at the sight of it on my finger. The bling factor exceeds my expectations. Oddly, it fits my personality. Yellow diamonds this vibrant are rare and costly. It makes a statement.

I'm taken.

He wants me. And he wants everyone to know I'm his.

I can't deny our physical attraction. I suppose the situation could be worse. My parents could have married me off to someone I have no attraction to. As luck has it, Matteo and I seemed to enjoy the physical side of our secret relationship.

I turn slowly, taking a breath before I confront my parents. They don't have to know Matteo and I already know each other.

Dad stands and walks to me when I enter the room. "I know you're going to protest, Alena."

"Really?" Sarcasm drips from the word. "I wasn't prepared for this. You could have warned me." I raise my voice.

"Me? What of you? You're the one with the bad reputation," Dad spits in my face. "What Italian?" he huffs, referring to my comment earlier to put Matteo in his place.

"What did you do to make him angry?" I ask. Now that I know Matteo is a don, there is more to this arrangement than Dad says.

If the look of amusement in Matteo's eyes can be trusted, tonight unfolded as Matteo expected. It looked to me like he enjoyed making my father fuss over him. "What did you do?" I enunciate each word and wait for his response.

"I bought a property that he has been working to buy, and I beat him to it." He shuffles his weight on his feet, imploring me to be merciful. "He found out about it and came to collect it, and he made it clear he wanted you."

"Me?"

"It was an anonymous tip. An email. It was encrypted. It could have been from anyone. It was a great idea, so I looked into it and offered more."

My father looks pathetic. My father wields power, but tonight, he's powerless. He's submissive. I pause. Silence fills the room, forcing him to talk.

"I acted on the tip. I didn't share the information with my boss." His last sentence puts me in a precarious position.

He didn't buy the building for the Russians. He was buying it for himself and business associates behind the Don's back. He sits at the right hand of the Don as his advisor, and if the Don finds out, he'd be killed. He's a traitor. His life is ruled by greed.

This is becoming an increasingly complex and messy situation. Izzy has feared my father over the years. But today, Izzy is the Principessa to the bratva. Her father is the don, and her husband will be the next to take over in his place.

"The Don doesn't know about this," I murmur the words as the reality of the situation sinks in.

My father's devious behavior and betrayals are revealed. He had to make a deal with Matteo because Matteo knew his secret. I marry

Matteo, and my father lives. If I refuse, Don Sidovo will have to kill my father to punish a traitor.

My father needs me to keep his dirty secret.

"Izzy is my best friend, and you want me to keep a secret from her?"

This is rich. I can't do that.

Can I?

"She's my best friend, Dad. How can I betray her? She's been lied to her entire life. She's been nothing but loyal to me and to you," I yell in anger and enunciate the word 'you.'

"I supported you and her for years. She lived with us for free, and I bought that condo for you. It's all been paid for," he argues. "You can lie to her, and you will," he says sternly as his eyes burrow into mine. He leans in, and his face is inches from mine.

My Dad's eyes drift like he's tired. Mom bids for him to sit by her on the sofa, and as when he turns, his shoulders slump.

"It's business, Alena. You knew you'd be married off to someone," Mom interjects. Dad sits beside her and runs a hand down his face.

I wonder how often he's done deals that the don doesn't know about. Do others hold my father's secrets?

"How am I to keep my Russian friends when I'm sleeping with the enemy—the Italian?" I ask.

"That's one steamy bed if you ask me," Mom says, then uses her hand to hide her smirk. It appears my mother recognizes a sexy man when she sees one.

"What did you mean about a hot Italian at dinner?" Dad asks, now that he's calmer. Mom moves her hand on his leg as a sign of support.

"Nothing, I attempted to make Matteo jealous." I shrug. I'm entitled to my secrets. No one will die over me having sex with Matteo.

"If you bothered to notice the look on his face, he did notice," Mom adds.

"Yeah, well, it's getting late. I'm exhausted," I say, turning to leave. I realize I don't possess the mental capacity to fight right now. There is so much I have to process.

Dad and Mom stand and walk me to the door. Dad holds my coat for me.

"Good night, Alena," Dad coos, as if all is forgotten, and kisses my forehead.

I never dreamed he would call in an IOU on everything he's done for me. I never realized before today how much I took for granted. I come from a life of privilege. Sure, Dad could have gotten into trouble over the years and ended up in prison. The syndicates fly under the government's radar and use mostly legitimate businesses for steady income. They do illegal things, but Dad sits at the top, where his hands remain relatively clean.

I slip into my coat that's being held before I sling my purse over my shoulder. Mom opens the door for me, and after she's closed it, I hear it click as the lock slides into place.

I walk to the vehicle that's running in the driveway. It's a somber, reflective time for me, and I'm happy to have the long sidewalk to collect my thoughts.

I never knew he did deals on the side. I wonder if this is why he's been stressed out lately, and it makes me curious if Kirill is aware of what my father has done. Kirill is loyal to the family, so I assume Dad didn't tell anyone, except Mom.

"I don't need you to follow the mystery man, Dima," I say as I enter the SUV.

"Why's that?"

"It's over," I say, for lack of a better excuse. I don't want to advertise that I've been duped.

I've had plenty of flings, but this is the first time I feel used. How long did Matteo follow me? How long has he known who I am? How did he discover Dad's deal?

I have more questions than answers.

"Fine. I'll inform Kirill," he says. "I wonder what I'll be assigned to next," he comments.

"I don't know, but you won't be driving me," I reply sourly as he pulls onto the road to take us into the city.

"What do you mean?" He looks into the rearview mirrors as he drives to the expressway.

"I have a feeling my next driver will be of Italian descent. I'm engaged to Matteo Borrelli. The Don of the Sicilian syndicate."

He all but slams on the brakes.

"Get the fuck out of here. What happened? You're only telling me this now?"

"It just happened," I replied wistfully. "I'm still adjusting."

"I wondered who pulled in behind me tonight. The tall dude, right?" His voice is calm, and I am concerned because he was a sitting duck in the vehicle. It could have been a hit team, for god's sake.

"Correct." I sigh in relief.

"The man with him had me roll down my window and checked me out before they passed."

"Did they?" I'm not surprised because men in Matteo's position always do.

"Yeah, I had an idea he was someone important. Shit, are you okay?" He says, turning briefly in his seat to look at me.

"I appear to be," I reply.

What choice do I have?

I look at the ring on my finger. It's heavy. I'm not telling anyone I'm engaged except for Izzy. I just started working, and I don't want them to think my job is a placeholder until I am married. Besides, I'd feel uncomfortable sharing the news with anyone at work. I'm the new girl in the office. I'm still on probation.

The car is warm, but a chill runs through me. I pull my coat closer to me. I wonder how Matteo had men on me. I thought I was immune to being hurt by the family's business associates and enemies. Sidovo wasn't here tonight. He probably doesn't know this deal was brokered. I find myself at the center of what could be the cause of the next mafia war.

I should be relieved Matteo isn't my father's enemy. He had every opportunity to kidnap or kill me for revenge. Instead, Matteo chose not to spill blood.

I have to assume he knows everything about me.

My privacy has been violated. I'll find a way to even the score for his deception. There were numerous occasions where he could have slipped the words out of his mouth, "Hi, I'm the newest player in the mafia world, and I want to fuck you."

He thought he was clever and played games with me while keeping his identity a secret. I need answers. I have to take matters into my own hands. I know who he is. He won't suspect me of having him tailed.

"Dima, don't tell Kirill anything. I want you to follow Matteo. He's been my lover, and I'm not in harm's way. Besides, I suspect my future husband will have an Italian guard on me soon. That protects me, and your time will be free to follow him. Will you help me?"

"Intrigue and stalking? Count me in." He gives me a funny giggle that reminds me of Uncle Fester in the popular TV series about a family who is dark and sadistic.

I love having resources at my fingertips. Matteo thinks he has won and will underestimate me, not that he has what he wants. I'm embarrassed that he's been pulling the strings of influential players behind my back.

"I want to know where he lives, who he meets, what his penthouse is like, and anything else you can obtain. I also want to know what women he hangs out with and who he takes as a lover."

"Got it."

He's made a fool of me once. It won't happen again.

Dima rolls to a stop in my parking garage.

Armed with my new attitude, I bid Dima goodnight. "Happy hunting," I say, void of emotion.

I'm expecting updates by morning. If Matteo thinks I'm taking this lying down, he doesn't know who he's marrying.

I change as soon as I get to my condo. I text Izzy to make sure she was up. She pings me back, so I pick up my phone and call her.

"How are you?" I ask. It's easy for me to get caught up in my life and ask her about herself as an afterthought. Tonight, my news can wait. What do I say? Is my loyalty to my friend or my father?

I would probably tell her if the secret involved Izzy herself. But since this doesn't affect her well-being, I decided to honor my father's wishes until I know more. I can't put my father's head on the chopping block.

"Everything here is fine," she says. "The baby is getting big. We're trying to pick a name for her. Dmitry is out of town for a few days. We should meet up."

"I'd love to. Maybe we can meet for lunch this week."

"Great. How is your job? Did you ever think you'd be gainfully employed?"

"Funny thing about that job…"

"What, were you fired?"

"No, worse."

"What could be worse than that?" Izzy's voice conveys her curiosity.

"Remember how I thought the interview was too easy?"

"Yes, that was weird. You didn't even do a drug test, and they hired you on the spot." She pauses, then adds, "That never happens."

"What if I told you my boss happens to be my new fiancé?"

"What? I don't follow," she says, confused.

"My mystery man is Matteo Borrelli, like in the don of the Borrelli Empire—from Sicily. He had to have known who I was and planned our hookups." I snap my fingers. "Damn. It makes sense now."

"What makes sense?"

"Remember my first day at work?"

"The elevator ride?"

"He just showed up, stopped the elevator, and we did it there."

"That's a bit kinky," she says. "Were you afraid of getting caught?"

"That's half the thrill, and he stopped the elevator. But I've discovered he owns the hotel."

"That's convenient," she says. I hear her padding around in a luxurious penthouse where Dmitry bought a few buildings next to them to expand. Izzy quit her job a few months ago to oversee the renovations and prepare for the baby.

"Rough night?" I ask, considering it's late, and I hear a few muffled groans as she moves. She has a way of flowing with how uncomfortable she is. She says every day is a new obstacle.

"The baby is moving. Things are stretching. It's not as easy as it looks. But enough about me. How did the mystery man in the elevator happen? Were you being followed? Did Dima know?"

"No, I told him I was alone."

"Good," she replies. "I think."

"You know, in summer, it would not have been so incredible. But the sex was intense." I chuckle at the steamy memory of how he choked me.

"I'm so happy you hit it off so well."

If she only knew.

"It would be easy for him to slip in and out of any floor in the hotel. He knows it inside out."

"He's acted like a stalker," she muses. "Are you sure you're safe with him?"

"He could have killed me or kidnapped me by now. Besides, if he bumps me off, make sure you get this incredible yellow diamond in the ring he put on my finger tonight."

Izzy laughs, then winces.

"Are you okay?" I ask.

"I'm huge," she replies. "The doula says my ligaments are stretching for the baby. It hurts. No one ever tells you all the fun facts about pregnancy. I've read books until my brain is fried. I'm glad we have her on call. Carrying and birthing a human is exhausting. This baby appears to take what she needs from me."

"Isn't that what they're supposed to do?"

"Thank you, really. Dmitry has been great. He tells me that all the time, but soon I'll be in slip-on shoes because I won't be able to reach my feet."

I chuckle. "I wish I could do something for you."

"I'm fine." She changes the subject back to me. "When is the big announcement? Do you have a wedding date?"

"I have no clue."

"Well, fill me in when you know more. I guess congratulations are in order."

"Thank you," I reply as I toss my bed sheets and slide into bed.

"Does my dad know?" Izzy asks.

I assume these alliances would typically be discussed among the leaders, but I'm not the don's daughter.

Maybe it's not a big deal?

My marriage was brokered faster than the amount of time it takes to move a shipment of fentanyl. Last week, I was told to get a job. This week, I'm engaged.

"No, actually," I reply, playing it off as if the arrangement was a spur-of-the-moment decision. "It appears Matteo wanted me, and when he found out who I was, I'm sure it made sense to make it official. I'm keeping it to myself for now. We barely know each other."

"Okay, just let me know before the news breaks. I can't keep it from Dmitry," she announces.

"That's fine," I reply. I like Dmitry. He'd do anything to protect me.

Matteo knows how to make allies and enemies. With me, he obtains an opponent's prized possession and a powerful alliance. My father made it easy for him to make a move on the Russians. This is not going to look good to Don Sidovo.

"Oh," she says. "Well, is he who you want?"

"It's how the games get played," I reply. "We knew I would be married to someone."

"That's true. That's so strange, though. You said you met at a sex club?"

"Yes."

"He didn't know you there?"

"We don't use real names. I don't see how he would have known."

There is no level Matteo won't sink to obtain me, buy me, or persuade me. Did he pick me out with a purpose? How far ahead does he plan his moves?

Am I marrying a psychopath?

"I'm sure I'm overthinking it," Izzy says.

I sigh in relief. How long can I keep up the charade that we've become engaged over steamy hook-ups?

"It's late. I better let you go," I say.

We bid each other goodnight, and I place my phone on the charger on my nightstand. I stare out the window and watch the snowfall. It's so pretty, and its serene presence calms me.

How do I wage a war with a man who will do anything to win?

Matteo wants me in a cage. He shows up when he wants and takes what he wants. So why bother to make it official? He had what he wanted from me. Why did he have to make me a part of the bargain?

He's older. I assume he needs an heir.

I wonder how long it will be before we're married. Once that occurs, I'll be locked into a lifetime of demands dictated by my husband, and I'll have to fulfill his every wish.

I hope some of his wishes are salaciously enjoyable.

CHAPTER 17

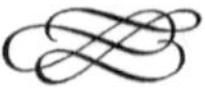

MATTEO

*I*t's the middle of the night in Sicily, and too late to call
Niccoló. I wish I had informed him of my plan, but life
sometimes moves quickly.

The mansion is so quiet that I hear the heels of my shoes click on
the terra rossa porcelain Italian tiles as I make my way up the large
staircase to the second floor. This house was bought months ago with a
wife in mind, so it's only natural that I wouldn't want to live in this
monstrosity like a tumbleweed forever.

Eventually, most bachelors take a wife. I'm sure Alena will know
what to do with the empty spaces. Federico is gone for the night, and
now I wish he were here. The mansion overwhelms me. We're not used
to such large homes in Sicily, where the sea and mountains limit
land use.

Federico is more than a chef. I occasionally have philosophical
conversations with him. He's intuitive, and I find him to be a good
judge of character. He's an integral part of my family, even if he's not
of my blood.

I hope he will watch Alena as I will be out all day and night, building my sprawling empire that will only grow bigger with time. I'm taking over for my father, and there are things I have to handle myself. I need to unravel his life if I'm to feel safe in mine.

I suppose I've started a list in my head, but I think it works best with a pen in my hand and a notebook. After tonight's dinner, my mind wanders off.

I'm a visual person. I prefer to see information in charts, graphs, and other mediums than to read wordy reports. I hold face-to-face meetings in secure rooms with no cell phones. I don't need distractions, and I can never be too careful.

Perhaps this is why I am drawn to Alena—the vision of her in the red and black bustier and stockings. The heels made the outfit complete. I had a boner stiffer than a lead pipe to prove its effective- ness. She was not afraid to commit to the themed night.

"Angels and Demons" is a great song, and as it turns out, it marks the first time I met a sexually liberating woman. I've always found sex to be liberating, but that was before I realized marriage was the end game.

She gave them the impression she was badass. I know underneath the finery she wore, she's an angel in disguise. I'm sure she'll soon conclude that I'm the devil she didn't see coming. She doesn't have a mean spirit, and I hope she will comply with the changes she'll be forced to make.

I've known beautiful women over the years, but not one can compare to her. I walk into my large, built-out closet, which resembles the one tailored for my woman. I undress and wish that she were here.

Soon, I tell myself.

It will take me time to get used to living here. Thankfully, Long Island is quieter than the city, but it is an adjustment for me. I love my Sicilian home by the sea. The rhythmic waves of the ocean helped me fall asleep.

I undressed and reentered the bedroom with the oversized king-size bed. A vase of fresh-cut daisies with lavender and baby's breath is on the dresser. Money might not buy me everything, but it helps to retain the best staff.

My burner phone rings. This is never a good sign at this hour. However, when Gio's name flashes, I inhale and exhale air before I answer.

"Have you given a thought about Finn? We forgot to discuss it today. We were busy dodging the law when we discovered your father's advisor dead, and then you had the engagement dinner," Gio's voice fades off.

Gio is not only my advisor but an attorney. He knows how to keep our men out of trouble and who to put on our cases should anyone end up in court.

"It can't be tied to us. Make it an overdose. Make sure he's no one important and that there are no witnesses. I don't want a band of angry Irishmen on my ass. I'm taking a wife. It would be nice not to have to look over my shoulder when I go on a honeymoon."

"Oh, a honeymoon? I thought Alena was only a business arrangement."

"I can't change the fact that the woman is as fuckable as she is insatiable. Besides, I need to put a baby in her. I need an heir."

"Sounds like you met your match if you ask me."

"I didn't ask you," I reply somberly. "Tell Antonio to make sure there are no fuckups. I'm all for keeping Caitlan safe. Some men don't respond to warnings. I have too much to worry about than to be involved with domestic issues. Take care of it, and I never want to hear of it again."

"I'm on it," Gio says before bidding me a good night.

This Finn situation is a nasty business. Irishmen love their dark ale and are known to be unpredictable. They also hold grudges forever. Forget about the Luck of the Irish. I'm a fucking Italian, and the Irish are a pain in my ass. They've been at war with a clan in England for years over a hit on a family member, and I have no desire to wind up in the same situation.

I slide into bed. I wonder what is going through Alena's mind now that she knows who I am. Her eyes flashed with delight when she looked at the ring. I've never been in a relationship. However, she's my Angel, and she deserves the most impressive ring. Besides, I want everyone to know that she's mine.

Where could we go for a honeymoon? Sicily is lovely, but we'd be overrun with my family around and dropping in to see my new wife. I don't have much of a lead on who might want me dead. So far, nothing has panned out. I'm like a dog chasing its tail. I'm running in circles, hoping our next lead doesn't meet with another dead end or a dead body.

What did Dad do? He was my father, but I didn't know him to be anything other than the ruthless and abusive man he was. I took the brunt of the spankings and beatings. Whenever he had a bad day, he took it out on me.

Was Dad the only target? Or does someone want me dead? I never leave my livelihood or that of my siblings up to chance. Logically, whoever killed him might want me dead as well.

Living defensively is the only course of action. I don't know how I'll break the news to Alena. She's never been in a gilded cage, but the danger that's lurking beyond my walls is real whether Dad was murdered or not. To me, the most dangerous time for a don is at the beginning and end of his service.

Death by poison is the sign of a coward or a woman, but weeks have passed, and I've not been able to ascertain anything. I'm frustrated, and it pisses me off.

My mind wanders to Alena and how she threw her tidbit about sex with an Italian in my face at dinner. She almost got me. If I didn't have her followed, I might have believed she was seeing someone else. I chuckle when I remember looking at her mother's face after the comment. I thought she would choke on her borsch.

Alena is a lively woman, and I doubt life will ever be dull. Can I make her leave all that she's known in the city and her life with her friends to be my wife and the mother to my children?

I need to go through Dad's papers. If I continue to ponder all of my problems tonight, I'll never get any rest, and I have to be alert now, more than ever.

CHAPTER 18

ALENA

I didn't get much sleep. The weight of my father's lack of good judgment disturbs me. Why would he go behind the don's back and take a deal for himself? I've never seen him angry at Alexsei. Is my father planning a campaign to unseat him? If he is, that means Izzy and Dmitry are in danger.

I'm curling my hair for work when my phone dings with a message.

I pick up my phone but don't recognize the number. Glancing at the message, I realize it's from my fiancé. The word fiancé is strange even though I knew I'd be married sooner rather than later.

How much time do I have before we are to be married? I'm just finding myself and don't want to leave the city. The presence of Matteo added excitement to my single life. I can't deny that I fantasized about him. What did I expect from him? Love?

Is he capable of love? I read the message.

Matteo: I'll pick you up after work for dinner.

Me: Fine.

I save his number, push the letters on my keypad, and type Mr. Grey.

Matteo: Vito is your new guard. He's waiting downstairs. Do not fight me on this. You've been irresponsible with your safety.

Me: Fine.

He was mysterious. Now, I find him to be bossy—and bordering on cryptic.

Yes, I should have been more careful running around town like I'm normal. Dad should have made me have a guard. It's funny because the last time I thought men might be after me, they were hunting Izzy. But in my defense, I had no way to know that my father had put me in danger. He pissed Matteo off, and now I'm paying the price.

Dima knows where Matteo lives and has emailed me the floor plans of his house. He picked them up from City Hall. It's a palatial estate. If I didn't know Matteo had the largest cock I've ever encountered, I would have assumed his home was to compensate for a small dick.

Lucky for me, that's not the case.

The ring on my finger reminds me that last night wasn't my imagination. My pussy glistens with the merest thought of him. He can drop in on me whenever he wants because I work for him.

I want to punish him and shock him like he did me. As the new don, I assume he will be highly cautious with every decision he makes. Each step has to be thought out, and he must have a plan to keep the organization profitable. He has to keep his men happy and confident in his leadership.

Chaos and distrust in the syndicate can lead to mutiny. I'm wise enough in the ways of the bratva to know that if there is dissension in the ranks, the don's life is at risk.

I wrestled with my father's secret, swearing to keep it under duress. What if my father is planning to take over the bratva? What if this was his first attempt to convince potential members that he could bring in deals? Dmitry is next in line to become Don. Is my father working behind the scenes with his own agenda?

I can't risk anything happening to Dmitry or Izzy. They are my family. My heart is heavy with concern. Izzy never trusted my dad. Did I miss something?

Once again, I find my future in a holding pattern. I know whom I'm marrying, but I don't know what my future holds. What does he want from me? Why did he have to have me?

I will be married to the Italian don, and if the bratva falls, Matteo could easily step in and take over. There would be a war, and I would be in the middle of it. I pray it will not come to that.

Matteo is as skillful at politics as he easily made me feel like his chew toy. It took him less than two weeks to recover his building and wrap me into the deal. Before meeting him, I would have gone with my parents' choice of a husband. Knowing what I do now, I don't trust my father's motives.

Dima texted me more information. I read what he sent, and I find it odd that there is no cause of death listed in Luciano Borrelli's obituary. I wonder how he died.

There were no wars at the time, and no shootings were reported in Sicily. It's not like he was too young to die. He was sixty, the age at which dons usually retire, one way or the other.

My next thought leads me to question Luciano's death. What if he was murdered?

And if he was murdered, who did it? Death is a retirement that doesn't include a pension. There is no trace of him on social media, and Dima didn't find any records that might be useful to me, like marriage certificates, children, or family deaths in Sicily. I doubt I'll ever see an authentic record of Matteo other than his passport.

I know how foreign countries work. To obtain any records, tons of paperwork and bribes are paid over the counter in fees and the untraceable ones under the table.

It's clear that Matteo has my safety in mind, and instead of being annoyed, maybe I shouldn't resist my guards in light of the current situation.

I finish my hair and pull a ribbed cotton Ralph Lauren dress over my head. I tug on black boots that zipper on the inside of my leg. The boots are shiny, a retro look from the 70s.

I'm marrying a man more powerful than my father. I smile because my father can't mistreat me anymore. Matteo will not tolerate him abusing me now that I'm under his protection. I saunter out the door and walk to the elevator, knowing there are perks associated with Matteo's status.

I arrive in the parking garage, and it looks as if this is the limo that we fucked in last week. Did Matteo send this vehicle to remind me of our midday tryst?

My dark red lips curl into a smile as the man, who introduces himself as Vito, opens the door for me.

"Good morning, Ms. Pasnov," he says without meeting my eyes.

"Hello, Vito."

He's dressed in a black suit. At six feet tall, he's shorter than Matteo, but he has dark hair and eyes that don't even give me a once-over glance. That's strange.

"I won't bite," I joke.

"I know. My job is to keep you safe, and the boss wouldn't like it if I am too friendly."

"Oh," I reply thoughtfully. I remember the night at the club, and Matteo didn't like Kirill being too close to me. I never considered Matteo's threats applied to men in his employ. Doesn't he trust them? It's clear that Vito understands what's expected of him.

Now, I worry about Matteo going off on someone over his possessiveness over me. And by "off," I'm assuming he would kill. I know first-hand how strong his hands are and the depth of darkness in his eyes, which is a darkness I hope I will never witness in action.

Vito drives me to work and is steady as people walk between cars sitting in traffic. I don't know how he can be so calm. I sink into the plush seat and watch the city come alive. Rush hour is always a bitch.

Vito parks the car in the hotel garage, and I wait for my door to open. I'm afraid it would offend him if I were to get out on my own.

He steps aside to let me walk by the door. He informs me to wait inside the door for him. I oblige. I don't want to be labeled as difficult, so I do as I'm told.

Vito joins me after he parks the limo and escorts me to the elevator. My entire morning has been filled with reminders of Matteo's presence. It's as if he's here even when he's not.

In the elevator, I run a finger over the gorgeous diamond. I forgot to take off my engagement ring before I left my condo. I carefully slip the ring off and place it into my zippered wallet. No one knows of its existence, and I'm not ready to be fawned over and asked a million questions that I don't have answers to. This way, I'll avoid the awkward situation altogether.

My guard walks me to the door and opens it.

"I'll never be far away," he says. He pushes a fob into my hand. "Press this if you ever need me."

"Is this necessary?"

"I don't take chances. If something happens to you, worse things will happen to me."

I meet his eyes. He means business. I take the fob. "Okay."

When I walk into the office, I am filled with mixed emotions. Thankfully, I have this job to keep my mind occupied for the next eight hours. I search the office for Penny and find her in the break room with a cup of tea.

"Good morning," she says with her chipper British accent. I'm decidedly a fan of accents. I'll have to learn some Italian words as Matteo whispers Italian words in my ear during sex, and I have no idea what he was saying, but I'd love to find out.

"Hi," I reply. "What's on the agenda for today?"

"We have a meeting with the vendor for the floating sinks in an hour. You should check your emails and get estimates on the pillows."

"Which one?"

"All of them."

"I remember we looked at thirty of them."

She walks toward me to leave the room, "That sounds about right. You're the newly hired. It's where we all started. This is your first job, and I'm sure you'll do well, but it takes time to become established."

"Right."

I walk behind her and veer off to a workstation where I log into my work email. I have to look at my phone for my password. I find it's always a pain in the ass. Whatever happened to having a desk of my own?

I read through my emails, and one is from the president welcoming me to the team.

Matteo. If I see or hear from him before dinner, I'm going to scream. I ignore the automatic greeting, respond to team members, and print out the list of pillows and sizes. They are from different vendors. It will take hours to work down the list.

The day went by, and as I'm still the newbie at work and haven't had any tasks to fuck up, and everyone is friendly. I feel like a glorified secretary, but I'm determined to stick it out and make a place for myself. I have an eye for color and texture. I want to prove I can be a team player and be of value.

I eat from the vending machine for lunch and pretend I'm busy on my phone for thirty minutes.

"How is work?" Matteo texts.

Me: Fine.

Matteo: I hope you can have more than one-word answers; otherwise, this will be a boring marriage.

Me: I doubt that very much.

Matteo: I don't see you as one to settle for boring.

He may not have spent much time with me, but he's right. Unfortunately, he's the one who added adventure to my routine life. If it weren't for him, I'd be home alone for the foreseeable future.

CHAPTER 19

MATTEO

I phone my brother before breakfast.

"Niccoló, how are you?" We rattle off words in Italian.

"Fine, fine. Everything is good here. How are you, brother?"

"Good. I'm getting married."

"I don't believe it. I thought I'd be the first to get married."

"Sorry, I beat you to it."

"Who is she? Gorgeous and witty, I hope."

"She is. Her name is Alena Pasnov. She's the daughter of the Russian syndicate's advisor."

"Not the Don's daughter?"

"His daughter is not Russian-born, and his son-in-law will take over for him shortly. Rumor has it he's married to his illegitimate love child, though."

"She's taken then, can't mess with that one," he chuckles.

"No, I wouldn't want to. We have leverage over the advisor, and as it turns out, Alena's best friend is the Don's illegitimate daughter," I add. "My marriage is a business deal."

I need an heir. I'll never give her anything other than a good fuck and shoot my seed inside her.

"How did the building deal go? The uncles are all waiting for you to fuck up," he informs me.

"I know. It's a done deal. You can pass the information on. Giuseppe and Luca have been bitching and complaining. Luca wanted me to use an ice pick on the old man."

"Figures, he's into dramatics." Niccoló knows him well. "But who knows what he's capable of?"

We're both silent for a minute.

"I have the building. Wu tried to sell it to the Russians, and he won't be an issue in the future."

"No loose ends, eh? Then the bastard got what he deserved."

"Mm, he did," I reply dolefully. "It had to be done to send a message. No one can say I'm weak."

"That's for sure."

"So, any news from you?" I wonder when he's going to propose to Chiara.

"No. Chiara has been busy with work. I think we're in a bit of a slump. She's tired and a bit depressed since Dad died."

"That's odd. No one liked the old fucker. If it weren't for the uncles, I would have danced on his gravesite."

"Yeah, it would have been a party. Well, he can have it in hell, as I'm sure that's where he is. He was mean. I can't imagine what you went through for us."

"Don't give it a thought," I say. "I want you to have a happy life."

He knows there are scars from him whipping my back. The wounds have faded with time but will never be erased from my memory. The old man loved to take his anger out on me. I gladly took the beatings to save my younger siblings. It was traumatic enough that Mom died suddenly.

Gio enters the breakfast room.

"I'll send more details when I have them. Is everything going okay there?"

"Yes, fine," Niccoló sighs.

"I have to go. Talk soon," I reply as we hang up.

"What's the word, Gio?"

"The matter with our Irishman has been handled."

"Great. As we discussed?"

"Yes, his last name is O'Donnell, but a million of them exist. He is a low-level person. I doubt he'll be missed."

"There is a Cillian O'Donnell that heads the Irish in the United Kingdom. Any relation?"

"He moves drugs for the Irish in Ireland in Dublin and small-town areas. He has quite the record with law enforcement. He comes up illegitimate. The last name is coincidental."

"What are the odds of that happening? Maybe I should play the lottery."

Gio chuckles. "Let me know if you win." Gio sits and pours himself coffee from the decanter.

"Great. Let's eat," I say as I observe Federico entering with a tray of breakfast foods and placing the plates on the table.

"Thank you, Federico," I say before I dig into my eggs benedict. Two perfectly poached eggs are resting on spinach and Italian toast. He delivers us both fresh espressos, one of which has a double in it for me.

I waste no time tossing it back.

"I'll peruse through Dad's papers that were left in his house. I doubt I'll find anything. What was on the SIM card?"

"Not much. The advisor called his kids, and there was a number used numerous times, but it's going to a burner phone that must be burnt. I was hoping we'd get a lead. There's no way to track who it could have been."

"Thank you for trying. Quick thinking on your part."

"That's why you have me," he says as he cuts his omelet into bite-sized pieces.

"Are the papers for the building in order?"

"Yes, all taken care of. The gala event for Councilman Addler is next month. You need tickets. I haven't been able to get you on the list.

Money isn't his only agenda," he murmurs in frustration. "He can't be bought easily."

I worked out in my home gym before Gio arrived. I finish wolfing down my food.

I push my chair back and stand. "Interesting. Maybe Alena will have connections. I'll work on it as well."

Gio stands to follow me.

"Eat. I have to go through my father's dusty papers. I'll be in my study. And get someone on Addler. There has to be dirt somewhere. I need leverage. I have to get his vote."

"Very well," he replies as he sits again and continues eating his sausage patty.

I walk to my study and pull papers out of a drawer. There are boxes in the corner of the room. Dad was a pack rat, and I'm afraid I'll burn my time and not find a damn thing.

"What were you up to, old man?" I mutter.

I pick up papers, straighten them, and glance over them one by one before moving them to another stack. I've been here for hours, and my calves hurt from sitting. I briefly considered using the indoor pool and sauna this morning. It's the only way to enjoy winter, I surmise.

I stand, contemplating my next move, and pick up the stack of papers to put back in a box when something falls to the antique rug under my feet.

I clutch the papers to my chest before bending to retrieve the one on the floor. It's folded. I open it with curiosity. I read the Italian words— I'll meet you tomorrow. Well, that's a clue. It's written in Italian, and it doesn't appear to be my father's penmanship.

The handwriting is cursive and slanted perfectly. It's too pretty to be the scribble of a man's hand, but my handwriting is atrocious. I can't make generalizations based on my limited handwriting interpretations.

Interesting. What was he meeting someone for? Why is it a paper note? Is it a secret? Was it for Dad or someone else?

I push a button underneath the middle of my cherry wood desk, and a fake drawer opens in the front. It looks like a decoration, but it's the perfect hiding place. I slip the note inside and close it. I dump the papers back into the bottom drawer.

"Gio," I call as I retrace my steps to the dining room.

"Yes?" He stands, stacking the breakfast plates with Federico.

"Let's go visit some businesses. I want to make sure everyone sees me and fears me."

"I'll call for the car," he replies, reaching for his suit jacket.

Minutes later, we're confined by privacy in the G-wagon. I share what I've discovered with Gio.

"That's odd. Antonio said the old man's security feed only shows them coming and going from the house. He had no visitors."

"Damn. Well, he had to go somewhere and meet someone. We don't store things in clouds," Gio states the obvious.

"I know. But all the same, it's annoying. Let's see if he had any meetings at our business locations. There is no date on the note, but the handwriting is elegant. I'm not sure we're looking for a man."

"Hard to tell. My mother writes like shit," he replies as he observes me.

"I do, too. I'm trying not to be biased. It could be a man or a woman."

"I'll instruct Antonio to give us a list of everyone he has a meeting with or a potential for a meeting to occur at all our holdings," Gio says, taking out his phone and texting.

I use my phone to text my fiancée at work. The word 'work' is like a cotton ball lodged in my mouth. I never actualized marriage. However, making an alliance through Alena will help me. All I want is for her to be a good mother to our children. I don't want her to have the stress of working. I'm the one who takes care of her.

I receive a text back, and my grumpy mouth cracks into a half-smile. She's amusing with her sassy retorts. We visit our new holding company; the last is my latest enterprise. It's a technology endeavor. Information is the key to power. We're developing a software app to be installed as a messenger on websites and phones under the ruse of being encrypted. The caveat is a back door will allow us to access the phone that uses it so we can obtain information on other businesses and sell it under a shell company so our opponents will never know it's been hacked.

I plan to sell it to all our known rivals in the city as a test. It's ingenious. I'll obtain information as it leaves cell phones. I have a huge warehouse of water-cooled computers, and I'll have the drop on all my enemies.

By the time we return to the city, it's time to pick Alena up from work. Vito walks her out the door and opens the door to the SUV.

I step out, and as soon as our eyes meet, I melt. My lips meet hers, and even though she resists, she can't hold out long enough. Her lips surrender to mine and return my kiss.

"Hello, Mr. Grey," she murmurs when I release her lips.

"Hello, Angel. How was your day?"

"Fine. And you?" She steps into the vehicle, and I want to slap her sexy well-rounded ass staring me in the face. However, at that exact moment, Vito hands me her winter coat. I take it and toss it in the back seat as I sit beside my fiancée. As soon as Gio closes the door, the driver drives off.

"Where is your ring?" I am peeved Alena isn't wearing my ring.

"Oh," her lips curve into a perfectly round O. "I didn't want a thousand questions at work." She slips her hand into her purse, pulls out a wallet that she unzips, and retrieves the ring.

I slip the ring onto her slender finger, pulling her hand to my mouth and planting a soft kiss before returning it to her lap.

The sound of her inhaling air causes my eyes to zoom to her face. She is surprised by my gesture.

"You haven't answered me," I reiterate.

"Yes, I understand," she replies as softly.

"Now that we have that out of the way, here is a credit card for you—an unlimited amount." I hand her the black card with her married name on it, even though our date hasn't been set.

"I don't need it." Her hands remain in her lap.

"I won't have you take a penny from your father. Besides, there are events that we need to attend that require one-of-a-kind dresses. Occasionally, you'll need a makeup artist and hairstylist. You're gorgeous. I love you in nothing at all, honestly. However, we're taking New York City by storm."

"What does that mean, exactly?" Her blue eyes glow warm upon my face, but she takes the card and slips it into her wallet.

"It means we're making connections and circulating in circles you've never seen."

"What do I have to do?" She's suddenly changed from a ferocious woman to one with uncertainty in her voice.

"Nothing unusual. But maybe you can soften people up as we greet them and help me gain access to the people I need to make deals go through. I'll be beside you to close the deals."

"What kind of deals?" Her eyes move over my face, and she observes my open trench coat, collared shirt, and tie.

"Nothing menacing. I need a height variance on the property I acquired. That's our first order of business. I'm the new don, and it's of utmost importance we obtain it to build another hotel."

"What do you need me for?"

"Councilman Addler's campaign fundraiser is a gala event. Half Masked ball, it will be up your alley, don't you think?"

She lets out a tiny laugh. "We dress up for this?"

"Yes, I have someone working on outfits. However, the fundraiser has been sold out for months. Find out if Izzy and Dmitry can fit us in at their table. They might have extras or know someone. They may have to boot someone to get us in. I have to be there. My success depends on my outcomes with Addler. He's known to hold out on these variances. I will head him off before he can deny my permit."

"I haven't heard about this event. How do you know they have tickets?" Her head is turned to observe my reaction. Her eyes are judging me, expecting me to have done something insidious.

"There is an RSVP list, and they're on it," I reply bluntly, giving her my most impressively mischievous smile.

"Wow. Well, I guess that's better than spying on their staff. Do you have men following people around the city?"

"Occasionally. However, that's a good idea. Technically, you're the only one I've followed in years. And it wasn't for business." I turn away from her to look out the window. I never should have let that slip.

Why am I blubbering? I don't show emotions.

"So, you followed me from Madame M?" Alena asks, but I know she's already figured out the answer. There's no reason to lie when I don't have to.

"Guilty," I reply with a chuckle. Being around her reminds me that I don't always have to be so serious. It's refreshing to have her as a companion.

"Oh, by the way, here is a new phone for you. I've cloned yours." I pull the phone out of my breast pocket.

She moves her lips to protest, but I put my finger on her to silence her protest. She moves her plump lips as if she'll bite me.

"This one is encrypted." I hand the new phone to her. "I even put the gold glitter case on it myself. It's necessary for our safety," I add.

"When did you clone my phone? How long have you known you were going to marry me?" She catches her breath. "Who are you?"

"Please hand your old phone to Gio." She pulls her phone out of her purse and slides it through the seats to Gio.

"I'm the don of the Borrelli family, and I'm going to be your husband. I will keep you safe at all costs. All I ask is that you keep an open mind for our marriage and future. And don't trust anyone or go anywhere without Vito. Do we have an agreement?"

"What do I get in return?"

I know she's asking to barter something. She's not greedy or needy. No, she asks with a purpose in mind. I'm curious to find out what it is.

"You get me and my empire," I state.

"Fine. Then, I want our marriage to be real, with no cheating."

There it is. My little Angel is jealous.

I turn my head to face her. My hand cradles her face.

"It goes both ways, my love."

Her blue eyes bore into mine and turned a paler shade of blue. What does this mean? I make a note to discover the secrets behind her pretty eyes. I've never known someone's eyes to change different colors, and I assume it might be connected to moods. I have to learn more about the Angel who brings a smile to my lips.

"Fine," she replies as if she's put out. However, I catch a tiny smirk on her face. She got what she wanted, and for some reason, she wants me.

I slip my finger over her lips and into her mouth. My cock twitches. Damn, she's so fuckable.

Gio pulls up to the restaurant and stops. I pull my hand away hesitantly. I have half a mind to fuck her, but it's my restaurant, and it would be awkward to arrive later when we've already pulled up to the curb. I exit the vehicle and turn, extending my hand to Alena.

She places her hand in mine and joins me on the sidewalk. She straightens her dress under her coat and stands next to me. I tuck her arm through mine and lead her into La Cucina del Padrino. My staff opens the doors, and the maître d' greets me by name and seats us immediately.

Alena is surprised at the speed at which the staff moves and is stymied by how all the staff nod at us. The head manager swings by our table and expresses his wish that our evening is a pleasant experience.

CHAPTER 20

The restaurant is elegant. There are numerous dining rooms, all themed. One has a Greek fountain in the middle of the room. We walk past another room with Roman columns that adorn the walls and separate the tables.

The guests are dressed like they are dining in Vegas, and the women's hairdos are spectacular. There is a quaint piano bar with a man playing the piano and a couple who look like they are on their first date.

I find it entertaining that the woman sitting across from the piano player is overdressed. Her date is wearing a dated suit. She has diamonds dangling from her ears, and her choker looks like an heirloom piece made of pearls. It's as if each is trying to make a statement to the other, but I can't figure out what it is. Are they trying to prove they have money, or is it an arranged date to appease mutual friends? They don't appear to have a spark between them. I guess we've all been there.

I'm underdressed. I should have gone home and changed into a cocktail dress. However, when we entered, heads turned. No one seemed to mind that I was dressed for work. Do these people have jobs or is this their evening entertainment?

We are immediately escorted to a table large enough for four. It sits toward the back of the main room. Matteo steers me toward the chair opposite him so he will sit where he can see the front door. I wonder why.

After we're seated, I turn my head to the left and check out the unusual circular room built of glass that obstructs my view of the piano room. I have a minute to observe the colossal wine room. Judging from the air-tight door, it's refrigerated.

The gorgeous glass spiral is filled with bottles of wine and champagne. The 360-degree staircase amazes me as I watch a man climb it. He effortlessly swings his body to swing the staircase until he secures the bottle he needs with his hand and returns to the bottom of the room. I've never seen anything like it.

Everybody tiptoes around as if they will be yelled at if they aren't efficient. Their white dress shirts are starched, and they all wear dark black slacks. The waiter at the table next to us announces the evening's specials and answers questions for the couple before he calmly walks away to obtain their drink order.

"What is the name of this restaurant? I looked at the sign, but it was in Italian. Is the word 'kitchen' in the name?" I slide the cloth napkin onto my lap out of habit.

"Yes, it's called The Godfather's Kitchen."

I gulp my saliva down my throat. "You're not a godfather, are you?" I whisper.

"It's a title, my brothers, and I thought it was funny when we decided we wanted to open a restaurant here. We're from Sicily, so it is a joke to us. Well, part joke and part a tribute to Sicily."

"Oh," I sigh in relief, but he never said if he wasn't the Godfather. I know there are other mafia families from Italy here, so there's no longer one man at the helm who controls them all.

"So, you own this?"

"Yes. My brothers are partners."

"Is that why everyone is scurrying around, and our waitress looks like she's waiting on God?"

"Probably." His voice is sexy as hell. He has a deep, confident voice that makes me want to come in my panties.

"They are afraid to look at you," I comment.

"Perhaps, but they'll get used to us being here. Tonight, we need to celebrate our engagement," he says as if it's important to him.

I don't know why he thinks we need to celebrate. It's a done deal, and I have to honor it.

Our waitress appeared with glasses of water and placed them on the table. Her hands shake. Her voice is strained. Her voice quivers as she speaks and tells us her name is Anna. Matteo orders champagne with appetizers to follow in fifteen minutes. I can understand her being nervous.

Geesh. I don't know how I'll cook for him if he's that exact. I'd crack under the pressure.

"Relax," Matteo comforts me. "I'm not hurting anyone," he murmurs.

He's not hurting anyone now, but what about tomorrow or the next day? Granted, if he has to act, they probably deserve it. It's not like the mafia commits reckless acts of violence to hurt innocent people.

"They flutter around you because you are powerful," I murmur.

"You're catching on. I knew you'd be good at this even if you didn't learn it from your father. Of which I should be grateful. He's not very good at the game," Matteo adds as if he's giving me a playbook.

"I wanted to ask you about that. Why did my father want that property you have?"

"It was his side deal, and he didn't want the don to know about it. Why are you interested in it?"

"Just curious."

Anna returns to the table, opens the champagne, and pours two flutes before she sets the bottle into the ice bucket at the end of the table.

"We need to make a toast." He lifts his champagne flute, and I lift mine.

"To new beginnings," he says, his dark eyes taking in my face before I meet his gaze.

"To new beginnings," I reply as we tap glasses, and take a sip.

"This is very good," I comment and take a second sip of the bubbles.

"It's a dry champagne from Italy. I'm glad you like it."

"I do like a great Italian wine. Your food beats Russian food any day of the week."

He chuckles at this. Seeing him lighthearted is refreshing, even if it's only for a minute.

"It seems like an incredible piece of property to go to such lengths to obtain it. I'm curious as to why it's so important to you."

"Your father swooped in and stole it from under me. I don't like being played, and that fucking Chinaman who owned it knew he would get more from your father than he would from me. Who first contacted who is still up for debate. However, I evened the score with both parties."

"You're sure my father took it?" I ask, wondering what else I'll learn from him.

"Yes."

"How?"

"The Chinaman's lips didn't lie. He enjoyed the fact he fucked me over. Or, intended to. But it's a deal that can usually be remedied."

"And what was this man's price?" I ask out of curiosity.

"Death, I guess," he replies bluntly and without remorse.

"You mean…?"

"One way or another, men in my arena know the rules—when they are broken, we take care of business." His voice is cold, and it's a new side to him I've never witnessed.

He can be ruthless.

I feel sick. Did he kill a man over a business deal? Granted, the Chinaman messed with a mafia boss and pitted two formidable opponents against each other. I realize it would have been worse if my dad had let Alexsei buy it.

He's Izzy's dad, so he and my husband would have gone head-to-head in a war. Dmitry is just as formidable as Matteo. I shudder to think how that scenario would have turned out. Neither of them would ever back down. This marriage put me in a position to make sure no ill will come between our families to preserve the peace. I hate to think that in the odd turn of events, our union might not be the worst arranged marriage. The Russians and Italians both have common denominators, mainly Izzy and me.

I thought I'd be married off to a capo. Instead, I'm the new queen of the Borrelli family. No wonder he wants me to make a good impression. Men can lose their lives over things I say and do. A shudder overcomes me. I'm not ready for the responsibility of the title.

"Are you cold?" Matteo asks, ready to hand me his coat, which is draped on the chair beside me.

"No, just wondering what my new life will be like. But first, I have a question."

"I'll answer if I can," he replies with a hint of curiosity in his words.

"Do you think my father has ill intentions, or was this a one-time occurrence where he's attempted to strike a deal of his own?"

"It's hard to tell. I haven't been in the city long. Why? Do you have doubts as to his integrity?"

"Possibly. I've never been involved in his work. I might be out of line. But I won't let anything bad happen to Dmitry or Izzy. We've been through so much. She's the sister I've always wanted."

"I'll watch him if that is what you want."

I pause to consider what he's offering. I'm sure he won't mind collecting information that will benefit him. Who do I trust more, my dad or Matteo? Matteo is direct, my dad—not so much.

"Yes," I state firmly. I'm resolved to protect those I love. It's the only way I can live with myself knowing what happens in the underworld where I was born.

As long as I have to keep my father's secret, I'm keeping tabs on him. I'm not as trusting as I was three weeks ago. I will no longer accept the status quo. The fact I trusted my parents blindly leads me to wonder how something else didn't happen that could have had a terrible ending.

I wonder how many chances I've taken with my life over the years. I can't believe Matteo cloned my phone, and I had no idea that technology existed outside of the movies. However, our phones always get funky updates, and I wonder what it entails. Is it really safe, or are we being spied on?

Perhaps this was Dad's first side deal to try to get ahead, and maybe he's learned his lesson. I'm not sure he's equipped to deal with the true sharks in the water. There are more powerful men who have more resources and are savvier. Dad's deal would have been uncovered in time. The city has many networks and loose lips sink ships. For now, I'll keep my thoughts about my father's potential motives to myself.

Trust no one, Matteo said. It's not a warning. It's my reality. I'm beginning to see the bigger picture of this seedy world. I'm better off under Matteo's protection. It's intimidating and exciting at the same time.

"Stop thinking so much," Matteo interrupts my thoughts. "This is supposed to be a happy occasion. The champagne is getting warm." He refills our glasses.

Anna returns, and appears to be more comfortable with us now that she had witnessed Matteo smile at me. Matteo asked if he could order our food, and I agreed. Anna says she'll return with the appetizers.

I sip more champagne.

"I'm amazed you've not run into trouble, but I'm glad I happened to come along when I did."

Anna returns, quietly slipping fried calamari and fresh shrimp before us along with the appetizer plates.

I let Matteo taste the food first. I'm starving, and the warm calamari melts in my mouth when it passes my lips. I wonder who they get their fresh seafood from. I wouldn't be surprised if it didn't fly in from Sicily daily. Matteo has an eclectic taste. He's a perfectionist. He thinks things through. It's a quality I admire about him. He's a man who knows his mind. He has an eye for detail, and it shows in everything he does—particularly my ring.

"I also have staff. You've met Gio, but I have a chef at the house. His name is Federico. I'm sure you'll like him. He cooks for us and oversees the house. He acts as a butler on occasion. If you have any questions on what to wear or where to obtain something, he's very knowledgeable."

"Good to know. Is Federico from here?"

"Sicily. He's been here before. He knows me and my routine. I trust him, and so can you. However, if a situation occurs that you don't trust, always go with your gut instinct. It's there to protect you."

"I can't wait to meet him." I slip more calamari into my mouth. It's not easy to eat with my hands in front of Matteo. I'm self-conscious and wipe my fingertips on my napkin.

I'm curious to know more but more concerned with my future.

"What am I to tell people at work?"

"Oh, well, you can leave it a mystery until the announcement comes out. Then the city will know."

"You mean, even you can't finagle an early release date?" I tease.

"I save my energy for bigger battles."

"Of course," I reply, suddenly feeling like I'm not a priority. How can I compete for his time? I'm just me.

The waitress clears the dishes and disappears without a word.

I hope Federico is friendly.

"Is everyone afraid of you?"

"No. Why?"

"You have a presence about you that speaks more than words."

"It may be that I've had to handle myself from an early age."

"Do you have a big family back home?" He's from Sicily, and most of his family will probably still reside there.

"Yes, and you'll love them. I'm the oldest. Then there are my younger brothers, Niccoló, Renalto, and Pietro. The baby is my sister, Chiara. My mother died at her birth."

"I'm so sorry. That had to be tough."

"It was. It made me tough. I don't know what I would do today if things were different. My father built this empire. I imagine I had no choice but to follow in the family business. I learned quickly."

"Of course, you were all over my dad's dirty deal. I don't think anyone gets the better of you."

"Touché." His perfect lips curl into a shallow smile. Far be it for him to let anyone know he's happy.

"Me? I don't know about that. I'm not savvy with games or politics. I love to decorate. It makes me happy. I like being creative."

Our food arrives, and it smells divine. He ordered Fra Diavolo for me and Fettuccini Alfredo with seafood for himself.

"The extra plates are for us to share if you like," he floats the invitation to me.

"Of course, I can't eat all of this. This place is amazing." I put some of my pasta on a plate and slide it toward him.

"It is. I hope you'll conclude it's the best Italian food you've ever eaten. I will have to take you to Sicily one day. The pasta here is home-made. My grandmother back home still makes it fresh daily."

I wondered how he knew I'd never been anywhere foreign except London, and I reminded myself that he knew everything about me. He probably knows what my favorite color of underwear is. I wonder if anything escapes his intense and intriguing mind.

He slides a plate of his food to me. We dip Italian bread in olive oil. I nibble at the bread before I twirl pasta on my fork.

"How old is your sister?" I ask.

"She's twenty and going to college in Switzerland."

"Do you like having a large family?"

"I can't imagine my life without them. We're very close. So, our wedding will encompass many invites and all the main players, coun-cilmen, and congressmen."

"We can't elope?"

"Don't you want a big wedding?"

"Most women dream of it, but I'm fine with something small."

"I will indulge you when I can, but this is a show of power and the merging of two houses. I need to meet Alexsei Sidovo and make sure there are no hard feelings. I didn't come to him first. He might feel slighted that I didn't. I'll tell him that we fell in love at first sight and that I didn't want to wait."

"To cover for my dad," I murmur.

"Yes, I have more to share with you, but not publicly. The walls have ears."

"Right."

How did I become entrapped in this clandestine operation?

Oh, my fucking father.

The man I trusted. The father, I thought, was so generous. Now, I realize he was only generous enough to hold it over my head and guilt me into complying with his demands. Matteo may want to take care of me, but I will keep my job. I don't want to be dependent on a man again. This week has taught me that there is a price to be paid for others' generosity. The worst part is that it's not the stranger beside me who used me, but my family. The realization was hard to accept as I was so angry at Matteo for playing games with me.

However, my parents told me my college and condo were paid for. I suppose I should find out if the condo is mine. It's probably another lie.

"I'm curious about something." Why not ask the man with all the answers?

"What, Angel?"

I notice this has become a term of endearment if I'm reading him — and not his other personality, which is dark and unforgiving.

"Is my condo paid off?"

"Yes, it was bought with cash. Why do you ask?"

"Just curious. Is it in my name?"

"Yes. Are you planning on running away to it when you are pissed off at me like last night?"

"Just curious. I've learned the value of checking the validity of things people tell me."

"You mean your father?"

"Especially him." I raise my eyebrows at the irony of Matteo being my confidant and my father being out in the cold. We have something in common.

Matteo's eyes linger on my face for a long minute as if trying to figure out what I'm thinking.

I hope I'm not an open book. I can't show feelings for him. I can't love him. I can't afford to trust the wrong person again. It's easier if I don't trust or love anyone but Izzy.

I will rely on myself. I will fit in with Matteo's world and make him proud of me. That's the role I have to play.

I observe Matteo as his eyes move around the room. Men in suits walk past the table and nod to him. He does likewise. I wonder if this is the meeting place for the Italians, but somehow, I pictured a small, out-of-the-way place like in The Sopranos. Granted, Tony Soprano was smaller, and it was a fictional story, but most of the big deals in the city are cultivated in tiny bowling alleys, pizza shops, and dive bars. I realize that places around the city are front operations for shady business deals.

I find it funny that they talk openly in Italian in front of people who are eating. Who knows what they are talking about? How many places around the city are under the Borelli shell corporations?

Matteo tosses a significant tip on the table before we leave. He helps me put on my coat before we leave. The staff opens the restaurant door, wishing us well, and Gio escorts us to the vehicle, opening the door for us. It's as if a movie crew has cued everyone.

I'm overwhelmed with how attentive Matteo was at dinner. He gave me his undivided attention, and I felt like a Queen being fawned over. I'm walking on a cloud between the attention and the humongous ring on my finger.

CHAPTER 21

MATTEO

We shared a tiramisu. Sharing dinner with Alena accomplished a few items on my agenda. We established a rapport. She understands the danger we're in and hasn't bolted yet.

Her father's bumbling with the building was like a red carpet for me to walk. The truth of her being in my life is not important. Maybe one day, I'll be able to open up. I have enough on my plate. I can't be the adoring husband she is worthy of, even if I can't stop thinking about her.

"Come home with me," I whisper along her neck as we sit beside each other in the car. She smells sweeter than the dessert we ate.

"I'd love to. However, I have to work tomorrow, and I'm sure it's a long commute from your place."

"I will let you off this time, but Vito will bring you to my home tomorrow, and then you'll live with me."

"Are you being possessive?" She challenges me as she turns her head to face me.

I'm sure she's wondering if my obsession is for her or her safety. Perhaps she feels that I'm aligning myself with her family for more men in the event of a war. I can't say I haven't thought about how convenient it was to meet. The pieces fell into place faster than I could have anticipated. I wish I had thought that far in advance. However, I was lucky.

"You are mine. Besides, we're engaged, it's expected. The safest place for you is under my roof. I have an army to protect you." I slide my fingers under her chin and tip her head backward, causing our eyes to meet. Under the streetlights, I find her blue eyes are lighter now. I know she's wet for me. I've decided that light eyes mean she's horny or happy. When her eyes are dark, it means I'd better look out. Her eyes are a mood ring. "My home is where you belong, Angel."

"Are you expecting trouble?" Her eyes darken, and I sense concern in her voice.

"A man in my position has to be concerned with safety around the clock. That's a given in our line of work. Now that I am the new don, I'm a target. Some people would love to see me fail."

"Who wants you to fail?"

"I'm not sure. I'm trying to figure it out. It would be reckless of me to send you out into a city of wolves without warning you of the danger. It would be unconscionable."

"That's why Vito gave me the fob," she murmurs.

"Yes. My siblings aren't after me. However, I have peculiar uncles."

"Who doesn't?" she quips at my remark, and I laugh. I can't suppress it. I glance through the window. Damn, Gio heard me.

Gio knows my laugh is as rare as a snow moon.

I'm not sure he'll let me live this down.

"If my siblings stepped aside, the uncles would have the most to gain. I'm not convinced of anything at this point. Gio and I are working on it."

"What do they want? Money?"

It's a fair question. What do they want?

"Who knows? History has proved that it is usually greed, jealousy, or power. I doubt anyone would be jealous of me taking on the mess my father left. However, I have deals that will work out in the long run. I'm not concerned over finances as much as I am about eliminating the traitor who knows too much about us."

"What do you mean?" She twists her adorable body on the seat to face me.

"How easy is it to penetrate a don and get close enough to kill him?" I ask.

"I have no clue. How did he die?" Her eyes are wide with fear.

"Poison. But you can't tell a soul," I warn. "Not even Izzy. The enemy doesn't know that I know this. I had my suspicions and had lab work done on my father before he died and after. I'm lucky I was there and could obtain this information discreetly."

"I never saw the cause of death listed in his obituary," she adds.

I'm touched she cared to investigate. I caress her face briefly and pull my hand away. There's no use in getting blue balls when I can stop before it becomes painful.

"You looked into me?" I tease her. She's a quick study. "I said it was cancer. No one needs to know otherwise. I told my siblings so they would be vigilant, but I'm the head of the snake. Someone would want to neutralize me if they knew I had this information. And, if I find a loose end that leads me to the person responsible, then they'd have to eliminate the loose end and me. My father was involved in something, and they wanted him dead. I lower my voice, "However, I have to get to the bottom of it."

I have more to lose now than I did two weeks ago.

The vehicle rolls along traffic as we head toward her condo.

"I didn't want to speak of this in public. Now you understand why." I sink back into the seat and peer out the window. The temperature is dropping outside. The windows are foggy.

"They would use me to get to you," she murmurs. Her assumption completes the circle. She's connected all the dots.

I remain silent. What can I say?

"Fuck," she exclaims. She flashes her dark eyes at me. "It appears I went from the mouth of the lion and into the den of another. How could you do this knowing the risk?" Her breathing is jagged, she's worked up, and she has every right to be angry. "Why in the hell did you do this to me? Did you know who I was at the sex club? How long have you been planning on using the bratva for added protection? You're afraid this will end in a war. I'm your human shield!" She balls her hands into fists and pounds my chest. "How could you?" she sobs as she continues to beat on me.

I remain calm and gently grab her delicate wrists. The wrists I held against the elevator wall as I finger-fucked her into oblivion.

I know she can handle the risk we're facing. It seems to me she's more upset being traded between two men without her consent. She's a victim in the dangerous game between powerful men in a treacherous game she's never been aware of until I came along.

"I love your dirty mouth. I love to see you riled up. I can't wait to have your lips wrapped around my huge cock again," I reply calmly.

Angry sex is hot. She will learn that my sexual appetite is fueled to epic proportions whenever she's near. I've never been so obsessed.

She's right. My enemies wouldn't bat an eye to take her to get to me. I'd gladly give my life for hers.

I grab her even though she pushes me away. My lips cover hers. It's a searing kiss, and my arms move as fast and as strong as a gale force in an ocean storm as I pull her into me. She resists me, but after thirty seconds, her plump lips are over mine. She moans. I return her enthusiasm and suck on her lower lip.

The kiss deepens as we grope each other in the back seat. She's locked in my arms. My cock strains against the zipper of my pants. She murmurs as her body presses against mine.

The fact that someone would take her and torture her to get to me chills me to the bone. I'm a selfish devil for dragging her into my world where the real devils exist.

She does not know the faces that hide behind fancy titles as the players weave their webs. Men like congressmen who fund human trafficking missions to fill sex clubs where the women are branded like cattle.

I hold her tighter than ever. I will never let anything happen to her. I vow it to God and myself.

Regrettably, we roll to a stop at her condo. Vito exits and stands, opening the door.

I help Alena out of the car. Her lipstick is smeared. Vito pretends not to notice. I kiss her and watch as Vito walks her inside the secure building.

"She's a handful. She's smart—I'll give you that," Gio states as he begins to drive.

"Yes, but it's more imperative that we find out what happened to my father. It's been over two weeks, and we don't have any clues." I run my hand over my jaw, which is rough as my day started before dawn. Whereas I would have loved for Alena to join me tonight, I let her have her last night at her place to adjust. It seems fair.

It's not the perfect engagement that Alena deserves, but I hope one day I can make it up to her.

I have to remain as lethal as I am nimble. I'm going to remain young and fit. I start each day working out at the gym at the mansion before dawn. I lift weights and run on the treadmill. Gio boxes with me from time to time. Niccoló is a real heavyweight, and he has a passion for it.

I have a young wife and many life events to look forward to. I have no intentions of being cheated out of the good life now that I've ascended to the head of the table.

"Gio, you have capos who tell you things. Can you hang out around them when they drink on their days off and see if any information comes from it without raising suspicion? I find it difficult to believe my father was doing something so secretive that no one knew about it."

"His advisor did," he deadpans.

It appears we've both reached the same conclusion. I mentioned loose ends to Alena. I know in my gut that the old man was privy to whatever became my father's downfall.

"Yes, I'll keep my ears open and see if anyone lets something slip. One would think there would be a trail of breadcrumbs with how things spread like wildfire around an office cooler."

Was it a business deal? Did he slight another don? Did a deal go bad? I may never know.

The fact he died by poison, and not bloodshed, is a surprising twist I didn't anticipate. No one else thought to check for foul play, but he went down so fast. I assumed the liquor would have rotted his gut like it did his mind. I guess everyone else did, too.

I'm going crazy trying to figure out what transpired when too many scenarios could have occurred. I'm frustrated that with all our technology, we still don't have a lead.

When will we get a break?

My worst fear is that my adversary might discover my secret before I learn their identity. I also have a Russian don that I need to befriend before he hears of my engagement.

ALENA

"Thank you, Vito." I look up to the handsome face of the man tasked with taking a bullet for me. He's ordered to protect me with his life. I hope it doesn't come to that, but now that I'm involved in the family business, I'm relieved he's here. "Have a good night," I say as I close my door, slide the deadbolt into place, and connect the chain for added security.

Who am I kidding? This door isn't even solid wood. How safe am I? Besides, every mafia movie ends with someone being whacked. The mafia is like the KGB. You can't escape them if they want you dead.

I slide out of my coat, toss it over a chair in the dining room, and prop my purse on the kitchen counter. Italians like coffee. I look at the coffee machine on the counter and pop an espresso pod into its empty mouth. I slide a to-go cup on the tray and push start. I unlock the door and look down the hall.

"Vito," I call out softly.

He walks toward me, having rounded the corner in the hallway.

"I made coffee and added sugar to it for you."

"You don't have to do that, Ms. Pasnov."

"We're going to be together for a long time. Please call me Alena."

"Only when Mr. Borrelli isn't around," he says, taking the warm cup.

"It will be our secret. Knock if you need anything."

"Thank you, Alena. You're very kind," he replies appreciatively.

"It's no problem—have a good night."

"You, too," he says, and I close and lock the door again.

It's a small token of my appreciation. The condo is quiet, and I'm surprised no one has complained about the foreigner walking the halls. I guess there are lurkers everywhere—it's New York City. Or have people learned to keep their noses out of other people's business?

As if that will ever happen. I chuckle at my joke.

I walk to the window and glance below. I love the light flurries falling under the streetlights of Central Park. Izzy is right. The location is good for traffic and lessens the chance that someone would attempt to abduct me at my condo. I can't fight Matteo on moving in with him. I will feel safer in his house and with him by my side.

I'm stunned by how much Matteo keeps hidden behind his sultry eyes. I wonder if he'll have to tell me lies. Who am I kidding? Of course, he will. He's a savvy businessman. I have no doubt he can be cunning. As much as I hate that he played the game perfectly with my father to get his building and me, I assume his acuity in certain situations will keep him safe. He exploited my father's weakness for his gain. He's a worthy adversary to anyone who dares to challenge him.

My father has no idea what he's gotten the bratva into.

I'm holding more and more secrets daily. At this rate, I'll be lying to Izzy about my entire life. I wonder how much she knows about the bratva she can't share with me. Does Matteo feel like he is living a double life? I'm beginning to feel like my life is getting away from me.

I undress, and damn Matteo for making me so horny. I pull on pajamas and rummage through my drawers for items I want to take with me as if I'm going on a long weekend stay at the Hamptons.

Only it's winter.

I toss essentials into the overnight roller luggage, making sure I have loungewear since tomorrow is Friday. I'll sort out work clothes later.

I reserve the room to toss my toiletry items into the bag in the morning. What is waiting for me at his mansion? He said I didn't need to bring much. He has staff who could pack my closet for me if I asked.

After I've removed the smeared lipstick, I wash the makeup off my face and stare at myself in the mirror over the vanity.

"Who are you?"

I wonder if I'll become lost in Matteo's world and be like that lonely woman at the piano bar in my forties one day, wishing I had a man who loved me.

Perhaps Matteo is preoccupied with the startling events he shared with me tonight. I know I would have a tough time sleeping at night knowing someone murdered my father and that I might be next.

Maybe I should be relieved that I'm a woman and that I am not expected to take over for my father one day. It sounds like Matteo always knew it was his destiny.

What is mine?

The mafia doesn't always protect a traitor's family. I doubt Matteo's father betrayed his family. I mean, the man had five kids. I want to think he wouldn't put them in jeopardy. But what do I know?

I remember reading about the mafioso killers I've seen online, and the one called The Icepick had a family. He was the mafia enforcer who used torture to gain answers. The only code he lived by was that he didn't kill children.

As if that makes him a model citizen. I huff. I'm in a pickle—the one wedged in a jar packed with others. We're all green, sandwiched together, and we can't run. I'm stuck.

My life went from opportunity flowering before me with a new job to one of obscurity and a life where I will live in the fray. I console myself with the fact that Izzy is in a similar situation—only her husband loves her, and they're having a baby together.

I hope my stomach won't always have knots in it. With any luck,

Matteo will find out who is behind his father's death soon, and our lives will return to normal. Only I don't know what normal is.

He made it clear our marriage is a business arrangement. I'd be delusional if I thought for one second he would ever fall in love with me.

I lift my phone from my purse in the kitchen and crawl into bed with it. I phone Izzy.

"What's up? Is everything okay?" she asks first.

"Oh, yeah. I hope it isn't too late to call."

"Not at all. How are you? How is the working girl?"

"Fine. I mean, I'm new, so what can I complain about? I can't stay up all night at clubs?" I chuckle at the irony of my life.

"Clubbing grows old after a while. I could tell you were looking for something more. You hid it well, but I could tell you wanted more out of life."

"You did?" I'm surprised she never mentioned this before.

"Sure. You're young, and you earned a degree. That's an accomplishment. Why wouldn't you want to use it? You're smart, pretty, and talented. It would be a shame to sit on it."

"I didn't think that much about it, then."

"And now?"

"My life has changed. I'm learning the job, and I ate dinner with Matteo at The Godfather's Kitchen tonight. Did you ever eat there?"

"I could never have afforded that, but it sounds interesting."

"It was," I reply, filling her in on the mansion's ambiance and describing the most incredible pasta I've ever eaten. "I hear you have a table at Councilman Addler's gala that's coming up." I decide to get to work and create an opening to do Matteo's bidding.

"We do. It's one of those things we have to attend. We must mingle at these affairs. How did you know? It slipped my mind. I hope Dmitry figured out what we're wearing. We need costumes."

"Do you have room left at your table? Matteo and I wanted to go. It would be fun to be out with you again. And you have to meet him."

"I definitely need to meet this man who has met your insatiable sexual appetite," she jokes.

"It was only a matter of time," I reply, playing it off. Gee. I'm pretty good at rolling with life as it comes. Is that how it happens? Will my lies continue to flow to the point I won't know what reality is?

"We haven't filled our table yet. Access to Addler costs a pretty penny. I can tell you that. This could very well have been called a Presidential fundraiser."

"Who knows where he'll be in a few years? Be careful what you wish for," I tease. I stow this information in the back of my mind. Is Addler going to be running for president?

This would make sense to me because he's from a family of politicians. If he's so picky with whom he takes money from, perhaps he's intent on looking like an angel when he has the scrutiny of every critic in the country running a microscope up his ass before he hits the presidential campaign trail.

What do Dmitry and Matteo want from the councilman?

"I don't think he's all that bad. He wants to keep the city unique," Izzy says.

"Opposed to change, you mean?"

"Just a bit," she chuckles.

"Have you mentioned my engagement to your dad?" I ask to know where I stand.

"No, you told me not to. I have to tell Dmitry before he hears it from someone else. I was waiting for Matteo to talk to my father—" She leaves the sentence hanging for me to fill in the gap.

"Please tell Dmitry because I don't want it to become an issue between you. I'll have Matteo meet with your father. I've been deluding myself with the notion that this is a normal engagement. However, I'm marrying the don to the Italian mafia, and it would be weird for us to share a table, wouldn't it?"

"My thoughts exactly. You know how the men get prickly over these types of things."

"I know. It would make it look like we're working together when we happen to marry men from the opposite..."

"Sides of Europe only, we're all in New York City," she finishes my sentence so eloquently.

We share a laugh filled with relief. I never considered that my marriage could change the dynamics of my relationship with my best friend. Navigating this will be a challenge if the bratva doesn't stand behind me.

"Is everything going to be alright?" I ask in a hushed tone. The gravity of the situation has hit.

"I hope so. Nothing can keep us apart if it's up to you and me." She speaks softly. She understands the implications of the situation as much as I do.

I don't know what's going to happen, Izzy. I thought I'd marry a capo.

"I know. Trust me, this has thrown me for a loop. However, I'll talk to Dmitry tonight. He's home, and I'll let Matteo call Dad."

"Thank you so much. You're the best, Izzy. Ironically, your mother ran from this life, and we're both into it up to our necks."

"I know. I hope she's not disappointed in me. However, I have nothing to do with my grandfather, Santino Morreti. He's never tried to reach me, and I'm relieved. I want nothing to do with him. He kept my mother from the man she loved, and she died over it. He's a mean man, Alena."

"I know. I'm glad he's left you alone. Do you ever think someone is following you?"

"No, I have good intuition about that. But who knows? I hope nothing is going on behind my back. I try to think ahead. When life in the moment scares me, I try to think of something that makes me happy."

"That's good advice. I'll remember it."

"It's late, but I'll talk to you during your lunch break tomorrow."

"Great. I'll talk to you then. Love you."

"Love you."

CHAPTER 23

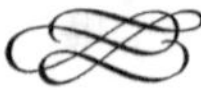

MATTEO

Gio and I talk on the ride to my estate. I'm not thrilled about Finn's passing, even though he got what he deserved. Gio and Antonio know how much I hate for my men to ask me for favors.

"I'm not fucking Santa delivering gifts," I complain to Gio.

"I know. It's one and done. Let's hope it all goes according to plan."

"Men like Finn, well, there's no cure for that. Addiction is addiction, and it eats people from the inside out and from the outside in. This is why I avoid taking drugs for anything, and I've never sampled the goods."

"You just sell them," he murmurs with sarcasm.

"True. We all do. They will circulate whether I have a hand in it or not. It's the status quo, and our government has its hand in the profits as well. It trickles down to every political campaign and drug rehabilitation program. I can't swim against these currents. I'd be out on a ledge, and my empire would crumble into ashes."

"That's so true," Gio says as we pass my guard gate.

My phone beeps.

Alena.

"It appears Alena is getting us tickets to the event, but Don Sidovo is expecting a call from me."

"Shit, we should have done it like yesterday," Gio mutters and runs his hand through his hair.

"You're sweating this as if you're the groom," I joke.

"Yeah, well, he could come out the door and shoot your balls off. If that happens, you're on your own," Gio states flippantly.

I let out a snicker. For being a man who doesn't show emotion, I'm in a good mood for the first time in years. I've managed to laugh and enjoy myself tonight.

"Alena is on top of the situation," Gio states.

I texted Alena that I would take care of it tomorrow. I also typed Good night, Angel.

"She told me she and Izzy are like sisters, and I hope our marriage will be accepted. I don't think there is an etiquette book for the type of situation I was in. Do I go to the father of the bride or the bratva's don? Tough call," I say, bemused by the situation.

However, it appears the don's first love was lost over politics, so I'm feeling confident he'll make the best of mine. I can hope. I've dealt with cartel leaders and gangs over the years. How tough will it be to meet the don?

Meanwhile, hours later, when I'm in bed and can't sleep, I admit I'm nervous. I've been ballsy, even reckless. I've put Alena and Izzy in a vice grip that could have serious repercussions. What would that be? I can't say. If Alena loses Izzy, she'll never forgive me. She's lost her parents this week, and I don't know when or if she will get over her father's business deal that goes against his oath.

She's been forced to keep secrets that no one in her position should be asked to carry, and it's why we protect our women from what we do. Our souls turn black, and we hope the women will love us and keep the family together. I won't do anything to put friction between her and Izzy again. One can only be loyal to a person who is trustworthy. Once trust is lost, the situation is irrevocably broken. I've lived this with my father, and I have no wish to carry the family legacy of lies and betrayal.

I can't come between my bride and her best friend. The only silver lining is that if we were in an alliance, Alena would be even more protected if something were to befall me. She was right. Having Russian support will make me formidable in the event I walk into a war.

In the morning, I received a text that the announcement and the picture Gio took of us at dinner would be in the paper. It's not the standard boring pose a photographer takes, but it will suffice. I need to avoid the gossip, which travels faster than wildfire. We're moving so fast that people will wonder if Alena is pregnant.

There's a thought. I wonder how she feels about that, but it's happening either way.

After my workout, Federico prepares breakfast, and since Gio isn't here yet, I eat in the kitchen so we can catch up.

"What would you like for dinner tonight, Matteo? I don't know what Alena would like."

"Thank you. However, I have no idea what to introduce her to next. For a woman of means raised in the city, I thought she would have every nook for great food on her GPS."

Federico chuckles. "You're different."

"No, I'm the same cranky don you've always known."

"Alena is a pretty woman. Gio showed me her picture."

"Did he?" Hm. I guess the three of us have lived lives void of women we'd feel worthy of, considering what we do. It doesn't escape my attention that my men have been discussing my future wife, and they both seem to agree on her being too good for me. This is a first.

Gio arrives as Federico and I finish our chat. I stand and pull on my suit jacket. Gio takes the trench coat Federico hands him, and we leave through the kitchen door and pass two guards who are walking the grounds.

They nod in acknowledgment, and I let myself into the limo. We arrive at Don Sidovo Long Island estate thirty minutes later. We stop at his security gate, and Gio has us buzzed in so we may drive onto the grounds.

The house is modern, off-white stucco with dark brown brickwork. The arch over the large front door is a northern touch, and the drive has been shoveled.

"I wish I had a drink," I murmur. The house is meant to exude wealth and power, and it does. The fact that the Russians are notorious for being ruthless is not lost on me. I know that on more than one occasion, a few were psychotic over the years, putting the fear of death in local citizens if they so much as walked past a house they owned.

"If I pull this off, I'm a genius. The Volkovs are international, and Dmitry's marriage to Izzy will make him the next don. I wonder when that will occur."

"There's no rumor of a date. I suspect after his daughter is born."

"Ah, yes, that would be a great gift for a grandchild to a man who's had great disappointments in life."

"You pull this off, and you are merging us with the largest Russian family in the world. Think of the new connections you'll have, not to mention the men behind him will support you too, should you need it."

"That's a valid point. However, I need to walk through that door." I slip the gun out of the holster on my belt and hand it to Gio, who puts it in the glove box. He slides his weapon in as well.

Gio opens my door, and I straighten my collar as if meeting my father-in-law. The difference between Alexsei and Alena's father is that I respect this man.

The door opens before Gio knocks, and the servant leads us into a room with scones and a light lunch displayed in a palatial solarium overlooking an indoor pool at the back of the mansion. A man in a black suit who looks like a pro boxer with a stern face grunts when he frisks us for weapons.

"Gentlemen," a voice greets us. "Please, come. Sit. Lunch is served."

I turn, and there before me is the man I identify as Alexsei.

"Thank you for your generosity. I'm Matteo, and this is Gio."

He shakes my hand, and our eyes meet. I like a man who doesn't have what I have coined "crazy eyes." Alexsei appears to be of sound mind and shakes Gio's hand after he releases mine. I wait for him to lead us to the table.

"These pies are called Coulibiac. They are puff pastry shells filled with salmon filling. They're delicious." He enters the solarium and sits.

We sit as well.

A butler places water before us, and I notice iced tea on the table.

"What is on your mind, Matteo? My daughter said it was important that I meet with you today."

"Thank you so much for arranging time to meet. I'm sorry for the short notice."

"It happens. I was young once. I try not to do so much in a day now. What can I do for you?"

My heart races like the engine in a getaway car.

"I had no idea whom to speak to first. I am taking over for my father, Luciano Borrelli, and I've fallen in love with an incredible woman under your protection. I went to her father, and it occurred to me that I might have offended you as we are both men in positions of power."

He sits back in his chair, a sober, reflective thought on his face. For a man in his late forties or early fifties, he's aged well, considering the stress of the job that I know all too well.

"Continue," he says as he places a pie and fruit on his plate.

I follow his lead, as does Gio. I figure it's only polite.

"I didn't want you or anyone else to assume that we have an alliance when I marry Alena, especially when we've never met. I don't want our marriage to imply things that might misrepresent the situation. I know how these things will be construed in our world, and I do not wish to offend you. As I said, I have no idea how to proceed with my marriage and the fact that Alena and Izzy are best friends—family, even. I can't come between my wife and your daughter."

I've made my plea. It's always better to act and ask for permission from men like us. But it never guarantees a favorable outcome.

"You know, Mikhail has been off lately. I couldn't put my finger on it. Now, I know it is over this situation with his daughter. He's alluded to the fact that his daughter has fallen for someone we might be leery of, but he had no choice with her affair of the heart."

Mikhail Pasnov might be Alena's father, but he's a worm. I never intended for him to come clean, but to cast a shadow on me is a slight I won't forget. He's become consumed with power, and now I understand why Alena wanted me to keep tabs on him. I have a feeling he might not be long in this world with how he's escalated things between us and is now disavowing me for marrying his daughter.

The don is quiet—my fate is in his hands.

"Manuel, please bring Vodka," he says before he takes a bite of his meat pie.

The butler carries a tray of shot glasses and a bottle of chilled vodka.

The don swallows and speaks. "I was once young and in love. The love of my life, one might say. But she was mine, and she was gorgeous. I only married for duty, which was a bed of thorns that did not end well. She resented my first love. I have looked into you, and you are a man of honor. We have commonalities for the women we love. Alena took care of my daughter while she was homeless and attending school. She did so out of kindness to my daughter, never knowing who she was and wanting nothing in return. Alena is family to me. I owe her a debt that I couldn't repay before, but it is owed all the same. I love my daughter more than life itself, so I offer you a trial alliance for this love. I cannot come between Alena and Izzy. It would break Izzy's heart if there were a falling out when both women are so happy."

The don pours three vodkas and hands two of them to us.

"Here's to love. May we have a blessed union."

I am overwhelmed by the amount of love this man has for his daughter. I choke back the sentiment over a love lost and love gained. I did not know of Izzy's unfortunate beginning, and I understand why it's been kept private. He cherishes his daughter's happiness above fear and hate.

We toss back our vodka, and Alexsei delivers a hearty slap on my back. "Besides, I hate the Morettis. I'd do anything to see that man in the ground," he mutters. "This will be one stake in his heart." He nods, and it feels like the click of a loaded gun.

Does he want me to whack Don Moretti?

We enjoyed our lunch and left the next joint business venture up for discussion. We stand. The Don shakes my hand, welcoming me into the fold, and even shakes Gio's hand. He walks us to the door, and once I step into the chilly air, I breathe a sigh of relief.

"I feel better now," I chuckle as we walk confidently to my limo.

"You got lucky. Alena seems to be the center of what is becoming a contentious relationship between you and her father," Gio says as he slides behind the wheel.

"That little fucking weasel. Alena asked me to keep tabs on him, so she doesn't trust him either. Alena won't sacrifice Izzy when her father is in the wrong. She's a sweet woman and loved by the Don. I think Alexsei loves Alena more than her father."

I wonder if Alena knows how Alexsei feels about her.

"Well, she saved your ass today," Gio says with aplomb.

"That she did." My marriage with Alena has to be protected at all costs. "I assume I should do something nice for her. Let's drive by Tiffany's. Women like jewelry, don't they?"

"Does a man like a warm pussy?"

"Hey, that's my wife," I snap.

"I didn't mean her, Matteo. I meant in general."

"Noted," I reply.

This woman is getting the best of me. Everywhere I turn, her presence is felt. When I met her, she wasn't pretentious, and she didn't impress me as the type to play games with people's heads. She was transparent and straightforward, which was new to me. She's down to earth amid the finery she wears.

One would never know that she's generous to a fault and caring. I never considered her as important as her mafia princess friend, Izzy. I guess I still have a lot to learn.

CHAPTER 24

ALENA

I walk out of my condo, pulling luggage behind me. I hand Vito a cup of coffee and lock the door.

"You shouldn't be doing this, but it's nice you do. Just don't let Matteo see you doing it, darling." Vito takes the coffee, but I insist on rolling my luggage so he can drink it without spilling it.

"Okay. So, how is the weather today?"

"Bad as usual. But the car is warm. Busy day today?"

"I have no clue. I'm still figuring out what I'm supposed to do. It's more busy work than I expected."

"Well, the hotel floor is closed and looks like shit. I hope you get it fixed soon. It hurts my calves walking on the concrete floors. It's like I've run twenty miles a day on that shit."

"I'll see what I can do," I reply as I slide through the open door of the warm vehicle. He tosses my luggage in the trunk of the SUV. I wonder how many vehicles Matteo owns. He must be in the limo today. It's always best to show up like you own the world when you meet with another Don.

I text Izzy on my way to work. She advised me her father is meeting Matteo today for lunch. I hope it goes well. For the first time since I met Matteo, I worried about him. I love Alexsei. He's more of a father figure than he is a hardened criminal. As a don, he is no stranger to being betrayed by his family. Izzy and I hold a special place in his heart. Perhaps he and I have more in common than I thought. I hope I'm wrong about my father, but my gut tells me I'm correct in my assumption and that he might be planning to take over the bratva. If that is the case, Matteo just fucked up his plans with our engagement.

I breeze through the doors at work. Penny greets me.

"Oh, my," she exclaims. Her parted lips are poised as if she is without words.

"What? Is my lipstick a mess?" I ask.

She shakes her head no. "Your ring! My god, it's stunning. I had no idea you were serious with someone. Who is the lucky man?" She pulls my hand to her face and eyes my ring like a juicy steak.

"Someone special."

"You're not telling me who he is?"

"For now, I want to keep it to myself," I reply, and I wouldn't be lying. I don't have a wedding date. Besides, I don't want my new coworkers to think I'm rich because I'm not. Matteo is. I didn't earn it. I hate the fact that I need his credit card. Who knows what my father did to scrape together money for a property in the heart of the City? I'm not sure I want the details, but I am concerned about his finances. Why else would he want to take over the Russian empire?

I know his attempt would be futile. Dmitry's syndicate with his brothers is enormous. They opened the door to overseas resources, and it's made us stronger. Alexsei loves his daughter, and what is his is hers, even though Dmitry will run it.

"Well," Penny drops my hand. "It's gorgeous. Flawless. Your man has money—that stone was not made in a lab," she says, resigning herself to the fact that I'm not giving her any more details.

"How do you know?" I ask to throw her off.

"It's a unique dark yellow. They are rare. Sure, most people can't tell the difference in stones, but I have a knack for it. I used to work at a diamond clearinghouse," she drops this on me. Now I'm shocked.

"It's not such a big deal. It was boring as hell, but I made connections, and that's how I got to where I am today."

"That's cool. I never knew."

"Of course not. You're not in human resources where all that is stored," she replies as we arrive at the break room.

"I think I'm good. I have emails to go over. Has the carpet for the hallways been picked out yet?"

"I wish. The floors out there are disgusting. I mean, why can't concrete floors be perfectly smooth? Did you see all the plaster on it from when they did the drywall? I mean, ugh." Penny stirs milk in her now hot tea.

"Yes, not to mention that walking from the elevator must be bad for our knees and joints. What's so difficult about picking out carpet?"

"Carpet sets the tone for the entire floor," Sophia says as she passes us. She is wearing a Fendi dress, and her high heels are enviable. I'd break my neck over if I stood in them. She's tall, so now, she's towering over us. Is this her way of making us look small?

I glance at Penny. She glances down and brushes past me with her cup of lukewarm tea that she pulled out of the microwave before it dinged. I'd hate to be Sophia's assistant. Penny is sunny and lets snide comments roll off her like water off a duck's back.

She can handle mental cruelty. Me, not so much.

I follow them to the room where Nathan and Cindy discuss the carpet. On the table are squares of samples and some rolls of fabric. We gather around the table, and Sophia breezes into the room.

"Do you have news to share, Alena?"

"No," I reply calmly.

"Oh, I think you do. If that stone on your finger is real, I'd say you have a fiancé." She eyes me as she walks around the table. She's trying to intimidate me into spilling my secret.

Now, everyone in the room is looking at me.

"Geez, that's a rock," Cindy says, adjusting her glasses.

"I'm not one to drool over bling, but damn, Alena, that's got to be heavy," Nathan chimes in.

"I'd like to keep it to myself for now," I reply demurely.

"Fine, well, we have work to do," Sophia states before sitting at the head of the table and fawning over carpet samples.

Whew. I dodged that bullet.

We managed to pick out the gold and red carpet. I find it ironic that it would also fit an Italian's taste and a Russian's. This leads me to daydream about my wedding. I wonder when Matteo's meeting is and hope that I'll be able to have my best friend as my maid of honor. I never considered the possibility that I might have to choose between my father and my best friend. I do not intend to speak to my father, which complicates a formal wedding.

Is it possible to get married and not have my parents there? Who will give me away? I'm sure Alexsei or Kirill, if I asked.

I'm in the break room, hitting the button on the vending machine and waiting for a bag of chips to fall off the hook, when my phone beeps. The bag takes forever, then drops. I quickly retrieve it and pull my phone out of my jeans. It's casual Friday at the office, and for once, I'm glad I didn't have to fuss over what I would wear.

I lift my phone and am disappointed when it's Izzy, not Matteo.

I open my chips and read her text.

Izzy: How are you? And did Matteo give you a ring? I forgot to ask.

Me: It's a brilliant yellow diamond that wasn't made in a lab.

Izzy: How would you know?

Me: Co-worker, but I'm still mum on the lucky man.

Izzy: Good call. I know you're probably nervous.

Me: Shouldn't I be nervous?

Izzy: It's normal to be nervous over weddings. Do you have a date?

Me: No.

Izzy: I gotta run. TTYL

Wow, that was short. When she becomes a mother, I doubt I'll get even a few minutes of her time in a week. I'll be by to see her often. I wonder if the gala event is a go, and if so, it might be the first time the four of us get together.

I text Kirill.

Me: Dad pulled the trigger. Did you hear?

Kirill: I've been meaning to call but was afraid to intervene. Concerned.

That's cryptic.

I walk to the hallway, pacing. Vito observes me and allows for distance between us to give me privacy.

"Kirill," I say when he answers his phone.

"What's up with this quick engagement? Your father just told me. I wasn't good enough—did you have to go with an Italian? Like your life needed to be more complicated."

"What do you mean? What did my father tell you?"

"Is this the man you were fucking? If so, you're being played. He must have known it was you that night at the club."

"That's not true. He followed me home afterward."

"Sure, he would say that. Your dad doesn't trust him."

"Well, that's the pot calling the kettle black," I huff.

"Are you implying hypocrisy?" he asks confused.

"Nothing. Forget it," I reply to avoid escalating the situation until I know what side Kirill is on. I can't let him in on my hunch. I have to have facts, and I need more of them. One incident can be explained. However, a string of them is not going to suffice.

I pop a chip into my mouth, then another. They are so damn addicting. My stomach grumbles. It hates me. I really should pack a lunch. The others usually bring food. We have a habit of short lunches and working the other thirty minutes.

"You don't sound like yourself," Kirill says.

"I'm adulting. What do you want from me? I have responsibilities," I reply hastily.

"That's true, I'm sorry. You're one of my best friends, and I want to be happy for you."

"Thank you."

"Are you happy?"

"I have to go, Kirill. I'll call soon."

Am I happy?

Izzy was right in her assumption that I wanted more than to be eye candy for a capo. I might look like I'm into the social climbing aspect of my world of socialites, but I don't need designer clothing to be complete. I like it and know how to shop, but now that I've become engaged to Matteo, I'm out of my element. He's still a few levels above me in how he holds himself and how confident he comes across.

I'm not sure I can pull that off, but I hope one day I can.

After calling contractors for the carpet and submitting the purchasing orders for pillows, I walk with Vito to the elevator.

"The carpet has been ordered; it just happens to be on the agenda today," I inform him.

"That's great. I can't wait. Is it nice?"

"I can't imagine anything done under the Borrelli name that isn't exquisite," I reply.

He laughs at this. "You know Matteo better than you think," he says.

We drive to Long Island, and Matteo texts me to see when I'll be home.

I call him.

"How is my fiancée today?" he asks first.

"You still have your head, or you wouldn't be talking to me, and I'd be a premature widow, so I assume it went okay?"

I hear him muffle his chuckle at this. That means it went well. I'm relieved, but I am curious if this is above board or if it involves clandestine operations in dark-lit rooms.

"Better than okay. And I have you to thank for it."

"Okay, I'll be there in…"

Vito shouts, "Thirty minutes."

"Very well. Federico will serve dinner when you get here."

I'm about to say he doesn't need to wait for me, but he's already hung up. I'm sure it's better to speak about family things face to face. So many things can happen with interpretations in a text, and who would know if we're compromised?

CHAPTER 25

MATTEO

$\mathscr{I}$’ve never been excited to see a woman arrive at my
mansion. I’ve thought of Alena off and on all day and have
had my fingers over the keys on my phone pad to text her half a dozen
times. I’m pacing the tiled floors, anxiously waiting for her to enter.

"Relax, Matteo. Dinner is perfect," Federico says as he sets the
formal table. I walk behind him. I don’t know what to do with myself.
Will Alena like the house? Will she feel comfortable?

"I don’t know what’s changed since Alena’s been in my life, but I
hope the heart palpitations stop."

Federico chuckles. "It’s love."

"I don’t do love," I growl. Any other person would cower under my
retort. Only Federico and Gio can brush off my denials without
retribution. Men outside my home would not dare comment. However,
my home is the only place I can be myself and let my guard down.
Even at that time, I rarely shared details about my women with anyone
other than Gio.

"Then why do you have a gift for the lovely Alena?" he murmurs as he breezes back to the kitchen.

Gifts. Hm. Before today, I've never paid attention to what a woman might want to be gifted by a lover. Alena has a way of bringing out my generosity.

As I follow Federico into the kitchen, the door blows open, and the cold air mingles with the sweet scent of her essence as she rides the wind. She smiles when she sees me in front of her.

"Let me help you," I say, rushing to help her get out of her coat.

"Thank you," she says, slipping her purse off her shoulder and letting me take her coat.

"Do you want a minute before dinner?"

"Oh, no. I'm starving," she replies, and as if on command, her stomach grumbles. "I had chips for lunch."

"That's not right. I'm sure you can order food. Is Sophia a problem?" My eyes narrowed at the thought of her being an issue when once I thought it would be fun to pit them against each other.

"Oh, no. It's habit or laziness. I'm still getting into my groove."

"Well, you have my card. Use it, not your money. I'm putting cash in your purse tonight. You can't walk around without it, even if everyone uses cards today. I want you to eat."

She studies my face, and I'm afraid I might have been too harsh.

"I'll work at it," she suggests.

Federico is thinking, and it hits me they've not been introduced.

"Oh," I say, taking her elbow to turn her to our chef. "This is Federico."

Alena extends her hand. Federico takes it into his own. "I will make you a lunch to die for from now on."

"You don't have to do that," she protests, but I know Federico does what he says. Otherwise, he wouldn't work for me.

"Nonsense. He loves to cook, and after you taste the meal he made tonight, you'll never be so quick to refuse," I say, putting her coat in the adjacent mud room.

"I hope you like pot roast. I know you just had seafood, but it's cold out."

"It smells incredible," she says. "The aroma of whatever you made fills the house. I smelled the meat and carrots when I walked in." Her smile at Federico makes me envious of the attention she's giving him, and I'm jealous that he's smitten with her.

Great, my chef and servant is now her ally.

"Thank you," Federico replies before he turns to lift the covered serving tray off the counter and leads the way to the table decorated with dripless candles for ambiance.

"This is incredible. Thank you both so much. I've never come home to dinner prepared for me like it's a special holiday, except for the engagement," she adds.

So, her parents put on the show for me this week. I assume it's only fitting since I'll be the one to take care of their daughter, but in reality, they did it so her father could avoid being bathed in betrayal.

The meal is on the table. I pull the chair out for Alena. "Wine?" I ask as I grab the bottle of chilled red off the table.

"Thank you. Do you mind if I start?"

"Not at all." I pour the wine as Federico disappears. If I know him, he's probably making dessert for her.

She helps herself to the serving utensils, puts slices of beef on her plate, and scoops veggies onto it. She wasn't joking. She is ravenous, and she begins to cut her meat. I sit adjacent to her.

She takes a bite of the tender beef and moans.

"This is ah-mazing," she exclaims as if she's describing an orgasm.

"I told you," I say as I help myself to the food.

"I want to hear about Alexsei. How is he?"

"He's fantastic. I'm not so sure your father will be in any shape to walk you down the aisle."

"I don't want him there at all," she exclaims, and her eyes turn as dark as the clouds that blow in with a Northwestern snowstorm.

"Really?"

"Of course. I was pissed at you for keeping your identity from me because you should have told me sooner."

"It's true. I'm sorry about that. I went for the dramatics. I did like the secrecy, and the thought of the two of us fucking all over the city still excites me," I confess. I'm growing hard as the words tumble from my mouth.

"However, my father's situation is alarming," she adds. "My father warned me not to trust you."

"You are right about that. He went so far as to tell Alexsei that he didn't trust me!"

"No," she exclaims, and her hand flies to her mouth.

"Yes, and it took me by surprise. I don't like surprises."

"We can agree that he's on our shit lists. How did Alexsei take it?" She confirms my belief that she has no clue about her father's dealings.

"Alexsei finds me honorable, and I'm sure it's only a matter of time before he questions your father's loyalty."

"I can't sit on the sidelines. I have to warn Izzy and Dmitry."

"Carefully. However, you're right about this. Alexsei adores you."

"Really?"

"Yes. In fact, you're the reason that my head is still attached."

Her eyes grow wide at my comment.

"What? I went into the lion's den. We met at his house."

"Wow. Well, he wouldn't have had you there if he didn't trust you, so I'm sure it's not as bad as you make it out to be."

"I'm not a man to be concerned over much, but it started intense, as you can imagine, and then, we became allies. He's repaying a debt he owes you for caring for his daughter."

"He said that?" She gave me a perplexing look.

"Yes. I can report that it was heartfelt as well."

"Izzy is my family, and I must warn her. Once someone betrays another, it's only a matter of time before they do it to you and those you care about."

"That's pretty profound. I have to agree. Let's drink wine."

She lifts her glass and taps mine before taking a long sip.

We demolished dinner, and Federico served us homemade cannoli with chocolate chips for dessert.

"I have to show you around. Follow me," I say, standing. I walk her through the spacious mansion. I show her my study, which doubles as my man cave. "You can read the books, but this is my room. It's off limits to everyone but for Federico to clean and Gio. I use it to smoke a cigar and drink bourbon occasionally."

"It's very manly." Her eyes roam the room, which is dark wood and leather with a tinge of cigar smoke. "You don't smoke in the house without opening the French doors, do you?"

"I won't if it bothers you."

"Doors open, please."

"Noted, let's head upstairs." We walked up the massive staircase, and I led her to our bedroom. I've never shared one before, and I was caught off guard when we were both stopped near the bed. It's the white elephant in the room. I'm speechless.

"Oh, my luggage is here," she says, dissipating the tension in the sleeping arrangements.

"Did your father mention the details of our arrangement? No. Why?"

"We're to share the bed and room, and I hope you aren't opposed to having a child next year. I need an heir."

CHAPTER 26

"*A* baby?" I stutter. My palms are clenched at my sides and become moist with sweat. The surprises continue to over-whelm me. I want children. I never dreamed it would be so soon.

"I'm afraid becoming the don has requirements, and it's expected." I turn to him. His face is void of emotion.

Where do I fit into Matteo's life, and will we ever be safe?

"What else is in this arrangement?" My face is placid, waiting to see if this is another decision that will be taken from me.

"We've agreed neither of us will take other lovers. I'm a man, and I have needs." He turns to me.

My cheeks grow warm under his intense gaze. I know his needs too well. I have my own. Turning him down last night was difficult, but I needed space to adjust to the changes that were pelting me with rapid fire.

"I need to put a baby in your belly. We'll start after the wedding. Izzy is having a baby. Wouldn't you like to have your children together? I never expected to have an alliance with the Russians. It helps us both. You and Izzy can remain close. I'll do some deals with Alexsei, and together, we'll be unstoppable." His voice is filled with purpose and promise.

A Baby is a huge decision. I wonder if our children will look like me or a combination of us both. His dark hair and my blue eyes would be unique, but no matter what color of eyes or hair, I would love my child to the best of my abilities. He wants to start immediately, and he's older than me. Most men in the family have children before they are thirty.

He takes my hands into his. "I've never wanted children before," his voice hovers softly in the air between us.

He's asking me for a baby. Surely, this means I'm special.

Walking through the bedroom door had me longing for his touch. My ovaries are salivating as my mind remembers our insatiable lust for each other. I want him to throw me on the bed and fuck me. My chest heaves at his request. The thought of him coming in me has my pussy quivering in anticipation.

"Tell me you want my child, Alena." His words melt my heart. He's a man who doesn't ask. He takes. This is his way of asking me to give him what he desires.

"What about our safety? The baby's?"

"With an ally now, we're safer than ever. The gala event will make a statement." The lines at the corner of his eyes lighten as he implores me for the answer he desperately wants to hear.

I'm sure it's a relief to know he has reinforcements should a war start. With my father's shenanigans, it might happen sooner rather than later.

His hands are soft. I don't pull away. When I look into his eyes, desire burns inside of me. I need to feel the itch between my legs. My loins warm by his request. It's as if I need the human connection now more than ever. He is my family. He didn't have to ask me—he chose to. In this past week, decisions have been made for me that left me feeling helpless. I'm touched that he's considerate enough to discuss the life-changing decision before us.

"I will give you a baby, Matteo," I whisper as I move my hand to caress his face. He leans into it before pulling my hand to his lips. He places a tender kiss on my hand. I'm stunned by the intimacy he's demonstrated.

"Thank you," he murmurs. My knees are weak. It's not like a don to show emotion, and yet he has. Perhaps he's capable of love.

He releases my hands and moves my luggage to the closet. I follow him. The tender moment has passed.

"The house is yours to decorate. Do as you see fit. Only..."

"Your study is off-limits, I get it." I give him a weak smile.

He sets my luggage inside a closet that takes my breath away. I will only bring a few of my favorite items from my condo because this closet is impeccably designed and full of red-bottom shoes, formal gowns, and business suits. Everything has its place. Recessed lighting illuminates the clothing, and at the top is a shelf with designer handbags.

"How did you manage this?" I ask. I'm sure he's taken care of everything here and that it will fit perfectly.

"I know people. You are an extension of me."

Meaning—he expects me to represent his name when I leave the house. It's back to business as usual. The tender moment has passed, and the letdown at his change in demeanor leaves me with a hangover. I'm alone again.

He takes a look around at his handy work. His shirt is fresh, and his silver cufflinks shine under the lights. His slacks fit him to a T. I eye his firm buttocks. He's a fine specimen.

He turns to me. "I picked up something for you today."

"You did?"

"Yes." He walks to the cabinet in the center of my closet and pushes something, and a jewelry box comes into view.

"It seemed something was in order for my bountiful day." He lifts something and walks to me. He opens a square box, and inside is a silver bangle bracelet that appears to be a lock, as one side of it is narrow. It fits into the larger side as he snaps it around my wrist.

I lift my arm to observe the new piece of hardware that reminds me I'm his property. It has a stamp of the jeweler on it, and it occurs to me that he didn't have his staff pick this out.

"I hope you like it." He unravels the cuff of his dress shirt and shows me he's also wearing one. How thoughtful and romantic.

"It's beautiful," I murmur. "It's very thoughtful."

His phone rings, and he pulls it out of his pocket. He nods to me and states he's heading to his study as he leaves the room.

I take a deep breath. I need a hot soak in the mammoth bathtub.

I take my time and enjoy a bubble bath. His mansion is humongous, but it's cold. I can warm it up with a few area rugs and add colorful accents to the rooms.

I wash my hair, sinking under the warm water, and when I pop up, the bracelet catches the light and sparkles as if it's winking at me.

I'd be naïve to think our life will be idyllic.

My father's words haunt me. Why would he tell Alexsei he's suspicious of Matteo? Matteo has treated me like an equal, and aside from the games at the beginning, he's been as transparent as a man can be in his position.

When my fingers show signs of water wrinkles, I stand, grabbing a thick towel that I wrap around my hair. I grab another to dry my body as I exit the tub.

"There you are," Matteo states as he leans against the doorway without a door. My nipples turn hard under his gaze. He unbuttons his shirt and slips out of his shoes.

I feel my heart beating faster in my chest.

"I want you on your knees," he states as he walks toward me naked. His large cock is stiff and throbbing.

I dry off quickly, pulling the towel from my head and letting my hair cascade over my shoulders. I drop the towel that is between us as his lips take mine by force. His kisses are hard and demanding. He's a man who knows what he wants, and he wants me to suck his cock.

I sink to my knees and grab his cock with my hand. I stroke him slowly, watching my painted nails move over his cock pleases me. I slip him into my mouth, and he moans as his hand fists my wet hair, and his pelvis moves to my rhythm.

I'm slick between my legs, ready for him to take me. I glance up, and his eyes are watching my lips that move over his bulging cock. I suck him and run my tongue over his head in a swirling motion that leaves him gasping.

"Turn over with your ass in the air," he barks.

I comply, thankful for the large fluffy mat beneath me. I am on my hands and knees, and he circles the head of his cock inside my pussy.

"You're so wet for me," he murmurs before he grabs my hips and slams inside me. I feel my body produce more juice at the thought of him coming inside me. I brace myself before he slams into me again, causing me to wince in surprise. I'm tight, but his giant cock stretches me to accommodate him.

He slides inside me as his palm pushes my lower back, and his other hand curves around my hip to pull me toward him as he creates a rhythm that slows. His cock strokes me and waves of pleasure wash over me, causing me to tuck my chin toward my chest. I'm helplessly spellbound as saliva drips from my lower lip.

He consumes me. My nipples are stiff peaks, and my breasts jolt back and forth as he pounds me harder and harder. He slides his hand over my belly, and his finger strokes my clit, and we climax together as my screams of euphoria fill the room.

He holds himself in me as if he's willing a baby. When he's satisfied, he pulls out and pulls me to him. He lifts me into his arms and carries me to the bed, where he tosses the bedding back.

"You must be tired. I have to work." He kisses my forehead and disappears into the closet. He pops out minutes later, and I watch him leave the room dressed in a matching jogger outfit.

I am tired, and my body is satiated. It's been a long day. I close my eyes and try not to think about what will unfold next. My father plans a hostile coup, and my fiancé needs an heir to solidify his empire.

* * *

I wake in a room where heavy drapes filter the morning light. It takes a few seconds to remember I'm in my new home. I look to the other side of the bed, and it is empty. I slide my hand over the soft bedsheet and find it's cold. I wonder if he came to bed last night.

After brushing my teeth, I flip on the recessed lighting that illuminates my new wardrobe. I run my fingers over the tops of the hangers, and the clothing moves gently against my fingertips.

I walk to the casual clothing area. After working all week, I rejoice in a weekend to explore my new surroundings. I pull my hair into a messy bun and descend the huge staircase, listening as I walk. I hope to hear someone speaking so I can discern who's home. Is my fiancé here? Without him filling me in on his calendar, I have no idea when he works.

When I pass the dining room, I know the kitchen is next. My feet are clad in no-skid socks, so I don't make a sound.

"Ahhh," Federico exclaims and smiles. He walks to me, putting his arm through mine, and leads me to a seat behind the marble island that serves as a workspace and an eating area. "Good morning, Principessa." He puts his hand out, indicating I'm to sit. "What would you like for breakfast? Coffee Americano or espresso? Eggs? Waffles?"

"You don't have to wait on me. I can do it myself."

He flings a hand to his forehead. "Mio Dio!" he exclaims.

I giggle at his Italian expression. "What?"

"You are not behaving like a principessa. You are to be waited on like the princess you are," he states as a fact.

"You mean the princess I'll be after the wedding? I'm no one, really."

"Oh, my, it's true! I heard that you were modest and full of kindness. You are too good for your own good," he mutters as he walks to a large machine with an Italian name sprawled in bold font along the metal front.

"Where did you hear that?" I wonder who has been talking.

"I can't reveal my sources. Matteo wouldn't like us talking. I think you need to have a real espresso," he adds quickly, changing the subject.

"Great." I accept his offer because the idea makes him happy. He begins to fiddle with the machine in the opposite corner of the kitchen. I think he's excited to show me he can make a perfect drink.

The coffee grinder's growl and hum fill the air, and the smell of freshly ground beans greets my nose. I watch as he maneuvers the attachment, twists it into the machine, and slips a cup under the spiral that resembles two metal units that spit out coffee until it's a stream that fills the cup halfway.

"Sugar?"

"Yes, please." I teeter on the edge of my chair and watch as he dedicates himself to the tiny spoon, sprinkling sugar into the cup, swirling it twice, and placing it on a saucer. He picks up an aluminum shaker labeled cinnamon and dusts the top of the froth with the brown powder before crossing the expansive kitchen floor and sliding it before me.

He stands on his side of the island and waits.

I lift the drink to my lips. The cup is warm to the touch. I use the tiny handle on the side and take a dainty sip. It's incredible. It's the best espresso I've ever sipped.

"This is fantastico," I say, using one of the few Italian words I know because it's like English.

"Ah, bene," he replies. "What will you eat? Matteo will not be happy if you skip meals. He was very angry you had chips for lunch yesterday."

"It's a bad habit. What do you feel like cooking?"

"Anything you want. I have it all."

"I'm hungry. Would it be okay to eat poached eggs on toast with smashed avocados? It sounds very princess-like to me." I smile as I finish my espresso before it's cold.

"Splendid. It will take only a few minutes. What do you have planned for the day? What do you want for dinner?"

"I have no idea. Is Matteo home?"

"He's been in his study with the door closed since dawn."

"Do you live here?"

"I live nearby. I'm here twelve hours a day, every day. I get out when Matteo is gone for the day to shop and run errands."

"What about your family and friends? That's too many hours."

"I am happy to be here. I came with Matteo as I've been with him for years. I'm a retired chef, but we are from the same neighborhood in Sicily. He pays me very well. I can't complain. My work was my life, and now I'm here."

I want to ask more questions but refrain from doing so because I don't want to appear nosy. Learning more about my husband-to-be will take time.

Federico serves me breakfast on a white plate decorated with parsley garnish and silverware wrapped in a stiff napkin. He makes another espresso for me. I eat and thank him.

"It's my job. There is no need for that," he replies.

"Nonsense, what do you recommend for dinner?"

"I can make fresh dough and put together Caprese pizzas with fresh mozzarella, thinly sliced tomatoes, and balsamic drizzled on top."

"My mouth is watering," I reply. "Where is Matteo?"

He nods toward the house's interior, and I set off searching for the King who owns it.

CHAPTER 27

MATTEO

*A*s the sun beams into my study, I assume Alena is up. I flip the note I've tossed between my fingertips back into its hiding spot inside my desk. I could take the note to a specialist for analysis, but it would be useless without something to compare it to.

I look up at the muted TV hanging on the wall. The news is displayed with a running caption of international news before it switches to the local channel.

The name Santino Moretti catches my eye. I find the remote to turn the volume up. "Breaking news" is the banner at the bottom of the screen.

The anchorwoman says, "Santino Moretti was arrested for waving a loaded gun in a crowded pizzeria. He is out on bail. No more details are available at this time. It is speculated that he is the head of the Moretti syndicate, which has ties to waste management and recycling facilities along the Eastern Seaboard. There were overdoses in the city today, and the body of a young man was discovered after family members in

England requested a well-being check by local officers. An investigation is ongoing."

"Moretti, what is it about you that has your name popping up twice in two days? What should I know about you?" I mutter before a soft knock lands on my solid-stained oak door.

I move to open it.

"Sleeping beauty," I tease.

"Good morning. I wanted to know if we have plans for today. It's a Saturday." Alena's face exudes youth and vigor as she clasps her hands in front of her.

Her hair is on top of her head, and she has a stick through it. How that occurs, I'll never know. She's breathtaking as she stands before me in a black sweatsuit. I stifle a groan as her large boobs fill the top, and her curvy hips will soon support the weight of my baby.

She's young and doesn't have lines from years of worry on her forehead. Her eyes are bright, and her face inquires whether I'll spend the day with her.

I wonder about bringing a child into my world. I've wrestled with it since my uncle brought it up in Sicily. The world is dark enough without my hand in making it darker. Will I fuck up a child and become my father?

When I see Alena, she dispels my worry. She's an angel, and any child with her as their mother will know her love every day of her life. Is that such a terrible thing?

No, it is not. Perhaps that is why I have only considered this with her in my future.

"One minute, I have to turn off the TV." I return to my desk and flick the TV off.

I return to her as she leans her back against the door jamb, one foot crossed over the other's ankle. She's sexy as hell. I close the door behind me.

"Are you off today?"

"We'll see how it goes." I hope today will be void of drama, but being in the business as long as I have, I have no expectations. I will be interrupted by something that will put me in a bad mood. It's the reason I never smile. I have nothing to smile about. I put out fires, and someone creates a new one. The city never sleeps, so I rarely sleep through the night.

"What would you like to do?"

"I don't know. What do you do? I've never had a serious boyfriend," she says as she slips her hand into mine. I walk her to a cozy room with a fireplace.

"Thank God. If you did, he'd be a dead man walking."

She stops walking, and I look at her face, filled with fear.

"There's no ex-boyfriend. No harm done. Let me light a fire for us." I lead her into the cozy room with dark green walls. The brown leather sofa is comfy and has an amber throw made of baby alpaca wool.

Alena sits on the sofa's edge and watches as I open the damper and methodically stack wood before lighting the kindling underneath it. In less than a minute, the fire is a steady flame, and heat spills into the quaint, private room tucked out of the presence of anyone who could pass by.

"How is your job going?" I ask Alena now that the room is glowing with heat.

"Good. I'm getting into the routine. My new friend Penny noticed my ring, but I didn't give any details."

"Why not?" I snap with the quickness of a twig in a forest—the current in the air changes.

Alena's face turns pale.

"I'm sorry I was so direct. Is there a problem?"

"Not really. I have no details to give anyone."

"I think a June wedding would be nice, don't you?" he asks as he stirs the fire with a poker.

"It would give your family enough time to get there," I reply.

"What about you? Friends or family to invite?"

"I don't want to see my father. I wish he hadn't broken my trust. Could he be setting you up for a bad deal with Alexsei?" She pulls her feet under her as she sits on the sofa, and I pull her toward me as I sit at the end.

I stare into the fire. What is the long con that her father is working toward? "I'm not sure, but we can't trust him. Someone will have to give you away." I look at her face, and I realize she's not surprised. "Has your father broken your trust before? You don't look surprised."

"I was surprised the night of our engagement dinner—which was an ambush," she adds. Her words are sharp. I shouldn't have surprised her like that. I let my childish needs prove to her that I knew more about our fragile beginning overrule my better judgment.

"Again, I'm sorry."

"Dad hasn't seemed right in some time. I thought I would have been engaged after college, but my parents said they were waiting for Dmitry to take over to see how the dust settled first. I never had a reason to be concerned about what my father was doing until I met you."

"Why is that?" I turn my eyes to the methodical flicker of the flames in the fireplace.

"I'm not sure. He was working and didn't eat dinner with us. He seemed angry. He was off. I'm afraid he might be planning to take over the bratva."

"I had the same thought. Who could be working with your father?" I ask with intrigue. She has an imaginative mind. Perhaps she's picked up on how my world works after growing up in a mafia family.

"I'm not sure. You know how it is growing up with everyone being a relative. Kirill, the man from the bar, and I are best friends, and he's tight with Dmitry. If he knew what my father was doing, he hid it well. We need to warn Izzy and Dmitry."

"I agree. Are you comfortable doing that?"

"I have to do it," she whispers as the fire's flames dance in front of me. I wish there were more information. "Besides, if Kirill knew more about my dad, he would have known your name, and he didn't. So that means I haven't been watched closely. Perhaps he has his men on others. It doesn't make sense." She slips her arms through mine and lays her cheek on my shoulder as we contemplate the situation.

"I'm new to the situation. I can't risk my neck on an assumption. However, you can throw a red flag in front of Izzy, and she'll take the warning. What do you know about the Moretti family?"

She shudders against me. "They are wicked. The don, Santino, is Izzy's grandfather. He forbade his daughter from marrying Alexsei when they were young and in love. He even faked her death when she left town so no one would look for her. She ended up dying in New York City in a car accident when Izzy was young."

"That's tragic."

"It was. I mean, Dmitry and Kirill had to discover all this through tiny snippets of information. We wonder if it was a hit, or was it her grandfather who knew where her mother was all along? I guess we'll never know," she concludes with a pause. "Dmitry is quite the hacker—without him, I doubt anyone would have been able to piece it all together. We all added something to the mix. We worked together to unravel the truth as we know it, but when Alexsei met Izzy, he said he knew she was his."

"Interesting. So, Dmitry is a good hacker, you say?" My mind naturally goes to my new messenger app. I wonder if it's something I can share with him. "So, what happened to Izzy?"

"Yes, he is, and Izzy's Aunt, who was her mother's friend, raised her. Izzy has nothing to do with the Moretti family. Alexsei's wife disappeared after Izzy's wedding. I'll never know what happened to her after the bomb went off in the fountain."

"You're kidding me. I remember reading about that," I reply, trying to recall the article I read. "I bet we both know what happened to Alexsei's wife," I say, knowing Alena has come to the same conclusion. "A woman who sells her husband out has got to be swiftly dealt with, and I'm not talking about a one-way ticket to Siberia. No wonder Alexsei has a soft spot for you and Izzy. Vultures have surrounded the man."

"True. I know better than to lie. My father knows the consequences of his actions. I won't betray Izzy or Alexsei."

"You are right. I would expect my family to come forward if there were a traitor among us." My phone beeps, and when I pull it out of the pocket of my jeans, which cost thousands of dollars, I see it's Gio.

"I have to call Gio," I say. Alena moves so I can stand. I excuse myself before I walk to my study and close the door behind me.

"What's up, Gio?"

"It appears Finn is the body they found from an overdose this morning, and the Irish are sniffing around. The O'Donnells in London were inquiring as to his whereabouts."

"Fuck!" I yell. "I told you to make sure this wouldn't come back to us. What the hell is wrong with Antonio?"

"He's blinded by love," he grumbles. "How the hell should I know?"

"Get on him and make sure no evidence leads to us. We're in an alliance with the Russians. We can't be kicking up shit with the Irish. I don't want to piss Alexsei off. He has enough on his plate," I state without a filter. I trust Gio, but I like to think things through before I speak.

"I know, I know," he moans. "I'll visit Antonio. Do you still think he can be trusted?"

"Unfortunately, I believe Antonio is in love. Men are capable of doing stupid shit when they are in love," I mutter.

Thankfully, Gio is smart enough not to comment on this statement. I am learning what it's like to have feelings for Alena. My heart races, my palms are sweaty when I'm nervous that my presence might not be welcomed. I'm in a state of worry over her safety, and my cock is hard, wanting to fuck her every ten minutes.

"How long before the Irish start kicking in doors?"

"No clue. Without proof, they can only speculate."

"Well, make sure there is no proof. If there is, you know what has to be done." I hang up the phone. I ball my right hand into a fist and smash it onto the desktop. Fuck. Now, my hand hurts. I have to wait for an update.

I returned to Alena and offered to show her the wine cellar I had built in the basement. It's not like the ones in Italy, but it's as close as I can get.

I lead the way to the door that looks like a closet off the kitchen and hold her hand as she walks down the cold steps. I explained to her what regions the Italian wines are from, and she picked a bottle. She says we're having pizza for dinner. I marvel at her fascination with my impressive collection, and we return upstairs, where Federico has a light lunch prepared.

In the past few hours, I've felt every emotion on the spectrum. Anger, rage, disappointment, and inklings of what I believe is love. If this is one day, how will I survive a lifetime? My heart is in my chest when I observe Alena. I imagine her belly swollen with my baby, and my cock grows hard, contemplating the process to make that happen.

After lunch, I escort Alena back to the fireplace and kiss her softly on the neck before I move to her lips.

"I have to have you now. Only you, Alena. I am going to fuck you hard and fast. I will fuck you until you scream my name," I mutter against her ear. We shed our clothing, and she lays on the long-haired bear-skin rug in before the fireplace. I run a hand over her head and let her hair down. I caress her face and peer into her eyes as my lips cover hers. I continue to drop kisses down her neck while I grab her firm boob and suck her nipple between my teeth. I nibble on it, and she presses her knees together.

I cup her between her legs, forcing her to spread her legs, and a moan escapes her lips.

"You are mine." I run my hand over her boobs before I bend, clasping her hips as I move between her legs. I suck her swollen lips as her juices flow. She's ready for me, but I will take my time. I slip two fingers inside her and flick her clit with my tongue, stroking it hardens under the pressure. She raises her hips.

"Fuck me, Matteo," she rasps with an uneven breath.

I align my cock to her opening and thrust into her. I'm hit with an adrenaline rush as my hard cock moves into her tight canal.

I want her pregnant, and the thought of the prospect makes me delirious as I grab her hips and fuck her harder and harder. Each stroke is faster than the last.

My balls pound into her firm ass, and I love the sound of it and the fact that we are skin-to-skin in every way imaginable. I hear her say my name before she lets out a long scream. She pushes me over the edge. I shoot my seed into her warm and willing pussy.

CHAPTER 28

ALENA

When I talk, I wonder if he's listening. After dinner, Matteo disappears from his study. My gut instinct tells me something is happening.

I roam the halls on the second floor to see how many bedrooms have ensuites when Izzy answers my call.

"What's up?" Izzy asks in her perky voice.

"I can ask you that," I reply.

She chuckles. "We're cuddling. I thought you'd be too busy with Matteo to call this weekend. I imagine your knees are hurting," she teases.

"Izzy!" She laughs at my pretense of shock. "Seriously," I continue, but she knows me too well.

"I thought you'd be sexing all weekend," she says, and I assume she's moved into another room as I don't hear the TV in the background.

"Well, it's been incredible, I can't complain. I've never had a man who does the things he does to me. It's as if he loves to pleasure me."

"Wow. That's incredible. How do you feel about that?"

"It's different. I've never felt this way about anyone the way I feel about him. I'm vulnerable for the first time in my life. It's scary."

"The other men you dated were assholes. Vulnerable is good. It's the only way you can ever know real love. The type of love my parents shared," she adds.

I chuckle. "What men? I've never had a man before."

Izzy snickers. "You're right. Did you hear Santino Moretti was arrested today for brandishing a loaded gun in public?"

"No. Really?" I reply, but I can't say that I'm shocked. "Has he lost it?"

"I don't know. I hope he never finds out who I am. I don't want to be near him. Dmitry looks forward to meeting Matteo at the gala. I was able to get a gown that fit. Imagine that."

"That's great. Matteo has something ordered or being made. I'm not sure. I've never been to anything as fancy as this."

"It's different than the red carpet. We're in good company. It's going to be the most popular affair in the city this winter, and we'll be together for it. It will be fun. Besides, with Dmitry and Matteo at our side, what can go wrong?"

"Don't say that. We know what can go wrong!" I all but yell with anxiety as I remember the bombing at her wedding. "But you are right. The fact we get to attend one of the most prestigious events in the city, and I'll be with you will make it a great time. I'm sure my days at the clubs are over unless Matteo takes me."

"Oh, I know they are," she replies. The tone of her voice tells me Dmitry is just as possessive.

"I will tell you more when I see you. I'm calling to give you a message. Please tell Dmitry that my father needs to be watched."

"What do you mean?"

"You never liked him, Izzy. Read between the lines. I can't tell you specifically; I don't know, but his hands are dirty. Be careful."

"We'll talk later and get caught up, but I'll pass it along."

"Thank you. I have to go, but we'll see you at the gala."

"You bet."

"Ciao," I reply. She says, "Goodbye" with a chuckle.

I hear Matteo calling for me, and by the time I reach the staircase, he informs me we have an appointment in the city tomorrow. I'm being fitted for the masquerade gown.

"What does it look like?" My heart flutters thinking about a beautiful gown for a themed event.

"You'll see," he says. "I take it you spoke to Izzy?"

"Yes, the message was a bit cryptic, but she understands the unspoken words. I can't inform her of specific details, and we don't know what he's doing. Right?" My eyes question him. I don't think he would keep information regarding my father to himself.

Would he tell me the truth if he knew it?

"Yes. If I knew something, I'd have to divulge it to Alexsei. I can't tell him something on a hunch that is against a man he's trusted for years. The warning needed to come from you."

"I think Izzy is a good judge of character. She hid whenever my father stopped by my condo."

"Time will tell," he replies as he escorts me to the top floor of the house.

"What's up here?" I ask.

"Are you always so inquisitive?" He mocks me as we climb a narrow spiral staircase at the end of the second floor.

"Maybe," I tease. I reach for Matteo's arm as the steps are narrow.

When we reach the top, we face a huge room with wood flooring worthy of a dance studio. The wall along the left is filled with one large window after another, and the sun is setting on the foliage outside. At the end of the room are numerous rectangular stacked verticals, and they are paired down the higher they extend with curved windows, creating a picturesque cathedral effect. Brown and off-white stones fill the wall, providing a perfect frame for the stunning water view. We're not far from the shoreline.

There is a pool table, a mini-bar, and a long sofa with a coffee table.

"Is that a bathroom behind the bar?" I ask, turning to see his face in the evening's light.

"It doubles as another master bedroom. It might be useful for guests."

"I counted six large bedrooms today," I state.

"This is seven."

"I'm relieved I'm not expected to clean and dust."

"That's the idea. You're my principessa."

We turned in for the night, and I lay naked in bed as Matteo fussed over something with the mattress. There's never been a night we're together that we don't make love.

Matteo pulls straps from under the bed and lays them on the bed. He kisses my body and wraps a soft Velcro cuff around my wrists. His hands slide down my body, and when he reaches my feet, he binds my ankles.

"What are you doing?" I'm slightly alarmed, but he wouldn't hurt me.

"This is an introduction to bondage. I'm going to torment you with pleasure, and when you're ready to come, I'll fuck you, but you're not touching me."

"That doesn't sound like fun," I smirk.

"Trust me, you'll enjoy this."

The sounds of his words give me chills, and my nipples harden under his gaze. His staff moves without detection, so I'm not surprised when he lifts a wine glass from the nightstand and takes a sip.

Then he leans over me and feeds me the wine. It's sweet and warm. A drop touches my lips, and he sucks it before he kisses me. This kiss is different. It's gentle, and his warm lips linger. He uses his fingers and dribbles wine down my abdomen. I close my legs defensively and yelp because it surprises me.

He moves to align himself with my body and bends his head, licking the wine drops one at a time. I am slick between my legs. This is torture. I moan and writhe under the pleasure.

I twist defensively.

"You're not going anywhere." He gives me a mischievous smile, and I hate him for making me vulnerable. My body craves him, and my heart feels things I've never experienced. Can I trust him to hold up his end of our marriage deal?

His soft hands move over my body, and he pauses for more wine. He feeds it into my mouth, and we kiss as the warm liquid slides down my throat. The act is incredibly sexual. I long for him to slip his huge cock inside me.

His mouth devours mine. I tug at the restraints to touch him, and I long to grab his hair, but I know it's futile.

His lips move to my neck, and he runs a hand through my long hair. Our eyes meet, and my heart hurts with the feelings I have been suppressing. I'm afraid to trust, but I know that the trust we're building is a foundation for our future, and I want him to love me.

His hands continue down my body, moving methodically and slowly. I inhale as if I could come on command, but I want to feel his cock in me.

His fingers slip inside me, and I gasp. I tug at the restraints.

"Fuck me, Matteo."

"No." His dangerous tone is followed by eyes that flash at my demand.

"Yes."

"This is making love, Alena. I will take my time. You are the only woman I've ever had in my bed."

My heart melts. I'm special to him.

He moves his lips between my legs and sucks my juice like it's as sweet as the wine he fed me.

Mother of God, I can't take it anymore. Goosebumps cover my body, and the hair on the nape of my neck rises. I lift my hips off the bed to grind into his face.

"I'm going to come."

"Don't come," he orders.

"I can't help it," I gasp as I feel my body levitating above the bed. Pleasure consumes me. My head is empty and void of thoughts.

He fingers me and sucks my clit—working in tandem. I twist and pull at the cuffs again.

My clit hardens. I'm about to come as his cock slams into me. My orgasm erupts, and a shrill scream fills the room. It's my scream, and it continues as I come again and again.

Matteo, as he leans over me, drives his cock deeper into me and flicks the wrist restraints off. He rides me slowly at first. Then I hear his breathing change. I see his face contort as his head tips back, and his loud groan reaches my ears. He pumps me one last time, and he's breathless. I never knew a man could come twice.

When he moves off me, he frees my legs and pulls me to his chest, where he cradles me in his arms and brushes my hair off my face.

"My Angel," he murmurs. We fall asleep, and when I wake up, it's dark outside. Even in his sleep, his arms are wrapped protectively around me.

* * *

The morning passes quickly after we eat breakfast. Federico flutters around, fulfilling my every need—espresso, lattes, breakfast, and the dinner menu for the week. Then Matteo whisks me out the door to the limo, where I greet Gio and notice another man in the front seat with him. I send Matteo a questioning look, and he ignores me. I assume he's being overly cautious.

We arrive at a private dress shop where we are buzzed in, and inside, on a wall, is a neon sign with the name Mariuccia Cavallo.

"She's in Italy now, but she's making a wedding dress for you," Matteo whispers in my ear.

"What do you mean, making?"

"You know, using fabric and beads and thread to make an article of clothing."

"Matteo, that's crazy. It has to be expensive."

"It's enough money to buy a few houses in Southern Italy, but I want you to have a one-of-a-kind dress. They will take your measurements, and occasionally, you'll be invited for private viewings of her latest collections. She has clients, and you have a personal assistant here to help you."

"Like the ones I've gone to in the city?"

"No. The store is closed for you. It's by invitation only. Each piece is tailored to fit you, and what you buy won't be sold in New York. She only sells to her clients. You won't find her clothing in stores or on clearance."

"Wow," I murmur. I observe clothing on racks with shoes to match. This is more upscale than the little stores I took Izzy to.

"It's not uncommon for jeans to cost five thousand dollars."

I protest, but his lips silence me before my assistant for the day greets us with champagne.

The drink goes down quickly. A dress is brought out. I'm told it's backless and made of wool. The bottom is wide and flowing. The fabric's print is black with cream swirls. A tux with a jacket that matches the material of my dress is suddenly carried in front of Matteo, along with black pants.

We move into the dressing rooms to try on our clothes. A team of women has me raise my arms and check the dress's length and bust. The bra is built into the undergarment with a hoop like the old-fashioned dresses to keep the shape of the dress perfect at the bottom. I have to kick the hoop so it flounces the dress out before I walk. I'm gobsmacked.

It's exquisite. After our fitting, I was led around to pick out what I liked for day wear, and then they brought out a few options for a wedding dress. The dresses weren't finished, but I was shown pictures of the sketches. Cinderella would be green with envy at the choices before me. I made my selection, and then we moved on to formal wear and walked the shop.

I select a few evening dresses, and we leave to return home. I fall asleep on the way. We enter the house, and I'm foggy but hungry. Federico coos over me as he provides us with a late lunch.

Overall, it was a successful weekend with my new fiancé. And, as life tends to go, it's one step forward and one back.

Monday dawns with Vito driving me to work. It's dark when I get up to fix my hair. Matteo left me a note he's in the gym. I don't have time to see him as I race down the stairs to eat in the kitchen and converse with Federico. He slides a stylish bag my way, and inside, I find it's a lunchbox disguised as a large purse. There is a thermos, a bottle of water, and silverware.

My lunch. "You didn't have to do that."

"I wanted to. Besides, Matteo wants you to take care of yourself. So do I," he adds before making my latte. I want to hug him as he's so kind to me.

I eat, and Matteo breezes by on his way upstairs.

He kisses my lips and tells me our announcement was on page six yesterday.

I assume the wedding date is June.

However, a knife can cut the tension when I arrive at work. I locate Penny. "What's up?"

"You never mentioned you are engaged to Matteo Borrelli."

"And?"

"He was Sophia's lover before she came here for this position last year. She envisioned herself as the one to wear that ring," she states emphatically, pointing to the rock on my left hand.

"Fuck."

"Darling," she drawls out her voice like Cruella de Vil. "Let me see that ring. You never mentioned Matteo. However, did you meet?"

"It was a coincidence," I state. Oh, God. Will the world know it was a sex club?

"I bet," she replies, popping the 't.'

Her hands are cold when she picks up my hand, which is heavy with the ring, and bends over to examine the diamond.

"Matteo has the best taste. Why he picked you, I'll never understand. I assume he's in grief over losing his father. They say don't make hasty decisions when one's had a major life event." She drones on. "The order you placed on Friday can't be delivered in time, so you'll have to find an alternative. The tile company is running late today. I told them you'd be happy to stay late and lock the office behind you. They can't be on the floor without supervision. The work order has to be signed. They are doing a bathroom today as a test. We have to make sure it's perfect."

"Of course."

She turns all my achievements into a mudslide of shit.

Matteo never mentioned that they knew each other. What are the odds that they are both from Italy and speak Italian?

My head is swirling. Matteo texts, but I'm too angry and busy to reply.

I take a few minutes to wolf down Federico's Italian sandwich. It's made with homemade bread that resembles pita bread, but it's light and airy. As the leafy green lettuce protrudes from it, I take a bite and taste the fresh turkey and cheese. Both are thinly sliced with a touch of mustard to the mayo spread, which is utterly delicious. He must have baked a turkey while we were out yesterday. It's that fresh.

I hear a commotion, and Matteo is leaning against a wall supporting my tiny office's partition.

"Why haven't you responded to my text?"

I quickly swallow and take a swig from my water bottle to wash it down.

"I'm sorry." I stand.

Vito is behind him, looking helpless.

"You can't go without answering me."

"I'm sorry. I'm sure you have more important things to do. I was so busy..." my voice trails off as he raises his hand to quiet me.

"From now on, you answer," he states like the mafia boss he is. All his orders are carried out immediately. I realized too late that I have to follow the rules as well. "I was worried about you."

"Matteo, my dear," Sophia appears in the narrow excuse of a hall-way. He turns and greets her. She kisses both of his cheeks, and I'm enraged. She buries me in work out of spite, and now, she's kissing my fiancé.

"Sophia, I trust everything is running smoothly. The floor has to be finished on time."

"Oh, that. Yes, your protégé is incredible. She's a hard worker. She even volunteered to work late tonight so I could leave on time for our dinner. You know how subcontractors are unreliable."

"Unfortunately, I do." He raises an eyebrow, and I can't tell if he's amused or overly kind to the woman he burned with a surprise engagement to someone else. I observe Matteo. What is he playing at? Why are they having dinner? He never mentioned it to me.

"Can I have a word?" I ask Matteo as Sophia stands devouring him with her eyes.

"Sure, Angel. Excuse me, Sophia," he says as we walk past her and into the hallway where Vito gives us the room. This is why Vito's presence didn't raise any eyebrows. Sophia knows who he is and where he's from. She must have assumed he was here for her or to protect his interests.

Matteo twists me into his arms, and his lips are on mine. I put my hands on his chest to ease his crushing presence that steals my oxygen.

"You never mentioned Sophia."

"That's my oversight. I'm sorry. I had a busy weekend. We're having dinner to discuss the project. Did you volunteer to work tonight?"

"Well, you know, gotta be a team player," I say as if I'm on a cheer squad for a Taylor Swift rally.

"Okay. Let me know if there are any issues. I have to run. Is that all?" He gives me a once-over, and I almost orgasm. He undresses me with his eyes, and I feel the heat building between us.

"Yes. I'm fine. See you later." I turn to go, but his hand clamps on my wrist, and he pulls me into his chest, holding my hands in his.

"Not so fast," he breathes before his lips cover mine for a deep kiss. "I didn't come here for nothing," he says before disappearing down the hall and leaving me wanting him.

I presume Gio is waiting for him downstairs. And, just as I thought —he knows how to access the entire building. I'm sure he's only seen when he wants to be seen.

Considering someone might want him dead, I'm a bit giddy over his supernatural abilities.

Izzy texts and congratulates me on my engagement.

Me: Thank you.

Izzy: I didn't know you were getting married so soon.

Me: June isn't soon.

Izzy: Page Six has your wedding date in March.

Me: March? There has to be a mistake. I thought it was June.

Izzy: They don't make mistakes. I hope you picked out a dress and have connections for a venue, or is it a destination wedding?

Me: I have to go, but I'll call you with the details.

Am I getting married in a few weeks? This is happening too fast. My head hurts thinking about what has to be done. How can I work and plan an impressive wedding?

Did Matteo plan the wedding without me?

CHAPTER 29

MATTEO

’m miffed. Sophia told me Alena was working late, but my fiancée didn’t. Doesn’t Alena know that her plans concern me? Doesn’t she value our time together? Does she have so little regard for our arrangement that she didn’t text me about this change?

I was heading to check out a business, but I had to see that she was okay. I suffer withdrawal when she leaves the room, so an entire day without her humbles me. I’m jealous others are with her—and I’m not. I’m happy she works with women and that Nathan is into men.

I’m irritated sitting in traffic and over Antonio’s botched overdose situation. I hope to God there is no evidence of our hit. I’ve never worried much about these things, so I guess there is a tinge of appreciation for my father, who carried the stress of the job for the rest of the family.

Without Alena, my dark world would creep into my soul and hold me as a prisoner forever. It would be a living hell. Am I being selfish in taking her?

Yes.

Am I selfish for wanting to have a family with her?

Absolutely. I'm fucking up her life and putting her in more danger. The funny thing is that she had no idea her father was putting her in the crosshairs. Would the don believe her father acted alone in his ploy of deceit?

She is my Angel and the light of my life. She makes me feel things I've never felt before. With her, I'm happy. I haven't been happy since my mother died. Sure, I love spending time with my family, and we laugh and carry on like most, but Alena awakens feelings that have been walled off forever.

Perhaps the hatred for my father made me unworthy of love, and now that chapter is closed. They say new doors of opportunity open all the time. Ironically, it was a door to the sex club. Our meeting was by chance, but now, I shudder at the thought that we might not have found each other. She can resent my control, but she'll never be free of me. I refuse to let her go.

I never thought my life would be a happy one. Alena is in danger every time I'm seen with her. Soon, my enemies will discover that she is my weakness. As much as I try to hide my feelings, I can't deny my love for her as she consumes my thoughts.

The day passes as I work in my office at a warehouse. Alena texts me about the wedding date.

I need to hear her voice, so I call her.

"What is wrong, my Angel?"

"A month? I thought we discussed June for the wedding," she exclaims. She's upset. I assume a bride would be anxious, but this is deeper than wedding jitters.

"June is a perfect month for weddings, but we needed to move up the timetable. March will be great. We'll have it in Florida, where it will be sunny," I say, trying to finesse her into the timeline I've set. "I have a mansion on the beach."

"Florida? How am I to plan this?"

"You aren't. I hired a wedding planner. She planned some singer's wedding—JLo or something like that. I can't keep up with American pop stars."

This causes her to pause.

"JLo?"

"That's what I've been told. Only the best for you, Alena."

"I don't have a say in who I marry. Now, you have the wedding planned. Do I get to make any decisions over my life?"

"The most important one, yes."

"The baby."

"Yes."

"You're getting everything you want whether I agree or not. Was it a request for a baby, or were you going to sabotage my birth control if I said no?"

Interesting. She's managed to box me into a corner.

"I was hoping you would say yes."

"You didn't answer my question," she continues.

"Can we discuss this at home?"

"Sure. And we'll discuss Sophia as well. You never said I was working for your ex-girlfriend. Or that you are having dinner with her tonight."

"My ex-lover, I don't date."

"Yeah, well, call it what you want. That woman is not nice."

"That's why you are wearing my ring—not her."

Silence reigns for thirty seconds.

"Oh," she whispers.

"Right. If that's all, I have to go," I reply.

"Okay," she says and hangs up.

"The little woman is not happy with you." Gio chuckles as he nods to the man with a face of tattoos.

Juan, the leading gang member in my territory, is sitting. Otherwise, his pants would fall to his ankles. His jeans aren't cheap, his sneakers are expensive, and the yellow color attracts attention. His organization runs our drugs.

His look is his brand. His subordinates respect him, and he loves to show off his wealth. We're not all that different. I show off my wealth as well.

His teeth are capped, and the three gold chains on his neck are his trademark. He's El Loco—Crazy Man.

"She'll calm down," I reply confidently. "What do you have for me, Crazy Man?"

"Addler owns a rental building. We're always calling the city as he never does repair work, and it's dangerous." His legs are spread as he slouches in the chairs. His hands rest on his legs. "It's not safe to live there, man. We've seen his assistant talking to the city's investigator. He took an envelope, and no one came by anymore. We call and call, but without an attorney, there's nothing we can do. Ain't no one got money to fight him. I'd love to tap him."

"He's a slumlord?" I state. Why is this surprising? I should have known.

"Are you sure, Juan?" Gio asks.

"Sure. I know who they are. I have pictures, too. I ain't stupid. That's how it works, man. They've not been seen lately, but all the Locos know it." He pulls a jump drive from his pocket and steps forward. Gio puts his palm up so Juan will drop it into his hand.

I nod. El Loco stands, and I shake his hand. "Thank you."

"We're good?"

"We're good," I say.

"I gotta bounce," he says, flicking his wrist to cause his chunky gold bracelets to jingle. He reaches the door and joins two friends who are waiting for him.

"Gio, print the pictures. I'll use them to bribe the councilman. Strange. I expected Addler to have a mistress."

"He might. Maybe we haven't found her yet. I can have him tailed."

"This is good for now," I reply, sitting behind the stately desk. The office is tucked away in a corner of the warehouse we use to keep our drywall inventory. It's out of the public's eye.

Nothing much happens around here that isn't mob-related. And for those who don't belong here, they are looking for shit to steal. The locals know that if they steal from us, we'll hunt them down and kill them. Stealing is against our code—we enforce it by any means possible.

This is another reason Mikhail Pasnov will be taken out. Alexsei is a smart man. Mikhail stole something that should have been taken on behalf of the Don. The deal was a crime of opportunity, but if I found him in a day, others could, too. It was too easy to trace his company to the title.

Pasnov needed help to do what he did, and I'm confident questions will be asked, and they will be tortured in the process. But rest assured, Pasnov will be implicated in the matter. He never dreamed I'd be in an alliance with the Russians. I can't knock off the Don's advisor, but the Don can.

I want him taken out before my wedding. Alena doesn't want him to give her away. This would also be suspicious and lead to questions. I prefer it if we're not involved. We won't lie for him. Besides, I'd never risk my neck for that piece of shit.

After he inferred he's suspicious of me, he's on my shit list, too. I can be a patient man at times. And I know this is a situation that calls for restraint.

After paying bills and checking in with our accountant, who stopped by, Gio drove me to dinner to meet with Sophia.

I text Alena.

Me: How was your day?

Alena: Fine.

Me: You are working late?

Alena: Yes.

Me: I'll see you after dinner.

Alena: Got it.

I wish I were fucking Alena on the drive back from the city at this very moment. My meeting tonight is for Alena. I have a solution to her work situation. I anticipated Sophia would go off; since I didn't know when the news would break, my timing was off. I would have had the situation under control if I had the details of the announcement sooner.

I'm obligated to tell Sophia in person about the office changes, and I need to do damage control. I don't want her to become a problem.

Gio escorts Sophia to me. I stand, and we kiss each other on both cheeks as is our custom.

"Matteo, you didn't have to pick such a nice place," she eyes me hungrily.

"Of course I did. I know how you love to frequent the most popular places," I reply as we sit.

I have my eye on the front door of the Oriental restaurant. Gio sits at the bar to run interference if necessary. I'm becoming increasingly nervous with each passing day that doesn't contain a bullet meant for me. Am I overthinking the threat?

"You know me so well, Matteo. It's why we're perfect for each other. I can look past your affair with Alena. She's a kid. You need a woman," she purrs as she slips her hand through my arm resting on the table. A waiter delivers two Manhattans. I lift mine and take a sip. I needed this before I arrived.

"We're not an item, Sophia. It's been this way for some time. I only have eyes for Alena. She will be my wife and the mother of my children." My voice is firm.

"Maybe this wedding is part of your scheme to obtain something. I know you'd never truly marry someone else," Sophia nuzzles into my ear before she takes a sip of alcohol. "I've been your only lover over the years. It's been off and on, but I know you always wanted me to be your queen."

Her arms slide up my suit jacket.

"Sophia, I'm engaged. This is inappropriate."

She chuckles and slides her foot up my leg. My God, she's taken off her shoes. I'm unprepared for her hand to reach my cock, and between the smell of her overly pungent perfume and the fact that I never once considered her marriage material, my cock remains flaccid.

"What's the matter? Do I need to get on my knees?"

"There will be no begging, Sophia. I am transferring you to our London office."

She pulls away, and if her eyes could kill, I wouldn't have to worry about dying from a bullet wound.

"It was implied. We've known each other for years. I gave you my virginity."

"You took mine as well, if I remember correctly," I reply calmly. Glancing around the room, I discover that some guests have been disturbed by her raised voice and are now looking in our direction.

I was never convinced she was a virgin. She knew too much at fifteen years of age. A beautiful woman and an only child, her mother often looked in the other direction at her indiscretions. Sophia is self-centered. She's used to getting what she wants as well.

She massaged my cock again, forcing me to grab her hand and place it on the table. "One more touch and you will lose a hand."

Her eyes grow wide with shock. She begins to speak, but she has nothing to say.

"I've never been so humiliated in my life," she finally spits out, dumping the cloth napkin on the floor as she stands.

I texted Alena to leave work now and have Vito bring her home. I don't want her to be a sitting duck should Sophia return to the office.

Hearts can be pawns, but love is the ultimate checkmate.

Alena is my queen. I am her king.

<h1 style="text-align:center">CHAPTER 30</h1>

ALENA

atteo arrives home earlier than expected. He blows in like a nasty head cold. He's terse with one-word answers. He doesn't look at me. I'm on pins and needles. This is the first time I've witnessed him in such a state.

What happened with Sophia? Did he eat? Did something happen? He wears a frown on his forehead, and the gruffness in his voice is intimidating.

Federico asks him if he is hungry, and he says he's lost his appetite. He asks Federico to bring him a bourbon, and then he disappears into his study, ignoring me.

Gio storms past me. I give him a wide berth.

"What happened?"

"Not today." He snags the bottle of Bourbon from Federico and follows.

The study door bangs shut, and the house is quiet again.

I turn to Federico for an explanation. He shrugs his shoulders. "It must be very bad. He might tell you when he's ready, or he might not." He shrugs and makes a plate of food.

I understand that there are situations where it's best to keep me in the dark. However, tonight, it looks like it might have been more than a dinner with Sophia that pissed him off.

"He's back from the city too soon to have eaten. He sent me a cryptic text to leave work and come home immediately."

"More guards arrived on the estate before they pulled in," he says.

"What does that mean?"

"He's expecting trouble, I presume. One never knows. The world we live in—it's more of a mental game than a physical one at times."

"Oh, I didn't know that."

"Quiet time makes one wonder, is the enemy waiting to make you think you are out of danger before striking? Or do they poke at you constantly and drive one insane? Sitting around brooding isn't good. But jumping into action without understanding the situation is worse. Time is the devil's workshop. Too much time on one's hands to sit and contemplate all that can be taken from us is cruel but good psychological warfare. What is real and what isn't? One often doesn't know the answer until it's too late to change the outcome."

"You're very wise. You are a great friend, Federico." I hug him. He's surprised by the overture.

"Matteo will not like this," he says as he gives me a quick hug before he pulls away and quickly walks to where he puts my dinner on the counter. "It's only soup and a panini. I hope you don't mind. Since Matteo went out to dinner, I assumed you were together, and you both ate."

"It's fine. He had dinner with my boss, Sophia."

"Ah. The woman who is a siren. She lures lovers to her as if they are shipwrecked sailors with no intention of committing to any of them. But she is always vindictive when they move on."

"What do you know about her and Matteo?"

"She's always wanted Matteo's money and power. Now that he's the don, she thought she'd be his wife. He's back in New York, and she was probably waiting for him and wanted to strike up an affair. How did you end up working for her?"

I sit at the counter as Federico cleans the coffee machine.

"It's strange. I think Matteo orchestrated all of it. He learned who I was after we met anonymously, and it stuck with me as odd that I was hired so quickly when I had no work experience."

"He is a man who likes control and is very good at thinking ahead."

"It will serve him well. It seems my father doesn't think ahead or about consequences," I mumble as I lift the spoon filled with soup to my lips.

Federico listens without asking questions, which relieves me. However, I'm upset that Matteo ignored me, and I do not know what happened tonight. As his wife, I suppose this is my first of what may be many bad days ahead.

I eat quietly, contemplating what Sophia might have done. She wants him. I'm sure she used their shared history to lure him back to her and probably hit on him. Did Matteo entertain the idea?

I trust him. He's the first person I would run to if I were in trouble. He is a logical thinker and savvy with his skills regarding people from all walks of life.

I don't have to know much to know that men in the mafia know the streets, the addicts, the players, and the gang members. Only a few can seamlessly move between them all and high society. Matteo fits in anywhere, and that's an attribute that will make him a good leader.

"Oh, your attire for the gala arrived. I put the outfits in your closet. If there is an issue with the fit, let me know. I have a number of well-known makeup artists, or you can do your face yourself. I wasn't sure what you'd prefer, so I booked her and a stylist."

"Thank you. I forgot all about it. It's this weekend already?"

Federico saved my ass by booking the glam squad I need to look my best at the event. All eyes will be on my husband as the new don, and now he'll be linked to the Russians. It will be quite the event. It's more a show of wealth and power. I want my husband to be proud of me. I can't have him disappointed because I'm not prepared for my new role.

"Yes, it's this weekend. You are sitting with Izzy and Dmitry. That's quite the statement. It should be fun. Do you dance?"

"I doubt I can waltz."

"Matteo is a great dancer. You are in good hands."

"Will he be in the mood for the gala after tonight?"

"He will drink tonight, and tomorrow, he will do what must be done. I'm sure your presence will put him in a better mood."

"I'm not so sure of that."

"You are too hard on yourself. He loves you. He tries to hide it, but I know."

I texted Dima before going to bed. I asked him if Sophia had left for London. He replied that she had had a man on the side.

Dima: Apparently, he doesn't date.

Me: Thank you for your service, Dima. There's no need to dig up details on him anymore. I'm good.

Dima: Very well, Alena. Good luck.

It is still dark when I hear someone bump into our bedroom door, and Matteo tumbles in. Immediately, I hop out of bed to help him. I hold his arm and steer him to the bench at the end of the bed. I take his shoes off. He stands, and I help him undress. He reeks of alcohol. I hope Gio isn't driving home tonight.

"Are you okay?"

"Fine," he mumbles as his words are slurred.

"Right," I reply as I pull the bedcovers back, and he tumbles into the bed. He doesn't speak words I understand, even though they are English. He gives up and waves a hand through the air as if it doesn't matter.

I pull the covers around him and return to bed.

When I leave for work in the morning, he is still sleeping. I'm even more perplexed when Sophia isn't in the office. She's always here before us, and we all look at each other, wondering where she is. Penny gives us an order to continue working amid the confusion.

We need to schedule the installation of floating cabinets in the bathrooms, and we're seriously behind on the tile work. I schedule the crews to install the carpet and hope they won't take over a week to finish the job.

I eat the panini Federico packed for me. It's prosciutto and cheese. I pull out a to-go container with slices of melon.

I texted Izzy to see if she was ready for the big weekend event, and after that, I called Federico to inquire about Matteo.

"He's rough. I gave him a shot glass of alcohol to help his hangover."

"Do we know anything?"

"No."

Shit. What the hell is going on? He can't keep me in the dark forever.

I haven't heard from Matteo all day, which is odd. He always knows where I am, and he never seems to be far. Today, I'm feeling the frostbite of Siberia. I don't know if he's alive or dead. He hasn't reached out to me. I won't chase him. I assume he'll come to me in his own time.

Men are like that. They like distance, especially when they are in a bad mood. I wish he trusted me enough to confide in me.

Does he love me?

I might have read too much into the fact that he always knows where I am. I can't decide if it's his need for control or his way of showing affection.

Vito drives me home after work. I'm exhausted from worrying about Matteo.

By the time we reach the house, I find Matteo dressed casually, and for him to not be in a suit is peculiar. I assume his hangover kept him home.

He greets me with a kiss on my forehead and helps me out of my coat. We sit down to a roasted chicken and vegetable dinner that smells delicious.

"How was your day?" he asks, breaking the silence.

"Sophia wasn't at work."

"Ah. Well, she won't be. I've transferred her to our London office. Who will run the project? We're behind as it is."

"I've given it some thought, and you enjoy decorating. I want to see your plans. If they meet my expectations, I want you to complete the project."

"I appreciate your vote of confidence, but I'm new. No one will listen to me. I'm too young, and it's too much responsibility."

"Are you trying to talk me out of this?" His eyes question me.

"Not exactly. I'm looking at the situation realistically, and that's my opinion."

"I thought you would tire of the commute when you moved in with me. Instead, I worry over the long days you work, and you don't complain," he replies.

"It's what normal people do, Matteo. It's what I would be doing if we hadn't met. Things snowballed between us. And the wedding is in March—I never agreed to that."

"It's important now more than ever to get married as quickly as possible. You need to be under my protection."

"What's happened?" I chew the chicken slowly. It's delicious, but I don't enjoy it as I'm still upset over yesterday's events.

"My brother, Niccoló, has a girlfriend, and she was murdered last night. She visited her father in Southern Italy. He works the docks for us. She said she would return on the evening boat. She didn't answer her phone that night. Niccoló went to check on her and found her dead. It looks like a home invasion."

His words are slow and painful.

"Home invasion? I thought that was an American thing."

"It's uncommon, especially in Sicily."

"You think this is related to your father, and that's why we have more guards."

"Yes." Matteo eats a few bites of his meal and pushes the plate away. Federico swoops in and removes it from the table.

I lay my fork down, sip cold water from my glass, and sit back in the chair.

"You think the scene was staged," I reply as the reality of the facts sink in. A young woman is dead for no apparent reason.

"Probably. But we don't know who would do such a thing. She was vibrant and full of life. She was a nurse."

"A nurse who would know poisonous substances?"

"It's not difficult to research anything today," he says as if he doesn't believe she's capable of killing someone.

"I'm sure she's a lovely woman if your brother loved her, but was there any indication something was off? She might have been threatened. She could have been scared."

"She was late to my father's funeral, and usually, she's early as she can't wait to see my brother. She was very emotional. I didn't understand it at the time. We all hated my father. He was a mean man."

"I didn't know that. How was she lately?"

" Niccoló mentioned she was working a lot and seemed to be distracted."

"He knew her better than anyone?"

"Yes, they've been in love for years. He wanted to marry her."

"How do you get a reluctant participant to do what you need?"

"I find dirt on them or bribe them." He responds as if we're best friends on a dinner date. I'm relieved he is sharing his pain with me instead of drinking another bottle of alcohol.

"How is your brother?"

"Torn up. He's paying for the funeral. I'm sure he will take a long time to get over this. I hope our wedding will cheer everyone up."

"March is fine. I understand." My words are void of emotion. It appears fate has intervened again. The tentacles of the killer have moved closer to us. This is a hit on someone outside the immediate family but a beloved member who is close to them.

Matteo stands and takes my hand in his. "Let's go watch some TV and take our minds off this. There's nothing I can do tonight. I wanted to return home for the funeral. Niccoló forbid it. It's safer for us to remain here."

"Oh, Federico told me our costumes for the gala are upstairs. He lined up my support staff to beautify me. He's a lovely man, very thoughtful."

"You are the most beautiful woman in the world. You don't need anything but clothes to wear, and that's only because I'm a jealous man." He kisses my lips, and I am relieved he's beside me, now more than ever.

CHAPTER 31

MATTEO

I'm relieved Alena understands the situation and that the wedding will happen as I planned. With the news of Chiara's death, the enemy moves closer and is tying up loose ends.

Poison is a woman's way of killing. It fits that she would have access to the house and could easily slip it into something my father's drink or food.

Alena is right. The evidence points to Chiara, but why would she kill my father? She'd been to all our family functions and knew our routines. She remained undetected after the funeral. It never dawned on me that the enemy was from within, but it is a diabolical and ingenious plan. I'll remember this. The Trojan Horse is an infallible technique that is as old as time.

My adversary is cunning. However, the fact that Dad was murdered and that we may never find the man responsible for Chiara's death will leave a festering wound in my brother's heart.

I need answers.

As we travel to my office at the warehouse, we pass the hotel where Finn was staying.

"The Irish are here," Gio states as he recognizes the G-wagons and a few faces of goons who walked in the street.

"Fuck. Did you speak to Antonio?"

"Yes. And there is nothing that implicates us. The needle was in the arm he used. The fact that they are giving this so much attention means they are looking to pin this on someone. He was a junkie and a dealer. I'm sure the Irish are not surprised he's dead."

"They want to flex their muscle and see if they can scare up a witness," I murmur.

Gio's phone rings. He speaks in Italian.

"What's happening at the hotel?"

"The Irish are at The Plazza Romano. They grabbed men who were taking out the garbage."

"Send men, and make sure they are run off with a few broken bones. They are on our turf. We need more security to walk the grounds at night. I want our warehouses patrolled as well. There is a shortage of building supplies. We have aluminum and copper that are worth a fortune. When the price is right, we'll sell them. However, the Irish might use the distraction of roughing up our men to make us divert manpower there. It would provide the diversion necessary for them to hit our warehouses."

"I'm on it," Gio says. He calls Antonio, who is in charge of security and is still speaking when we arrive at my office.

Gio clears the building before I enter. The other guard in the limo heads to the gated entrance and will check anyone wishing to enter the area.

We're in a high-alert phase.

I texted Alena. I felt better telling her what happened in Sicily, and I could see the wheels in her head spinning.

Today, she's organizing the staff and creating a design to set us apart from the other luxury hotels. The Ruse Luxe is Volkov's International hotel chain, and I intend to follow in their footsteps. I have the family money to invest, and property value never declines. I want to propose to Alexsei that we buy out a Vegas hotel. It has to be on the strip, and one will soon go into bankruptcy. Together, we could offer them a deal that they can't refuse.

I sit in my leather chair, and Niccoló calls. Tomorrow is Chiara's funeral. I wonder if the Borrellis are cursed. Mom died, Chiara wasn't even married to Niccoló, and yet, she's dead.

"How are you, brother?"

"I'm not well. However, I have something important to discuss. I'll fly to New York tomorrow. I can't wait to see you."

"I look forward to it. Let Gio know when you're arriving. We'll have someone meet you at the airport. I must attend the gala tomorrow."

"It's business, I understand," he replies.

I wonder what is so urgent, and the fact that he's not comfortable speaking of it over the phone makes it imperative that he arrives in one piece. What has he learned? Will it bring us closer to catching the person behind Chiara's death?

I can't focus on fear. Its presence is a spiral into darkness and despair. Fear consumes happiness like a fire eats oxygen. Nothing good is left in its wake because it leads to depression and, at its worst— death.

I feared my father at first. Until I discovered that he was a weak man who got off on watching others' reactions to his violence and machinations to feed his sickness. Father pushed buttons and was a good psychopath. He constantly needed validation that he was the smartest one in the room.

I learned that the person who knew the most was the one who said the least. I've attended many meetings among high-ranking members of our syndicate. I've watched the men who remained silent, thinking they needed to speak.

I later discovered that they were absorbing information like sea sponges in a bathtub. They were learning how to read the others in the room. They knew the character of the men who surrounded them and the men under them. They understood what motivated people, making them respected leaders because the ranks had no bickering.

For some, it was money. For others— power, and some, recognition of a job well done. When men lose faith in their leaders, discontent festers.

I'm curious if the Irish are having internal issues. Is this why there is a sudden interest in Finn? Is it a diversion? And if it is, what is the underlying issue? I conclude it's a problem for another day.

Alena calls in response to my text. Her enthusiastic voice pulls me out of my melancholy mood. I informed her my brother would be arriving soon and that I didn't want her working past five. She agrees, and I'm relieved she's on board with safety concerns.

I'm looking forward to meeting Dmitry and Izzy Volkov. I've heard so much about them that I'm anxious to spend the evening with them. We'll be the talk of the gala as two powerful families sitting at the same table. It's the first time in history that the two powerhouses have been in the same building without an attempted hit.

Perhaps I should wear Kevlar under my costume.

* * *

Alena is excited when she joins me for dinner. She brought her portfolio to the table, enthusiastically pulled printouts out of it, and showed me her team's idea for the rooms. She even showed me the hallways lighted with sconces.

"It's elegant. I love the red and gold colors. Very regal. I want the indoor pool to look better as well. The plastic chairs are what I'd find in an inferior hotel chain. I want wicker loungers. I know the towels are a service and can only be white, but the quality needs to improve."

"Sure, that's easy to arrange. I'll take a look at it on Monday."

"Very well."

We retire to the family room, and I start a fire. Federico serves us cannoli and Frangelico. Alena feeds me a cannoli, and I find that even with the current events that have dropped on my doorstep, they haven't dampened my desire for her.

I use my finger to paste cannoli filling on her lips before licking it off.

I apply more, and she goes to move her tongue to clean it off, but my lips are on hers before she can accomplish her mission. She returns my kiss, her arms slide around my neck, and my world is complete.

I sip the Frangelico and dribble it into her mouth when I kiss her. She sinks into the couch's cushions, falling on her back and pulling me to her.

I run my hand through her hair, my cock presses against her thigh.

"If you're not naked in my bed in the next minute, I'm fucking you here," I threaten.

She squeals and bolts out of the room. I follow behind her and enjoy the curvy globes of her buttocks swaying as she runs. She reaches the stairs and takes the steps two at a time. My heart pounds in my chest as I jog to catch up. She'll be the death of me, and I couldn't be a happier man.

CHAPTER 32

ALENA

The wedding planner and two staffers arrive by mid-morning. Her name is Francis, and she's dressed in a stylish business suit. Federico delivered us scones, tea, and coffee in the cozy room where Matteo and I made love in front of the fireplace. The French doors let in the morning light, and Federico stirred the fire that had burned low.

Francis pulls out the floor plans of Matteo's house, and I'm stunned. It's much larger than I expected. It's on an island on the East Coast called Manalapan. The backyard is white sand that runs into the Atlantic Ocean.

"I suggest canopies to shade guests. We'll use white fold-up chairs, and the patio will be covered with a wooden dance floor. The DJ will sit on a platform and announce the wedding party and, of course, you and your husband. Mr. Borrelli informed me that it will be roughly three hundred people."

"That many? Well, he has a large family. We'll need hotel rooms for guests," I suggest.

"We're making phone calls. It will be the beginning of Spring Break, but the island isn't the place for that. The hotels are inland. We'll hire a shuttle to bring guests over to the house. What is your color preference for the wedding party?"

"As for colors, I guess anything would go with the white sand. What are the popular colors this year?"

"Wine shades go well outside." She opens a sampler book that contains wedding invitations.

"Oh, I like the marsala. It's deeper than burgundy. That would look nice in flowers on the invitation and cake. White china plates, white invitations with flowers at the top, and the marsala envelopes would be pretty." It all unfolds before my eyes.

I can see the event. I want it to be elegant but simple. "Oh, and at the end of the rows of chairs, I'd like white baby's breath with sage leaves. Can we have that draped over the tables on the patio and in the house where we'll be dining?"

"Would you like to eat outside? We can arrange that. We have banquet tables that can be decorated."

"What about rain?"

"We can provide tents."

I think about the expensive wedding dress and sand in my shoes. "How will I walk on the sand?"

"Many brides use ballet slippers or flip flops then change into heels for the reception. Do you have a second dress?"

"No, I'm fine with one. The beads and sequins in it are hand-sewn. I can't imagine wearing anything else."

"Very well." Her staffers are taking notes and speaking quietly to each other.

"Mr. Borrelli gave us a list of invitees." She hands me a list of names. "Please go over it this weekend. We'll send the invitations out on Monday. Given the short notice, we have to get them out immediately."

"I understand. My husband didn't want to wait." I smile as if he's impetuous, but nothing could be further from the truth.

Francis proceeds with the tickets, the sign-in table, and a list of DJs. I do not know who the best is, and I'm mentally exhausted now. I've not been conditioned to make one hundred decisions in two hours. When Francis and her staffers leave, Federico announces that lunch is served.

Matteo joined me, and we reviewed the list of invitees.

"I don't know. Izzy is all I have as far as family. I'd love to include Penny from work. I don't want a huge wedding party."

"How about my sister, Bianca, being a bridesmaid? She'll represent my side of the family. She'll love a shopping spree for new shoes and a dress."

"Okay. A maid of honor and two bridesmaids. What is your sister like?"

"She's sweet, like you. You'll love her."

I give him a side-eye. "I hope it won't involve a bottle per person."

"It will, but I'll behave. Gio will make sure we're safe. We'll take a limo around the city. What would you like for your party?"

"I'm boring. A day at the spa would be nice."

"That's tame." His face relaxes considerably. He's not been himself since we learned of Chiara's death. "It makes me happy you won't be in clubs with men looking at what's mine."

"It's about you, is it?" I tease, giving him a wink. He smiles at me. It makes me happy. He hasn't smiled in days.

After lunch, I nap, as it will be a long evening, and Matteo disappears into his study.

At four o'clock, the crew shows up. I'm in a robe, and they paint my toenails and fingernails to look wicked. It's a dark red that looks black but will accompany my dress and the gothic theme.

They wash and style my hair, braiding it before piling it on my head. After two hours of tugging, pulling, and gripping my chair, I look at myself in the mirror they hold before me and see the incredible updo. I look like a movie star.

I'm in awe of what these men and women can accomplish. They are worth every penny and give "glam squad" a new meaning.

Next, they help me with the underwear for the dress. My hands run down the smooth fabric, which is the softest material I've ever felt. I step into a new shoe brand and find it more comfortable than the name brands I've been wearing. I assume the shoes were made in Italy. The black leather molds to my feet, and I walk without discomfort. The gown flounces as I walk, and I can see the fabric's sheen under the bedroom lights.

The assistant pulls out a book and gives me a choice of looks for the evening. I pick a design with gold glitter to complement the blackness of my dress. I love gold and black together.

Matteo has his tux in another room and is dressing to give me the space needed to prepare, and I am relieved he didn't witness all that I had to go through to look regal. He might think he's not getting the prettiest fiancée if it weren't for the help of these experts.

My face takes a half hour, and the finishing touch is applying glitter to one side of my face and gently carrying a few for continuity to the other side of my face. My eyebrows are more dramatic to match the dark blue and black eyeshadow that tapers upward with an off-white color that makes my eyes look more prominent. The numerous shades of blue provide continuity and illuminate the blue in my eyes.

I stare into the mirror and don't recognize myself. I'm a woman who is much prettier than I ever imagined. My skin is flawless, and the mask around my eyes tapers off to the side like a natural mask tied behind my head.

I wish I could create illusions with color, but I'm limited to furniture and accessories. Izzy, on the other hand, knows clothing and fashion. She worked on Broadway and loves to design clothing. I wonder if she'll recognize me. We're meeting just inside the doors at eight.

My crew leaves, and Matteo breezes in. He stops walking when his eyes take me in. I twirl on my heels. The gown moves, creating a whoosh sound as I walk.

"You're incredible. You are the most beautiful woman in the world." He walks to me, takes my hand, and kisses it like we're in a Shakespeare play or a Medici garden party.

"You look incredible. I love the tux. I have to say your designer is incredible. The outfits are outrageous."

"Only the best for you, Alena."

I blush under this intense gaze. He undresses me with his eyes, and if he were to take me now, I'd be willing, but it would ruin my makeup.

"I guess we should be going?"

"If it's not, we're leaving anyway. Otherwise, I'd be tempted to cart your firm ass to the bed and tie you up for hours," his voice deep with desire.

"We'll make up for it later," I reply as I take his arm, and Federico helps me into my coat before opening the front door. Gio opens the limo door for me and goes to the passenger side. I assume he'll escort us into the affair.

The ride in the darkness is appropriate for a masquerade ball. The snow is picking up, and ominous shadows dance on the streets of Long Island as we make our way into the city.

I texted Izzy, telling her I had to update her on my wedding and inquire if they were on time.

My phone beeps.

"Izzy and Dmitry are on time and will meet us inside the doors on the right side of the museum."

"Great. I'm looking forward to meeting them."

"Did you ever think what would happen had Alexsei been offended by our engagement?"

"I try not to dwell on it. How did you like the wedding planner?"

"Francis is nice. I have no clue what the DJ will sound like. I chose to eat inside instead of on the beach. I can't imagine having sand in every crevice of my body should the wind blow in the afternoon. We'd be eating sand, which would ruin the surf and turf dinner."

Matteo chuckles as he pulls my hand into his.

"You're so thoughtful. See, I could never plan an event. I never thought about that."

"I've had to think of many things since I met you. My brain was in meltdown mode after work. But today, making one hundred decisions with so many options exhausted me."

"I'm glad you slept. You are ready for a long night."

"Yes. I hope it all goes well. I've never been to an affair like this. Izzy went to the MET, so she popped her cherry."

Matteo burst out with a hearty laugh.

"Really?" He recovers from his outburst and says, "The Volkovs do get around. I'm happy we have an alliance with them. I'm considering asking Dmitry to look at the tech company I picked up last year."

"He's the one to ask."

We are in line for drop-off at the event, and limos stretch as far as I can see ahead and behind us.

"I think the timing will be perfect when we reach the door."

"You're perfect," he says as he kisses my lips.

It took twenty minutes to reach the door. Matteo helped me out of the limo. Gio escorted us as the driver circled to pick him up later.

We walk through a metal detector, drop our coats in the coat room, and put his top hat back on his head. I turn and see Izzy. I wave to her as we walk through the crowd.

"You look incredible," I say as I hug her. Her belly is round and radiant in a yellow dress with a sweetheart neckline. The paisley red print overlays the dark material underneath. She holds a black and gold mask for her eyes by the attached gold stick.

"Forget about me. Let me see that canary diamond," Izzy demands as she takes my hand and eyeballs my ring.

"My God, that's huge! I love it."

"Thank you," I said demurely. "It's heavy, too," I joked. Then I turned to her husband. "Dmitry," I hugged him. "This is my fiancé, Matteo."

The men shake hands, and for a minute, I'm afraid Dmitry will be in enforcer mode. He's quiet. He's a reserved man.

I hope this won't be a war of two alphas all night. They are like two angry dogs; both are out for blood.

"Izzy, will you be my maid of honor? I have Penny from work and

Matteo's sister as bridesmaids. I hope you can still fly. We're getting married at Matteo's place on a Florida beach."

"Of course, I will be there. I need a dress big enough," she jokes as she glances at her silent husband. "Dmitry, their wedding is next month."

"Great. I love Florida." His cheek moves slightly. "We should head inside. I hear cocktails are flowing."

"What's your poison?" Matteo asks.

"Vodka, what else?"

Matteo chuckles at the obvious answer for a Russian. We walk inside and make our way to the bar.

"With the cost of tickets, we could have all flown to Russia for vodka," Dmitry murmurs, "and it would be better than this shit. But we do what we must, da?"

"Da," I hear Matteo. I wonder if he can speak Russian.

I turn my attention to Izzy and hold her arm as we walk through the crowd. It's a carnival atmosphere with gold and black helium balloons covering the ceiling.

A band is playing piano and violins. It's dark music, dramatic at times, and I envision it setting the tone for a sinister scene in a movie.

"Look at the ice sculptures," Izzy says as she glances at a banquet table with appetizers. I turn and see the sculpture of a Renaissance couple; he's wearing a striped shirt and tux, and the woman has a mask around her eyes. There is another sculpture of a jester.

"No expense was spared," I murmur.

Dmitry hands Izzy a seltzer, and Matteo hands me a dirty martini. Now that the men have a drink in hand, we decide to circle the room. The gowns are incredible, and the air is filled with the aroma of roast beef and perfume.

I feel naked without Vito and worry that no one is armed, and I assume everyone will be on their best behavior.

I overhear Dmitry and Matteo talking about computers. I'm relieved that the two have one common ground, as I'm sure they are both unprepared to navigate the new alliance forced upon them.

CHAPTER 33

I believe the councilman will eventually run for a congressional seat when he's bored with the city. He's on his second four-year term and will have to wait four years before he can run again.

He spared no expense on this event. The money raised could easily feed a third-world country for a year. Addler must have his eyes on larger budgets. He runs the district over Staten Island Shores and is working on converting an old landfill into a park.

It's a noble cause, but I'm not convinced it's feasible. I'm sure Santino Moretti is drooling over it. Moretti is in waste management. The public doesn't realize what a money-maker old landfills have become. Creating new ones is too expensive for cities as land is expensive. Converting an old landfill is cheaper and requires the help of mafia-held companies with the infrastructure to make it a viable alternative.

Everything in a landfill is recycled. Old landfills are converted to new ones that collect methane on every level, creating clean energy.

Items are recycled and composted. The various sources of energy they provide are then sold back to utility companies, which charge a premium for electricity as no distinction between clean energy sources and fossil fuels is made.

I don't see how the city can't close down a landfill without opening another. This is why I've always invested in land. Land lasts forever, like the sky. I'm not surprised multibillionaires are investing in space. It's the newest frontier.

Dmitry and I discussed my tech company, and I'm willing to share in its profit with his technological help. He'll speed up the process of the new app.

I take Alena by the hand and excuse us from our friends. I need a word with Addler. I find him shaking hands with strangers. Alena is as polite as can be when she interjects into the conversation about his work, which involves cutting red tape for state benefits to go to low-income families.

"Why thank you, Ms.?"

"Alena Pasnov, this is my fiancé, Matteo Borrelli. He's interested in helping more with your reelection. Do you have a minute?" She puts her hand through his arm and steers him away from prying eyes. It's a crowded event. He's expected to give a few minutes to his supporters.

"Ms. Pasnov, sure, I'd be happy to," he replies. Meanwhile, she steers him in my direction. I take him aside from the woman wanting to speak with him about a needle exchange program for the city and quickly state how I would like his support for my building when it comes up for a vote at the next meeting.

"I'm not into those issues. We need more public housing than hotels." His frankness is appreciated, but he's preaching to the wrong man. I'd love to punch him for being a pompous ass, but I need him.

I whisper into his ear, as the message is for him and no one else. "I have intel that complaints on your apartment building are never looked into. I'd hate for a fire to rage through your buildings. It would result in dozens of injured people trapped and dying from smoke and fire due to faulty fire alarms. The investigation would find you negligent. Your career would go up in smoke. If you vote on my hotel variance, I can ensure that doesn't happen."

The councilman's jaw drops. He quickly recovers with a smile on his face.

"I'll make sure I'm there to support you," he says through clenched teeth.

"Thank you. Nice affair, by the way." I smile and gather Alena to me as we return to our table.

"How did it go?" Alena asks.

"As well as I could hope for. It looks like we're in. He was shocked, but I can't be the only one who knows he's making money off low-income renters. That's why he's making it easier for them to gain the financial assistance they need. He's collecting a nice paycheck off it every month. You were fantastic. Thank you for helping."

"Don't mention it. It was kinda fun."

The music stops, we're on our third drink, and the appetizers have disappeared. The event emcee announces it's time for dinner, and we are to make our way to our table.

As I move through the crowded room, Congressman Nichols comes into view. I have a quick second to shake his hand and say my name before the crowd separates us.

Our table seats ten, and Congressman Savoy is seated with us. He's a benign player to date, but who knows for sure? If he's at the Sidovo-Volkov table, he has a connection to the Russians.

I understand Dmitry is taking over for Izzy's father, and I wonder when this change will occur. So far, I'm finding more questions than answers tonight, and I was hoping for the opposite.

I looked at the table of honored guests tonight, and Vincent Moretti's name appears on the list. It can't be a coincidence. I texted Gio to do a quick search on the Moretti children. Perhaps the old man had a meltdown waving his gun in public. Given the recent turn of events, I'm sure the councilman has no wish to be associated with him.

Addler's wife is nice-looking and works for a top law firm in the city. I don't recognize the other names announced as they all reach the podium, and everyone praises the councilman and all the worthy causes. I know they will benefit from his leftover campaign funds after he wins his reelection.

On top of our dinner plates is an embossed card listing the evening's ceremonial events—the introduction of the speakers, dinner, followed by dancing.

Izzy and Alena are talking, and I don't have the heart to interrupt her. I admire my future wife as she sits with her shoulders poised perfectly, and I obsess over her pert breasts, and I long to have her alone. I don't like large events. I hate public venues even more. They aren't safe. I feel naked without my gun.

The first course is served, and dinner music is played. I keep my eye on Addler and Moretti. It's easier to figure out the connections between people when it's an event as even the mafia mingles with the elite, and it's not subject to scrutiny as it's in an open venue that anyone can attend—if they have the funds.

Dmitry leans into my shoulder. "In the back of the room is Cillian O'Donnell. It's a long way for him to come for a fundraiser, don't you think?"

"I don't think I know. He's looking for someone to pin for the murder of his youngest son. There's a larger play going on. I haven't figured out what it is. Have you heard anything?"

"No. Only that he's set up a reward for information in his son's case. Ironic. Never gave a damn about the kid, he grew up a junkie, and now he's obsessed with the notion it was a hit."

"I find it sad."

Alena finally gives me her attention. Discussing the food took all of a minute. Then, she decides we will have a contest by rating the costumes that parade past us. I can't turn down a contest, but I have no clue how we'll decide who wins. I ask the server passing by for more drinks.

Across the room, I see a familiar woman standing a few tables away. She's tall with jet-black hair, green eyes, and a body that men will lose their hearts over.

I excuse myself and make my way to her.

"Fancy seeing you here. You didn't tell me you were in the States," I say.

"It's early spring break. A handsome billionaire picked me up on the slopes in France. I've been curious about New York, so I had to see what all the fuss was about," she says as she slips her hand through my arm as I escort her to the bar.

"How did you get in?" I ask as she orders a drink from the bartender.

"New acquaintances. It appears we're in an alliance with the Russians. That's scary," she replies.

"You have no idea. I don't know if I need to sleep with one eye open, considering I'm marrying into them, or if I need to keep a gun on me even in the bathroom."

She smiles. "I'm fascinated by the woman who changed your mind on marriage. I'm looking forward to having a sister-in-law."

"She's a handful, like you. Now run along to your billionaire and keep your ears open."

"Always," she says, kissing me on the cheek.

I veer off to return to our table, and Alena gives me the universal look that tells me I'm in the doghouse.

"Who was that?"

"Someone I know. How is the beef?" Our dinner has been served, and I have skillfully deflected more questions.

"Excellent. You would know if you were here when it was hot. How do you know the woman who looks like a model?"

"You wouldn't believe me if I told you," I say, acting coy to tease her. Honestly, I'm surprised my sister is here. She's studying special arts in Switzerland and is working her way into the circles where we need to make friends—with billionaires. As far as I'm concerned there are only a few who came by their wealth legitimately. Legitimate businesses have shady ways to bilk money out of unsuspecting consumers and business partners. We both have one thing in common—we are self-serving.

Alena turns enough to give me the cold shoulder after the visit with my sister, but I'd rather Bianca remains anonymous as she might be working an angle. At the least, she's making contacts.

My little Angel is jealous. I can't dampen the smirk on my face. She cares for me. Perhaps she loves me. I find it amusing, but I know I'll have to come clean before I'm allowed to fuck her again.

I notice men passing by, and their eyes go to my wife. I dive into my food like a starving man to avoid bashing in faces.

Alena pulls her phone out of her purse. She sends a text and leans into me. "Mom says Dad hasn't returned from a meeting tonight. She's worried."

"He might turn up. It could be traffic. Who knows?"

"I played it off. What do you think?"

I glance at Dmitry to my right. He has an excellent alibi if a top figure in the Russian bratva goes missing tonight.

"Jury is out on this one. We both know Alexsei will not let a traitor have a second chance. Besides, this event is the perfect alibi for all concerned."

"I agree. I feel bad if that's the case, but he created the situation."

"That he did," I reply. Things are heating up across the city. The Irish are intent on pinning Finn's overdose on someone. The Russians have a traitor at the top; I'm getting married, and then there is the death of Chiara.

I can't imagine she'd hurt anyone in the family. We loved her, and she was one of us. She was sweet and caring, and I welcomed her into the family because she loved my brother and made him happy. Now, I'm second-guessing her integrity. What am I missing?

Dinner plates are cleared, and the music turns to an upbeat song to encourage dancing. The emcee encourages the guests to dance, and the music is lively. I'm sure he wants to turn this into a festive party, so we all leave wearing a smile and nursing sore feet.

Great. However, it's time I show the men who have spent the evening eye-fucking my future wife who she belongs to.

I stand and pull her into my chest. She wants to resist me, but I overpower her without causing a scene and tell her she's to dance with me. If she doesn't, there will be a punishment.

"You wouldn't," she says, her voice enraged.

"Really? How well do you know me?" I insist.

"As well as you know me."

"Then I say we call a truce until later. Let's give all the men eye-fucking you a picture of a happily engaged couple. It's time they learn to keep their eyes on their own wives."

"And what of you?" she asks defiantly.

"I only have eyes for you," I reply honestly.

"The woman you spoke to at the bar was beautiful."

"Do you believe I would be interested in anyone else?" I ask with lust in my eyes. She's in my arms. I move around the dance floor as she tries to keep up.

"We have a deal, Mr. Grey." She didn't have to remind me to be faithful to her. I was committed the minute I saw her.

"We do, and I'll never break it. You are my Angel," I say as I kiss her crimson-red painted lips. I pull her closer to my chest. She's the sole focus of my attention. "Follow my lead."

"I'm trying," she replies as she steps on my foot. She giggles and buries her head in my chest. A chuckle bubbles in my chest, and she tosses her head back to see the smile on my face. We laugh over her awkwardness on the dance floor.

"I think you had too much champagne with dinner."

"It was the martinis. Remind me to stay away from them."

"Can you dance?"

"Nope," she says, overly enunciating the 'p.'

"So, who is she?" Alena asks.

"My sister, but don't announce it. You'll meet her next week."

"Bianca? Here? How did she attend?"

"Those are questions for another day. Are we good, my love?"

"We are."

"Great, because I didn't want you to be pissed all night."

"I wasn't jealous," she protests.

I know that her words are a cover, judging by the daggers she shot at me as I interacted with my sister. That was the real story. By the time we made our way around the large dance floor for two songs, my Principessa was ready to go home.

We leave before the event officially ends. Dmitry and Izzy left before us. Gio greets us at the door and scans the road as we walk down many steps into the cold night.

I hold Alena close to me to fend off winter's chilly wind when I hear a familiar boom and instinctively throw my body over Alena to protect her.

CHAPTER 34

ALENA

The loud noise sounded like a gun went off, and my heart skipped a beat. What was it? I can't move as Matteo and Gio tower over me protecting me with their bodies. I'm stunned. I had no time to react.

Gio straightens and says, "We're clear." Matteo then stands but checks and runs his hands over me as if I'm an apparition.

"What happened?" I ask.

"Backfire of a car," Gio explains.

"God, damn it. That scared the life right out of me." I grab my coat closer to me—as if it were a shield. The men rush me down the steps and to the waiting car. I guess they don't want to tempt fate. It's late. We're in the city. We only have Gio. It feels like we are being warned that we are never safe. I'm sure it was a coincidence.

Matteo fawns over me the entire ride home. He's visibly shaken. His brother's girlfriend was murdered a day ago. Now, my father might be missing, and the backfire of a car has us all on edge. Is this my future? Is the car's backfire a bad omen?

I've had too much to drink. I can't wait to get home. I'd be embarrassed if I was sick in the limo. I do not want Matteo to see me puking. It will ruin his perfect vision of me.

When we arrive home, I step into his arms, seeing that I am unsteady. He carries me into our home and up the stairs.

"You don't have to do this," I protest.

"Yes, I do. I'll have to limit your martinis. And mixing liquor is never a good idea."

"But the stuff you have from Italy is much better."

"It is," he replies. We reach our bedroom, and he lowers me to the bed. He takes off my shoes. I hear them hit the floor, and with how much they must have cost, I'm mortified they are in a heap and not placed on a shelf.

He senses my concern.

"The maid will clean the room in the morning."

"I don't feel good," I say, putting a hand to my head.

"Sit here. I'll be back."

Matteo returns with a washcloth. "Lean back," he says. I comply. My head hits the pillow before he returns and places a cold compress to my forehead. "Better?"

"Much, thank you."

"If you feel sick, let me know."

"I will," I whisper as I close my eyes, and the darkness swirls. Is the room moving?

I hear Matteo moving about the room, probably undressing. He returns to me, flips the washcloth, and helps me out of the dress.

I can only imagine the makeup smeared over my face. I must look like a freak show. I close my eyes and will myself to sleep off the impending hangover.

The sound of the wind batting the side of the house wakes me in the middle of the night. Matteo pulls me closer to him. I feel his hard cock on my buttocks. His hand naturally cups my breasts, and I'm filled with desire. The room is dark, and in under a minute, Matteo has caressed my body, making me slick for him. He pulls me on top of him.

I sit on his pelvis and take my time lowering myself onto his hard shaft. I lean forward and give myself room to pull to the top of his head, giving him a long stroke before I slide down his hard cock. My hands clench his muscular shoulders, and as desire fills me, my nails dig into his taut back. I find myself climbing the wave of euphoria that consumes me.

"Fuck me, Angel. Fuck me," his husky voice penetrates the darkness.

I move faster and faster as his fingers tweak my nipples.

"That's a good girl," he coaxes.

I come as he pulls my nipples until they hurt. My oblivion washes over me, and I hear my voice screaming.

I squirt on his head. I've soaked him. My wetness is the puddle between us.

"I can't wait to get you pregnant," he murmurs.

I nestle into the crux of his arm and lay my head on his chest, where I fall asleep again.

When I awake in the morning, Matteo is by my side and hands me a cold glass of water and two aspirin.

"How are you?"

"Better than I expected, but this will help." I swallow the tiny pills and hope my headache will go away. "No more martinis. My goodness. What was I thinking?"

"I think that's the point. You didn't want to think. It was a nice party. Dmitry and I have some things in common, and you and Izzy were like twins."

"I know," I smile as I get out of bed. "We tend to get caught up in ourselves. How long have you been up?"

"Hours. My brother used my jet here, and he arrived early."

"Really? I can't wait to meet him. How is he?"

Jet? Does he own a jet?

I gasp. When I turn, he's gone.

When I enter the bathroom, my face looks like the glitter fairy puked on it. How do I remove this stuff? I pick up makeup remover with oil and hope it works. I rub the clear substance over my face, and fifteen minutes later, I assume I'll have to let some of the sparkles wear off. Thankfully, I don't have to clean the floor. I'm sure glitter is all over the bedsheets and bathroom floor.

I hear men's voices as I go to the dining room, and Federico takes my breakfast order.

A handsome, tall man with dark hair approaches. I immediately recognize the family resemblance. Their stature is the same, and they share the same skin tone.

"I'm Niccoló. Welcome to the family," he says, taking my hand in his. His hands are larger and rougher than I expected.

"Thank you. I'm so sorry for your loss," I murmur.

"Thank you." He sits to Matteo's left. "I hear you were at quite an event last night."

"It was. How was your flight?"

"A jet to myself? I slept from exhaustion."

I know he's referring to his sleepless nights rather than the time change. Matteo mentioned he is having a difficult time. It had to be horrible to stumble into a bloody crime scene. I didn't want the details.

I eat, and we talk. Afterward, the men invited me to study with them. I send Matteo a questioning glance, and he nods.

I make myself comfortable on the couch as Matteo sits in his leather chair and Niccoló paces.

"I have a letter from Chiara. Her sister was able to slip it to me at the funeral in a room where no one would see us. She said Chiara told her to give it to me should anything happen to her. She promised she would. She had no idea what was in the sealed envelope."

He pauses, and his face is about to erupt in tears from the sound of his voice. "It's Chiara's confession. She killed our father. She had an affair last year. The man meant nothing to her, and she ended it. She was afraid to tell me. She loved me and was afraid of losing me. She said it was a stupid mistake. All she knew was that a Sicilian man with a Cosa Nostra tattoo approached her after work one night. He gave her the poison and told her he would be watching her and that they would kill her sister if she didn't do as she was told."

"That's barbaric," I exclaim and look at Matteo. He's not surprised, and I wonder if he's done something similar.

"It happens. Sicily is a different world," Matteo interjects.

"Chiara knew she was being watched. She was stressed and couldn't tell anyone. She sent the letter with directions to her sister. She was afraid her sister would be killed if she met with her. She felt as if she was being followed. This explains why she suddenly worked more and saw less of me. I knew something was off. I should have known someone would use her to get to us. Why is it the women in our life pay for our sins?" Niccoló's voice cracks. He sinks to the floor in grief.

"So, they knew of her affair and used her as a weapon against the family. She had our trust. It was easy for her to slip Dad something. Don't blame yourself. Niccoló. She was in a situation where she was going to die either way. She wanted to live, so she did what they wanted. She had no way of knowing that she was a loose end and that they would kill her whether she did it or not. She can identify the man who approached her, and it would lead to someone else," Matteo says. He walks to his brother and pulls him into his embrace. "You can't blame yourself. You have to find the will to live."

"Who did this?" I ask, feeling helpless as I sit on the sidelines.

"The Cosa Nostra could be working on anyone's behalf," Niccoló says as he finally hugs his brother and sits beside me. He buries his face in his hands. I move closer and put my arm around him to comfort him.

"I'm so sorry. Try to remember when you were both at your happiest time together. You can't let them destroy you." I try to encourage him to live and hope it will get easier as time passes, but I wonder if that's possible. He was dedicated to her and remains faithful to her memory in the wake of her death.

"I'll never love again. I loved her with all my heart. These men are cruel. Life is cruel, and love is not worth the pain it causes. You shouldn't marry Matteo. Alena is in danger. The Borrelli men are cursed."

"I know of curses and have repeatedly questioned it, but it doesn't have to end badly."

"I can tell you love Alena and that she loves you. They will use her to get to you."

"Unless I get to them first." Matteo stands and paces. "We might be overthinking this. What if it is related to the Cosa Nostra? They have no way of knowing we know they approached Chiara. Perhaps there was bad blood between Dad and Santino Moretti here in New York. Dad's advisor knew something, as Gio and I found him dead in his apartment. While we were there, we heard the paramedics and cops were approaching."

"You were being followed?" Niccoló asks.

"Yes, and we assume we are still being watched. Someone doesn't want us to know what happened between two families that have never been friends. But what set this in motion?" Matteo stares out the French doors and watches the snow flurries.

My eyes follow where he's looking. The sky is gray. Dark clouds are moving in. I get lost in their darkness that never ends.

My phone dings. I jump.

Kirill texts. I read it and relay the news. "It's my friend Kirill. He worked under my father, but he's been reassigned. He's under a capo now."

"This means your father isn't going to be found," Matteo states matter-of-factly.

"What do you mean? Someone is missing?" Niccoló asks but is trying to catch up with what's happening.

"My father works as an advisor to the don, and he's been making enemies," I state. "The story is longer than that, but your brother and I knew it was coming."

Niccoló turns to face me. "I'm sorry. Were you close?"

"No. However, I should call my mother," I state. I stand and look at Matteo. "Do you need me?"

"I got this," he replies. He touches my hand briefly as I walk past him. I feel electricity from his touch. His strength reassures me that we can overcome what lies ahead together.

I phone my mother, who rants hysterically. I can't understand a word she says. I remind myself to be patient. I saw this coming—she didn't. She's in shock.

"Who would hurt your father?"

"There are plenty of people, Mom. Dad was doing inappropriate things. He might have used Bratva's funds for his agenda."

"I don't know what you are talking about. We have bills to pay. We still owe on the house," she sobs.

"Mom, be calm. Don't do anything."

"I need to call the police," she says.

"Sure, but don't give them any information. He just didn't come home after work. Do you understand?"

"Yes, of course. I'm not stupid."

"Okay, keep me posted."

I get a call from the wedding planner and give her the updated list of invitees, and Federico pops into the living room, stating that it's time for lunch.

Matteo joins me.

"Where's Niccoló?"

"He ran into the city. He's going to meet with our trainer."

"What trainer?"

"We own some gyms." He sits and begins to eat.

"What kind of gyms?"

"The usual," he says, but he continues when I raise my eyebrow for more information. "Fine. We also do underground boxing, and Niccoló used to be very good. I didn't want him to go, but he said he'd find somewhere to box, so I gave him our guy. This way, I can keep an eye on him."

"This is about Chiara, isn't it?"

"He blames himself. What man wouldn't? It's his way of coping. It's better than beating up strangers."

"True. But still, he's so handsome. I'd hate to see that change."

"It's the way it is. He's a man, and he has a talent for it."

I want to ask what he does for the family, but I'm not sure I want to know.

CHAPTER 35

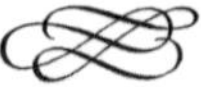

MATTEO

The variance went through as expected. Gio and I are sitting in my office at the warehouse. I pull a bottle of Bourbon out of my drawer. Gio pulls two cigars from his breast pocket.

Niccoló breezes in wearing jeans, a turtleneck, and a winter jacket. He loves military-style boots that lace up to his ankles. He's been a soldier and a boxer. I set a rock glass for him.

"I'm in training."

"When has that stopped you?"

"I'm serious—I'm following the rules, and sugar is bad. I never should have stopped working out. This is tough. Fuck, I hurt. I know I'll hurt more tomorrow." He sits and rubs his calves.

"I don't care to do more than my normal routine. I usually work out at home."

"It's called age," Gio says, lighting my cigar, then his own. We both take a puff.

"What about you, old man?" Niccoló says to Gio.

"I'm a minimalist."

"I'm talking about the gym, not your choice of furniture," Niccoló banters.

"I'm good. I don't care to have the shit beaten out of me unless the job calls for it." He takes another puff on his cigar.

"Just don't overdo it, kid," I say. I love my brother, and I would prefer him not to pursue this dangerous sport, but it's in his blood. Telling him no is like pissing in the wind. He's doing this because he has a death wish. He needs to recover from his grief, but instead, he's behaving as if he has nothing left to lose.

I'm sure I'd feel the same if something happened to Alena.

We smoke and drink, and Niccoló becomes less talkative. I should be relieved he's at the gym channeling his anger.

The week passed quickly. Alena is working. The wedding invites were sent, and everything seems to be running smoothly— although Niccoló's presence is a rarity. Judging from his perfectly made bed, he sleeps many nights at the gym. I gave him the top floor of the house, so he won't hear Alena and me fucking every night. Sometimes, I'm so happy that I feel like I'm rubbing my happiness in his face when I hold Alena's hand, and he walks into the room.

This weekend began with Alena's bachelorette party. Bianca arrived at the house this morning. The two hit it off as anticipated. Vito and another guard will take them to pick up Penny and Izzy for a day at the spa.

I have a minute alone with Alena before she leaves. "I love you. I want you to know I loved you from the minute I laid eyes on you. You're on my mind all the time."

"I don't know, Gio. Should they be out?" I watch as the limo leaves the estate.

"It was a backfire last weekend. For all we know, there are no threats. Your father's debt might have been paid in full with his death."

"That's too easy. Old business tends to turn up when it's not expected. We need answers. Did the syndicate act locally, or did Moretti order it?"

"Moretti is the don. I would assume it would come from the top.

However— some men don't follow the rules. Whether he knew or not doesn't matter. It won't bring Chiara back. There was a motive behind Chiara's murder because, without her, we can't prove who was behind this. Without a witness, there is no crime." I'm not too fond of Gio's answer, but he tells it the way he sees it, and I know we've both arrived at the same conclusion.

"She was killed to keep the Cosa Nostra out of this," I mutter, "and that would mean something is going on. They might be making a move to take us over." I swirl my mid-morning coffee in the cup. It's incredible coffee made from Hawaiian Kona beans, but it turns bitter in my mouth. War is never good. It takes lives and brings attention to us, and then we'll have the Italian government and the United States working together to hit our assets and round up men on the wanted list.

Fuck.

I hate the fact that this is coming to a head. The timing is unacceptable. "I hate the fact that someone is watching us. Do you have men on Moretti and his son? The old man is bonkers. He can't be trusted. We've never trusted the Cosa Nostra."

"That's true, and the old man is mean from what I hear," Niccoló walks into the living room. I didn't know he was home.

"What do you know?" I ask, turning to him as he walks in with a gym bag slung over his shoulder. He's been using my older Mercedes as I refuse to take the Lamborghini out of storage in winter.

"I guess so. I only know what I told you. I have no clue why she's on drugs. It's a hush-hush thing. She hasn't left the house in months. There is a rumor she's not sickly. I say we investigate and find out what is behind his fortress."

"That's creepy as fuck," Gio states.

"What's up with the son? I think I saw him briefly with Councilman Addler at the gala. I wonder what they are trying to gain with their campaign donation." Federico pops in with a tray of pastries and drinks. Niccoló eats a chocolate-filled croissant, and I'm relieved he's eating.

"The son, Vincenzu, is not the nicest man. I get the impression that he's preferred over his father. He's smart and has more common sense than the old man. He also likes boxing. I might run into him at some point. Maybe I will suggest we have a Sicilian cookout," Niccoló says sarcastically.

"We have the house being watched, and Mrs. Moretti has not been seen," Gio adds.

I receive a text.

"The woman is at Alena's dress fitting. I turn to Niccoló. Can you investigate Moretti's wife? We need to confirm the rumors."

"I'm on it," Niccoló says as he grabs a water bottle. "I'll use your tech company. You say you have the best hackers. Let's see what they can do." He gives me a salacious smile, and I know he's the man for the job. "I want to kill the man responsible for Chiara's death. I'll never forget finding her that way."

I feel for my brother. I've seen the crime scene photos, and since she was beaten and stabbed, her death was painful. The pictures looked like a botched murder. I'm used to seeing a ton of fucked up shit, but that is a murder where I would have puked. I'm convinced it was staged to look like a robbery. She didn't have anything worth stealing.

Niccoló leaves, taking a guard. Gio and I walk to my study, where I pace.

"You are driving me nuts, Matteo," he exclaims.

"I'm standing with my hands tied. There has to be something we're missing." I move my hand over my chin and tap my lip with my finger as I think. I move to my desk and pull the paper out of the drawer. "I found this in Dad's papers. Do you recognize the handwriting?"

"No, probably a woman's," he says. "Was your father seeing someone?"

"Not that I know of, but the old man was cagey. How can we find one Italian woman in New York City who might have crossed paths with my father?"

"True."

I received a text from Vito that the women were at the spa. My chest is consumed with tightness—and anxiety. This is something new to me. I pray today goes without an incident.

I checked in with Niccoló for an update, and even though they have hacked into hospital records, he can't find any records of Santino's wife, Gabriela, being admitted anywhere in the city.

I ordered him to continue digging and hang up. This task will keep him occupied, and keeping his mind busy is important. I'm worried he's on a path to self-destruction. I'm hoping the allure of him finding the villain will give him a reason to live. We always deliver justice. An eye for an eye. It's the law of our world and the oath we all swear to uphold. I feel the anger in my chest. Vengeance will be mine. I know we're getting closer. I need a few chips to fall into place, and revenge will be mine.

"That's odd. Why would a woman be medicated if she doesn't need it?" Gio asks. "She has kids. How could that go on?"

"Is Santino just being cruel, or is there a reason his wife is a prisoner in their home? And the kids are all raised and out of the house. He is in control of what happens in his house."

"I hope we're wrong. Either way, he's an asshole."

I'm too restless to sit here without Alena. We head into the city and take a guard to drive us. We check on shipments and make sure things are locked down at the warehouses. I need to keep my shit together now more than ever, but the circle of death appears to be moving closer.

Gio and I stop for lunch at a pub in our territory. It was probably not the best decision, considering we don't know what the Murphys, the Irish mob, own. They have a stronghold in Boston and are carving out their territory with underground boxing and gambling.

We're at the end of an incredible shepherd's pie when men enter. Their Celtic crosses and tattoos on their necks show they are part of an Irish clan.

I leave cash at the table, and we walk to the door. On the way to the door, one of the men hollers at me.

"You bloody well don't belong here, Borrelli. Stick to your side of town."

"Leave it," Gio mutters so only I can hear him.

"I didn't know you owned this joint," I reply.

"Get a map." The tall Irishman pushes his sweater up his arms. "And you best take care of your women. Cillian O'Donnell isn't happy about his son. You best be careful. When he's mad, it rains more here than in Ireland."

Rain? A metaphor for bullets? He's threatening me.

"Well, if he's unhappy, he should go to therapy."

He stands, causing the wooden chair to scrape as it refuses to slide over the old tile. My God! He's over six feet tall, and his chest could pull a hand-truck full of milk.

"Get out and don't come back," he says with an accent that makes him difficult to understand.

He raises an arm and curls his fingers as if he has a gun in his hand and is ready to pull the trigger. He pulls his fingers back and pretends to shoot.

We leave. I text Antonio to send more men to the girls, hoping the threat was for me and not them.

"The Irish are stirred up over you." Gio quickly calls for the G-wagon, which rolls around, and we slide inside, contemplating the situation.

"Call your contact with Cillian. We need a sit-down. Something is about to go down. Is every mob family in a state of rebellion?"

Gio is on his phone and makes the call.

"How do you see this meeting going?" he asks after he's hung up.

"No clue. One never knows. I assume he wants something from me, and this is his way of communicating."

"That's pretty fucked up," Gio replies.

"They have a fucked-up history of wars," I reply. Mom would have been proud I made good grades in school. I liked history the best. "We need to swing by the port. I have a shipment coming in. I want to make sure it's not hijacked."

"I can have men do that." Gio protests us going out of our way, but Alena and Bianca won't be home for a few more hours, and I feel incomplete without her there.

I instruct the guard to make sure we're not followed. I have Italians and the Irish crowding me. I wonder what stirred up this shit storm.

The guard and Gio exit the car, making sure it's safe. I walk into the postmaster we have on our payroll. He says things have been quiet. I walk to our dock and find my men in a small building, drinking coffee and keeping warm.

They are surprised to see me, but that's to be expected. I don't come here often, but today was an exception. I desire to do things that aren't necessarily productive, but the ritual of going down my checklist before a war gives me the illusion that I have control over something. And for now, it's a comfort.

I head back to the car with Gio, and we stop at a bodega because Gio needs some cigars. This store happens to have illegal ones from Cuba. He tells me he says a few words in Spanish, and they are pulled from under the counter. I stretch my legs and walk into the floral store next door. Flowers for Alena would make her day complete. I exit the store carrying a huge vase filled with two dozen red flowers.

"Get down!" is what I hear Gio shouting as a gunshot rings in my ears. One or more, I don't know. It was so fast I dropped the vase, and it shattered at my feet. Gio is on top of me. "Are you okay?" His hands run over my body, and he opens my winter coat to see what the wound looks like. I hear the wail of police sirens and an ambulance. "It nicked his arm. Let's get him in the wagon. We need to get out of here."

The daylight blurs. My arm hurts like a burn. I'm helped into the G-wagon, and the vehicle lurches forward under the weight of my guard's foot.

"The flowers," I mumble.

"She'll understand that, but she'll kill me if I don't get you home in one piece." Gio is visibly shaken. "Did you see anything, Andre? What kind of car was it?"

"It was a Hummer. I was parked illegally, so I stayed with the car."

"Fuck," Gio yells, applying pressure on my arm. The pain is excruciating. "Drive faster!"

I'm dragged into a room, and an IV is in my arm. Then, my head is in the clouds. I fantasize about being on my honeymoon and fast forward to Alena, pregnant with my baby.

I'm at home and in bed, and a few hours must have passed. The pain meds are wearing off. The fog has lifted. Niccoló is sitting in a chair by my bedside.

"You scared us. Thankfully, you'll be as good as new in no time." Leave it to my brother to try to cheer me up.

I look at the bandage on my arm. "Fuck, I have a hole in my arm, don't I?"

"They did a good job. You're lucky. It could have been your heart."

CHAPTER 36

ALENA

Something is amiss when I return home. Federico is making a tray of soup and tea.

"What's going on? Where's Matteo?" I ask. Bianca is quiet beside me. The day was perfect. I was relaxed and enjoyed time with my best friends.

"Follow me, Alena." Federico is always chipper.

"I'm coming too," Bianca says as she dumps it on the kitchen counter. I run up the steps, passing Federico, not knowing what I will find. I take the steps two at a time.

Gio and Niccoló are with Matteo, who is in bed. His left arm is bandaged.

"Please tell me it's just a scratch."

"If that's what you want to hear, sure." Matteo gives me a weak smile.

"What happened?" I glance at all three of them as Bianca and Federico enter the room.

"It was a drive-by. I was getting you flowers. I've never given you flowers. Gio was getting cigars. The guard stayed in the car. It happened so fast," Matteo relays the facts as if it's nothing.

"Who did it?" I ask as my eyes light up. Someone is going to pay for this.

"No clue. But we have a call into the Irish. I think they want something from me and are trying to leverage nothing into something." I take Matteo's hand, and he allows me to hold it.

"Are you going to be okay?" Bianca asks, moving closer to her brother's bed.

"I'll be fine. I'll have a scar." He shrugs.

"Well, thank God they didn't have better aim," she jokes.

"They sent a message. If they wanted him dead, he'd be dead," Gio speaks at last. "I'm sorry, Alena. I never should have let my guard down. It won't happen again."

"I want the person responsible for this!" I yell in frustration. We're victims. I hate being powerless.

I'm also pissed. I want to scream and shout with the anger that swells inside every cell in my body.

Matteo was shot and could have died. I'd be lost without him. I consoled myself in the fact that he's alive. However, the situation reminds me how fragile life is.

I'm so in love with him that I can't focus on anything else. I'll be by his side as long as he needs me. Sex is no longer fucking—it's become meaningful. Touch for touch, a caress in return for a caress. He makes love to me, and he's letting me in.

When we make love, our eyes meet, our souls kiss, and the euphoria is pure joy. So much so that I cry tears of happiness, and I don't hide the fact that my cheeks are wet. I love this man.

Federico leaves the food on the bureau and leaves the room. Gio and Niccoló excuse themselves, and Bianca kisses her brother on the cheek and tells him she's relieved he will be okay.

We're alone. I change into a jogger and crawl into bed with him.

"How are you feeling?"

"The pain pills are working," he teases.

"You know what I meant."

"I'm fine. And I'll get to the bottom of this. It was probably the Irish. I have the Morettis being watched, and it's been quiet at his house. Did you know his wife hasn't been seen in months?"

Matteo is wounded, but he still talks about work. That's my husband. He works nonstop. In his mind, we'll be safe once he solves the mystery of Luciano and Chiara's murders. I love him for his dedication. I've learned so much from him. I admire the man he is, even though he loves to show the world his rough exterior.

"No, I didn't know that. Are you sure she's alive? Her husband is strange. No, that isn't strong enough of a word. He's mean and spiteful. He's powerful, and powerful men can make things happen."

"Oh, I know that. She wouldn't be the first to die by suicide."

"Oh, so that's how you'd do it?" I tease him as I lean my head on his toned shoulder and lay my arm protectively over him.

"Come here," he says, wrapping his uninjured arm around me. "I couldn't wait for you to get home. Did you have fun?"

"Yes, but I missed you."

"I missed you more."

"It's debatable, but since you're wounded, I'll let you get away with it this time. But I'm taking care of you."

"No, I'm fine."

"You have no choice. We're camping out in bed until Monday."

"That means we have all day Sunday to fool around."

It's refreshing to see his sense of humor return.

"I was thinking we'd hang out and watch TV and cuddle. You're supposed to be resting." I nuzzle his neck and breathe in the smell of the light fragrance from his natural soap.

"That's not what I have in mind," he growls. It's similar to the sound he makes before he tears my underwear off with his teeth.

I check his temperature and play nurse for the remainder of the afternoon. Federico serves us dinner in our suite and picks the tray up before he leaves for the night. I thank him profusely.

I sleep past dawn. It's Sunday, and I find his bad arm draped over my midsection. Our legs are intertwined. I can't move. There is no way for me to move without waking him. I pretend to sleep, and he wakes up despite the fact I'm still.

He kisses my dry lips. "How's my angel?"

"Fine." I stretch, and he sits on the edge of the bed. "I need a shower. Would you care to take one with me?"

"I'd love to." I walk him to the shower and run the water. I wrap his arm with plastic wrap the doctor gave him. I don't ask if he went to the hospital. I assume he has a man on the payroll to handle these things. The plastic sleeve protects his bandaged area.

We step into the shower. I run the square bar of soap over his toned body. He insists on washing my back, and I let him. I admit it feels good, and he's gentle and romantic as he kisses me softly. I turn off the water and help him dry off. I know he's feeling better when he play-fully grabs at my boobs. I dodge him, but he manages to slap my naked ass.

"That hurts!"

"You liked it, didn't you?"

"Mm, the doctor said you have to take it easy."

"Fuck that. I'm the king, and what I say goes. Your pussy and your heart belong to me and no one else. Ever!"

He lunges for me. I scamper into the bedroom and hop on the bed. He tackles me, and it's game over. After more than an hour of having every inch of my body covered with kisses and having orgasmed twice, I want to make his day special.

"I want to give you a blow job. You're doing too much."

"Angel, I'd love to see your lips on my cock."

He stands by the bed. His veined cock is hard. I kneel on the floor and take him into my mouth. I lick myself off of him and ride my hand up and down his shaft as I flick my tongue over his head and take delight in the fact that he moans and arches his back. He's so long that I have to be careful not to suffocate. I love knowing I can pleasure him this way.

He has fists in my hair. I bob my head fully, taking him into my mouth, and move my hand faster and faster.

"Fuck," he groans as he explodes into my mouth, and I swallow. I lick him clean.

"That's so hot. You're amazing."

"I like doing that with you, only you."

His face softens as he kisses me deeply. "Let's get out of the house. I need some fresh air."

"Is it safe?"

"I have a temporary truce with the Irish. Gio texted me last night. We'll talk. We both want a peaceful resolution."

"Did you do something?"

"Not anything he would know of, but who knows?"

Matteo's phone rings.

"Yes, Gio. I'm resting." Matteo talks first, and then he listens to Gio speaking in Italian. "Fine. Pick us up in ten."

"What's going on?"

"Gio received a message. It appears Gabriella Moretti's sister wants to speak to us."

"Us?"

"Yes."

"Why?"

"I can't read a woman's mind," he replies, giving me a complex look.

"Well, you read mine very well, especially in bed."

"That's a talent I only share with you, my love."

"Well, Mr. Grey. I suggest we get dressed. Where are we going?"

"Eisenhower Park. It's not far. I doubt many people will be there when the forecast says the day will be filled with heavy snowfall. I assume it's a secretive meeting."

"I wonder what she wants."

"I have no clue. I'll be asking questions—you can bet on that."

"It's odd. The Morettis haven't reached out before. Can we trust her?"

"We'll find out."

"I don't know if it's worth the risk. Why can't she talk over the phone like normal people?"

He raises his eyebrows, mocking me.

"Oh, right. Fine, the park it is," I say as I tug my boots over my socks.

Gio arrives and is sitting in the limo. Along with him is another guard and our driver, who also doubles as a guard.

Matteo said he wasn't taking any chances. It could be a setup so the men can check out the park before we leave the armored limo.

The park is deemed safe. Only one woman is sitting on a park bench near a fountain. We approach her. She has a scarf around her face, and a winter hat adorns her head. Her black wool winter jacket covers her body. She's wearing leather gloves and appears to have an adequate lifestyle. But I can't make out the features of her face.

"Sit down casually," the woman says softly but sternly. She looks straight ahead as if we're here by chance.

"Who are you?" Matteo asks.

"I'm Lucinda, Gabriella Moretti's twin sister."

This meeting reeks of a conspiracy. The question is—who's?

"Twin?" Matteo asks. "I confess there isn't much information on your sister."

"That's true. You understand that. I don't have much time. I keep moving around. This nightmare has to end." She takes a breath and then continues. "When my sister was forced to marry Santino, I knew our lives were ruined. We live in his shadow, and we fear him. He's ruthless. He has no morals."

"Why are you here?" Matteo says tersely. His eyes survey the landscape for trouble as he pushes her to get to the point.

The driver and guard continue to canvas the area, but Gio sticks close to us. I know he has more than one weapon under his trench coat. After the near hit yesterday, he's not taking unnecessary chances.

"I helped my sister have an affair with your father, Luciano. I delivered their love notes. She would come to visit me, and I'd slip her out the back door. She'd be picked up to meet your father. Usually, hotels and off-the-beaten-path eateries. They were like teenagers in love. She was happy." She sighs. "I warned her she was playing with fire, but she didn't care. Her children were grown and out of the house. And for a few hours a week, she escaped her cruel husband. I assume Santino grew suspicious and had her followed. I'm not sure. When I saw on the news Luciano Borrelli was dead, I knew he found out about the affair. It was too coincidental."

She pauses and pulls numerous envelopes from her coat pocket. She hands them to Matteo, who sits next to her. I stand and pace before him.

"This is proof of their affair."

"Why give this to me?" Matteo opens a letter cautiously and looks at it briefly before tucking it inside the envelope. He then shoves the notes into his coat pocket.

"I'm in danger. I can't return to my home until Santino is dead. He has my sister drugged. He doesn't allow her children to see her. If the drugs to sedate her don't kill her, he will do it himself. She's losing her will to live. We're twins, and I feel her slipping away." She falls quiet as if her sister is speaking to her.

"What is it that you want from me?" Matteo is still. I'm concerned he's in pain as he sits beside her.

"The enemy of my enemy is my friend, Sun Tzu," Lucinda states. "You are familiar with it."

"Yes."

"He used someone close to your family to kill your father. He's paranoid. He will kill anyone who knows what he did, as it would start a war. He didn't want my sister, but he didn't want anyone else to have her. I stole those notes from her hiding place to prove their affair the last time I saw her and informed her of Luciano's death. It's the proof you need to do what you do in these situations."

"And then you and your sister can inherit. Gabriella's son, Vincenzu, takes over, and all is forgotten. An eye for an eye."

"I hope that's how it happens. Vincenzo and his sisters have had years of abuse at that man's hands. I was powerless to stop it. I am doing what I can to help now."

"You fear him," I state as I pace back and forth in front of my fiancé. "One would be foolish not to. He has eyes and ears everywhere. Be careful. I have to go." She stands.

I feel for the woman who has seen her sister suffer for years and was powerless to help her. Now, she's trying to save her sister at the risk of her own life.

I hug her. "I'm so sorry for what you've been through."

She returns my hug.

"I hear you are kind. I see that my great-niece is a wonderful woman. I hope to meet her one day. She's safe with the Russians. Santino is crazy, but the alliance of your families means you outnumber the Morettis."

"Does he know about her?" I won't risk saying Izzy's name in case Lucinda is wearing a recording device. If I learned one thing from Matteo, it's that I have to be more careful with whom I trust.

"I saw a picture of her with Dmitry on the red carpet. I knew she had to be related. Her mother loved Alexsei. She has his eyes and our features. I never said a word to anyone, not even my sister. Santino would kill her to punish Alexsei. It all happened so long ago, but Santino holds grudges forever. He will never let go of the past. He doesn't forgive or forget those who wronged him, even if it's in his head. The family doesn't support him, but no one can go against him. He is paranoid. I think the sins of those he has unjustly killed haunt him. He's going crazy."

"Thank you," I reply as my eyes tear. I quickly brush them away as she slips out of sight.

Matteo stands. Gio approaches.

"We better move to be safe."

"Agreed," Matteo says as he slips his arm through mine as if we were alone in the park the entire time.

We're safely in the limo heading home when Matteo informs Gio about the discussion with Lucinda.

Gio lets out a low whistle. "I never saw that coming. She handed you what you need to take him out."

"My father deserved what he got. He touched another man's wife, but using Chiara to do his job for him crossed the line. When Alexsei learns that Santino is still a threat to Izzy, I'm sure he'll side with us." Matteo summarizes the issues, and we all know the solution.

Santino Moretti has to die.

CHAPTER 37

ALENA

 ito picks me up in the G-Wagon and drives me to my mother's house. I sit in the back and call Izzy.

We chat, and I discuss the ups and downs of life in the mansion, leaving out the part about Matteo being hit with a bullet and the mysterious visit to the park.

I'm sure Matteo will resolve the issue with the Irish. Therefore, Dmitry doesn't need to know. I trust Matteo to handle the situation. Izzy is thrilled the baby is kicking, and I wonder when that will happen to me. I can't imagine what it would be like to have a human growing inside me.

"I assume my father will remain missing." I was upset, but I knew it was coming. Mom might not have known how much trouble he was in.

"I think so, Alena. I'm sorry. I don't know the details."

"I didn't expect you to know details, and if you did, you can't tell me. I need to prepare my mom for the long-term picture, y'know."

"Sure. The gala was fun." She changed the subject, and I'm grateful. "Did you have a good time?"

"Yes, I did. You looked incredible," I say. "You were glowing."

"No, you had the best gown," she insists. "And I see how much you and Matteo love each other. We're lucky women."

"Maybe. But the costumes were all Matteo's doing. He picked them out and had them made. They probably cost more than the tickets. Oh, I forgot to tell you my boss, Sophia, was transferred to the London office. I didn't have to say anything to Matteo."

"That's great. How is work going now that you've been promoted?"

"I plan to finish the hotel floor in time for the wedding. I have a great wedding planner. Did you get your invitation?"

"Yes, I RSVP'd to it already. When do you try on your wedding dress?"

"I think a week before the wedding. I need to follow up with the dress shop and Francis."

"It will be so nice to be in sunny Florida next month. I hope spring has sprung when we return home."

"Right? I'm ready for warm weather. I wonder if we're arriving a few days before the wedding. I might be able to get a tan," I reply, thinking of the possibilities. I've never been to Florida.

"I think that would be a great idea. Just don't overdo it. Lace makes me itch. Don't get a sunburn. The lace will cut your skin and hurt as much as a finger sliced in an immersion blender," she warns.

"I think Matteo will keep me busy with indoor activities," I snicker. I make a note to apply plenty of sunscreen daily. Maybe I'll stay under the beach umbrellas. I don't want to look like a red lobster stuffed in my gorgeous gown on my wedding day.

"I'm sure. You're in the honeymoon phase."

"I guess we are."

Vito parks in my mother's driveway. It sounds weird, my mother's house, her driveway. I'm not in denial over the fact Dad is gone. Mom is.

I go to open the door, but it's locked. I pull out my spare key, unlock the door, and push it open. I walk in and notice the mail is piled on the coffee table unopened, and there is a pile of bills.

"Mom?"

"I'm here." Mom is in the kitchen with vodka. She appears to have lived in her jammies and bathrobe for a few days.

"Let's get you a shower, Mom."

"No, I'm fine." She's had too much to drink.

"Mom, come on." I take off my coat and purse, drop them on the kitchen chair, and pull my mother up. "You'll feel better."

An hour later, Mom is showered and dressed.

"Where have you been?" As if it's my fault her life has fallen apart.

"I've had my hands full with Matteo's business and work. Why?"

"Who's going to take care of me now?"

"You will, Mom."

"Your father lost all our money. The house is paid off, but I have no income. The bills are too much. I can't pay them."

"We'll get an attorney or something. It's a problem for another day. Today, focus on cleaning up the house and getting some groceries. Has there been any news?"

"No. The police do nothing."

"Well, there may not be any leads. Who was he meeting with that night?"

"I have no clue. Where were you? It sounded like there was music."

"We were at the councilman's gala. Izzy and I were there with Dmitry and Matteo."

"Dmitry, too? And Kirill?"

"Dmitry. Kirill isn't high enough in the organization to be invited."

"Right. Do you trust him?"

"I doubt Kirill or Dmitry had to do this because Izzy and I are best friends, and the don wouldn't come between us."

I think she understands. I don't want to discuss this with her. What's done is done.

I hug my mom. "I'm sorry. I have my hands full. But we'll figure it out. Okay?"

"Da."

I cook my mom some food, and Vito drives me home.

Matteo greets me with a hug. He asks if I'm okay and lets me take my time to fill him in on my morning.

We walk along a path through the backyard, which, judging from the trees, will blossom into a pretty garden in the summer.

"Alena, I have a question."

"What?"

He stops and drops to one knee.

"Will you marry me?"

"We're engaged."

"Yes, but I never asked you. I shouldn't hold you to our contract. I'd rather have you decide for yourself. I love you. I'll ask you again, and I want an answer this time. Will you marry me?"

He's giving me a choice over my life, my destiny. My heart lurches. He loves me. And he's giving me a choice.

"Yes, I love you, too. I'll marry you, Mr. Grey."

Matteo laughs as he stands. He pulls me into his arms and kisses me.

"So, what are we doing about Moretti?"

"I'm having a meeting with Alexsei. This is all he needs to put a bullet in Santino's head. He hates that man."

"After everything he's been through because of Santino, do you blame him?"

"No. I don't. But I'd burn the city down looking for you, Alena."

I blush. I'm sure he would.

"When are you meeting?"

"Today."

CHAPTER 38

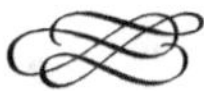

MATTEO

Don Sidovo meets me in a smoky room I use for our illegal gambling. My manager brings us vodka and chilled shot glasses and disappears.

"What is so important that I have to meet you here, Matteo?"

"I have information from Lucinda, Gabriella Moretti's twin sister."

At this, the don sits taller in the chair and pours us both vodka, which we toss back.

"Interesting. What did she have to say?" His eyes narrow with the hatred he has for the family. The family that tore him apart and destroyed his young life. I know he probably thought for many years about how he would kill his nemesis. He's been waiting for a legitimate reason to pull the trigger. And I am the person who gives him his wish.

"Her sister is drugged. It appears Gabriella and my father were having an affair. Santino found out and killed my father. I have a letter of confession from my brother's girlfriend, who was forced to deliver the poison that killed him. I also have a note in Gabriella's handwriting that matches this."

I pull two letters from my suit pocket and hand them to him. One is Gabriella's last love note, and the other is my father's note to her.

Alexsei holds the notes gingerly in his hands. He flips them open, and I translate what they say into English.

"This means we can kill him, and it will be justified. Granted, your father was wrong. He touched his wife. But he used an innocent to carry out the hit to throw us off his trail. We don't use innocent women. We don't kill women and children. And to drug his wife is unconscionable and demented."

I pour us another vodka. We toss it back, and our empty glasses click as they touch the table.

"Do we make it personal? Or do we make a huge splash that leaves it open to interpretation?" I'm curious how we can handle this without causing more issues. I already have one with the Irish. I don't need to make more enemies back home with the Cosa Nostra retaliating against my family. Nor do I want them shooting at us in the streets of New York to even the score.

"I'll think about it. Of all the ways I've thought I'd kill him, I never saw this day coming to fruition. When I was younger, I'm sure I would have killed him if I didn't believe his daughter was already dead. He's a skilled manipulator. It's as if he's a magician, throwing up smoke screens to present one story while the truth lies under the surface."

"He's a rabid man who needs to be put down," I concede.

"That he is. Thank you for the information. You've been very valuable in this and other matters. I thank you. I'll be in touch."

Alexsei and I stand and shake hands. His two guards escort him out the back door, where his armored vehicle waits.

I'm relieved that we've found the man responsible for my father and Chiara's murder. I'm sure there is a hitman in Sicily that I may never find. But we have the head of the snake, and for today—this is enough.

I have a bride who needs her wedding day. Then, I'll meet with the Irish and put their feud to bed. After that, Alexsei and I will plan our revenge.

For more of Matteo and Alena, download their bonus scene now!
https://dl.bookfunnel.com/kw9ef0mt2n

ALSO BY ZOE BETH GELLER

Visit https://www.shopzoebethgeller.com

Pre-order at my store and get your book first!

Mafia prequels are at shopzoebethgeller.com

Would you like to hear from Zoe? Join my newsletter today for cover reveals, updates, behind-the-scenes news, and free books!

https://geni.us/MafiaNewslettersignup

Dirty: A Dark Mafia Romance Series

Dirty: A Dark Mafia Romance Series (Micheli Mafia)

Italian King: A Dark Mafia RomanceBook 1

Dirty Vengeance: A Dark Mafia Romance Book 2

Dirty Bargain: A Dark Mafia Romance Book 3

Dirty Born: A Dark Mafia Romance Book 4

Dirty Deals: A Dark Mafia Romance Book 5

Volkov Bratva Series

Bratva's Bride (prequel)

King's Promise

Brutal Promise

Sinful Promise

Borrelli Mafia Series

Nanny for the Bodyguard (prequel)

Mafia King: Matteo

Vengeance and Vows

Scandalous Vows

ZBG Mafia Romance Group on Facebook

Maine Megaladons (Football Series)

Faking it with the Football Star

The Player's Obsession

Scoring with the Coach's Daughter

Maine Maulers Series (Pro Series)

Maine Maulers Hockey Series

Rookie in Love (now in audio)

Jagged Ice

Hotter than Puck

Benched by the Nanny

Puck in the Oven

Pucking the Team Captain

Pucking with the Goalie

Pucked Over by Cupid

Sin Bin Hockey Series (College Series)

Tyler: Hooked (Free prequel to the series)

The Sin Bin Hockey Series

Jackson: Against the Boards

Alan: Between the Pipes

Erik: Fire and Ice

Blayze: Slap Shot

Paavo: The Defender

Spencer: Penalty Box

Isak: Coach

Kaden: Game Time

Liam: The Enforcer

Jake: Roughing

The Sin Bin Hockey Series Box Sets

The Sin Bin Hockey Series Box Set Books 1-4

The Sin Bin Hockey Series Box Set Books 5-7

The Sin Bin Hockey Series Box Set Books 8-10

Zoe Beth Geller's Hockey Pond Reader/Fan Group

www.ingramcontent.com/pod-product-compliance
Lightning Source LLC
Chambersburg PA
CBHW060434310726
48977CB00001B/177